AG 15 '96

CALIFORNIA PI

D0195720

BILLINGS COUNTY
LIBRARY PROGRAM

F Schulte   c.2
Schulte, Elaine L.
Mercies so tender

M
So T

ELAINE SCHULTE

CALIFORNIA PIONEER SERIES

Mercies So Tender

ELAINE SCHULTE

WITHDRAWN FROM
Dickinson Public Library

DICKINSON AREA PUBLIC
LIBRARY
139 Third Street West
Dickinson, North Dakota 58601

LIFEJOURNEY
BOOKS

A DIVISION OF COOK COMMUNICATIONS

Life Journey Books™ is an imprint of Chariot Family Publishing
Cook Communications Ministries, Elgin, Illinois 60120
Cook Communications Ministries, Paris, Ontario
Kingsway Communications, Eastbourne, England

Published in association with the literary agency of
Alive Communications, P.O. Box 49068
Colorado Springs, CO 80904

MERCIES SO TENDER
© 1995 by Elaine Schulte

All rights reserved. Except for brief excerpts for review purposes, no
part of this book may be reproduced or used in any form without writ-
ten permission from the publisher.
Cover design by Paetzold Design
Cover illustration by Robert Papp
First printing, 1995
Printed in the United States of America
99 98 97 96 95   5 4 3 2 1

The California Pioneer Series

The Journey West
Golden Dreams
Eternal Passage
With Wings As Eagles
Peace Like A River
Mercies So Tender

*With gratitude to Loma Geyer Davies Silcott, who drove
me through the Missouri and Mississippi valleys, helping
immeasurably with the research,*

*to Charlotte Adelsperger, an exceptional encourager,
who so graciously shared her Kansas home,*

*and to Susan Richardson, an extraordinary bookseller,
who taught me a little about Southern cooking and a lot
about the South and Southern hospitality.*

*In memory of our
sisters and brothers
who brought His love
through the gathering storm*

Prologue

Benjamin Talbot settled into his high-backed horsehair armchair and scanned the *Alta California.* "World news," he remarked as he shook out the already misfolded newspaper. "Must not be anything of consequence happening here in San Francisco."

Across from him in their whitewashed parlor, his older sister, Jessica, glanced up from her sewing. "There is elsewhere in the country. Read on, Benjamin. Read on."

Benjamin scanned the upper half of the front page. Fortunately, there was nothing more about the atheist Charles Darwin and his absurd theory of evolution. Suddenly Benjamin's eye caught a small headline in the middle of the page: "Strife Grows on Missouri-Kansas Border."

His heart faltered.

As usual, Independence—where his son Adam and his family still lived on the old home place—was in the thick of border lootings and shootings. Everyone knew the Missouri River had long been a transition zone between the settled East and the lawless West, but now New England abolitionists were purposely settling in Kansas across from Missouri's "little Dixie."

"Let's hope Adam sends your reckless-mouthed granddaughter

Kate upriver to Weston for the time being," Jessica said. "At least he's considering it."

Benjamin looked up over the newspaper at his sister with indignation. *"My reckless-mouthed granddaughter?!"* It took forbearance not to mention that twenty-year-old Kate was also Jessica's kin—in fact, her great-niece. Or that Jessica was in no position to cast stones, since she'd been known to be reckless-mouthed herself.

"Our reckless Kate," Jessica conceded.

Benjamin harrumphed, then found the troubling article again. Under "Strife Grows Between the States," an even more discouraging subtitle said, "More Southern States Advocate Secession." And as if that were insufficient bad news, a nearby article concerned California's pro-slavery legislature. It occurred to him that from the very beginning of the 1860s, disheartening events had followed one another like black clouds before a gathering storm.

"I fear no one can stop the border fighting," Jessica said, her voice pained. "The rabble-rousers will only help to bring on a great calamity."

My concern precisely, Benjamin thought with a sense of doom. A civil war seemed inevitable, if not this year, then the next. May God help Kate and the others, and this entire nation!

1

The aromas of coffee, hot cornbread, and frying pork sausage mingled in the air as Kate Talbot stood over the big black wood-burning stove in her sister's farmhouse kitchen. She turned the breakfast sausages, enjoying the symphony of bird song that drifted through the open window.

Under an ample white apron she wore her yellow dimity, a frock that complemented her reddish blond hair and always made her feel especially comely. She was trying to recall when she had last worn the dress back in Independence, when quite suddenly a loud *pop-pop-pop* of distant gunshots rent the morning air.

"What is it?!" Kate asked, hoping the sounds were not what she thought. She set aside the skillet and started for the window. Outside, she heard horses whinny with fright. "Whatever's happening out there?"

"Shooting," her sister Sarah replied, hurrying along with her and then pulling aside the yellow calico curtains. "It sounded like gunshots."

"Just what I thought. . . ."

As they glanced out the open window, an eerie silence hung in the morning sunshine. The warblers in the black walnut tree by the window had quieted, and the dense woods that lined the long lane to Weston Road were equally hushed. Even the new spring greenery on the bushes and trees seemed motionless. Kate half-expected to hear shouts for help or to see someone stagger from the woods towards the house, but nothing happened. Slowly the birds resumed their twittering, and a rabbit bounded from the underbrush edging the woods.

Kate steadied herself. "It's over. Perhaps it was only hunters."

Sarah let out a deep breath. "Let's hope so. It makes me so agitated. Oh, Kate, I have a foreboding . . . a terrible foreboding."

Kate stared at her sister and realized she had to be calm for both of them. "You've always told me never to go by feelings. 'Never' was your exact word."

"I know it," Sarah admitted, "but having said so when I lived at home was different. It's not the same here."

Peering out the window again, Kate tucked a strand of loose hair into her upswept coiffure. To think she'd just fled Independence two days earlier to escape the border turmoil, only to find just as much trouble here in Weston. Not that there wasn't trouble all along the state border with Kansas, and not that she hadn't brought on her own swift departure. Anyone who spoke out against slavery in western Missouri was courting trouble. Worst of all, she'd known it after the Sunday service when she'd informed the visiting preacher that his stand for slavery was wrong.

She could still hear her voice by the open church door. " 'Do unto others as you would have them do unto you' is for people of every color! How can you hold for slavery?"

He had stared at her with shock, then finally asked, "How do you happen to know so much about Scripture?"

"I don't."

"Then mind those who do," he had admonished her and turned away.

Beside her, Poppa's face had blanched, and on the wagon ride home, he'd said, "Think before you speak, Kate! Boldness has to be tempered with wisdom, not to mention plain common sense."

"Und courtesy!" Mama had added, her German accent thickening. "Oh, my dear Kate!"

That night, someone had broken the windows of Poppa's mercantile and left a note saying broken windows were only a harbinger of trouble if he didn't silence his "reckless-mouthed daughter." Daily there had been more dire warnings, and in the nights, more damage to the mercantile. Finally even Kate knew she had to leave Independence, at least for a while, or the mercantile would be burned down.

She still held to her opinion about slavery, but wished she'd been more circumspect. *Speak in haste, repent at leisure,* she thought, and not for the first time. Now she could repent upriver in the town of Weston, though in the Bence household there was very little leisure for either her or Sarah.

She glanced at her older sister. Sarah was taller and leaner than most of the Talbot girls, and had a look of solemnity in her wide-set, light blue eyes. Likely the serious streak came from being the eldest in a large family, and was compounded by her onerous duties here in her father-in-law's house.

For a change, Kate spoke with reluctance. "Poppa will be upset to learn it's not as safe here as he'd hoped."

Sarah looked as somber as the plain gray-blue cotton frock under her white apron. "At least he'd be glad that trouble won't keep us from church."

Kate had already promised herself to keep her mouth shut at church, no matter what was preached. Trying to forget her rashness in Independence, she said, "Yes, he's a good deal like Grandfather Talbot in California, I suppose. Maybe it comes from having had a minister in the family years ago."

Sarah raised her thin brows, then nodded. "I'm glad they made us go. It didn't hurt any of us."

"No, it didn't."

"Besides, Sunday mornings are almost the only time I get out of the house," Sarah confided.

"I'm sorry to hear it."

Sarah took a deep breath. "Having you here and then Greta Davison inviting us to dinner makes this a real banner day. As if that weren't wonder enough, we have the box supper social tonight." She quickly added, as if wishing not to be a complainer, "You know, it's not like living in Independence and going to town whenever we pleased."

"No, I guess it's not," Kate replied. It couldn't be easy for Sarah, living in a house with her husband's disagreeable widowed father and two exasperating brothers. As it was, Sarah had made their box suppers at sunup, before her in-laws were up and about.

Sarah cast another long look out the window. "After that shooting, let's hope Stephen will still take us to church. In any event, we won't have his family's company there."

Kate returned to the stove and pulled the skillet back onto the burner. "I presumed not."

She'd arrived two days ago, and nothing concerning God or godliness had been mentioned by Stephen's father or brothers; even those who wished to say grace at meals did so in silence. As for "feelings," she had a bad feeling about all of them except Stephen . . . a feeling that Sarah wasn't quite safe here.

Kate slid the pan of cornbread up into the stove's warming oven. "Where's Stephen?"

Sarah stood at the plank kitchen table, nervously setting out plates and silverware. "Getting the buggy."

"Before breakfast?"

Sarah nodded. "Best if he does. That way his father and broth-

ers take it better, as though our going to church is already settled."
She glanced toward the window, and said with a trace of alarm,
"Here come the men from the barn! I'll start frying the eggs."

"Better you than me," Kate told her. She'd never again fry eggs
for Pa Bence or Stephen's two brothers, not after the fuss they'd
made about her eggs yesterday morning. Considering their
slovenliness, they were certainly particular about their food.

The back door opened, and Pa Bence stomped into the kitchen,
making a great noise for such a small man and leaving muddy boot
prints behind him. "What was thet shootin'?" he asked peevishly.

"We don't know," Sarah replied, her tone uneasy. "It was too far
away for us to see."

"Don't know anythin' much, do ye?"

Sarah pressed her lips together. "Not about that."

Kate forced what she hoped was a kindly smile. Pa Bence wore
his filthy buckskins, even on Sunday, she noticed. The only
improvement for the Sabbath was that he'd shaved off his grizzled beard last night before going to town. He might have been a
fine-looking man if his pale hazel eyes weren't so shifty and
bloodshot, and if he weren't always badgering and complaining.
He looked especially grim and sulky this morning.

Behind him, his eldest son, Aubin, wiped his boots on the outside stoop, making a big show of it. "Thought maybe you ladies
was out shootin' breakfast fer us," he said with a wide grin. He
wore his usual brown work clothes. At twenty-four years of age,
with his massive hulk and his bushy brown hair and mustache, he
looked nothing like his father.

"Now yer ma, she was a good shot," his father put in, "but it
ain't likely these two'd hit the outhouse with a bucket of
buckshot."

"Doubt they could hit the barn," Aubin said, then guffawed.

Pa Bence winced. "Quiet, boy!"

Stephen's father lacked a sense of humor and was likely suffering from the aftereffects of last night's outing at a tavern, Kate guessed. She only knew that he'd come from a hemp farm in "Kentuck," as he called it, married the owner's daughter, brought her here to the wilderness of Missouri for the promise of free land, and grown rich beyond his dreams—until the flood struck Weston.

Behind them came the youngest brother, Rodwell, grinning as usual. At twenty-one, he was a brown-haired replica of his father, a handsome rough frontiersman. "Thet'll be the day—Talbot girls out shootin' our meat!" he laughed. "Look at 'em, dressed up fancy under them aprons. Whooeeee! Makes a feller feel like dancin'—though they prob'ly think dancin's sinful."

He eyed Kate with bare-faced admiration, then put his arms out for dancing. "Whooeeee, Kate Talbot! If you ain't the sweetest thang with them gold-red hairs and big blue eyes!"

Gold-red hairs and big blue eyes! Kate's mind echoed with dismay as she edged around to the side of the stove. In her twenty years, she'd had a few boys and young men after her, but none had ever been quite as blunt about it as Rodwell, and she certainly did not wish to encourage him.

"Whooeeee, Kate!" he called out again. "Ah do believe you're a right sassy gal under them infernal good manners! About time someone showed you how to cut loose."

His father clutched his forehead as if it hurt fiercely. "Stop thet whoopin' an' yammerin.' "

"Whooeeee, Pa!" Rodwell yelled. He laughed, then stretched up his neck and scrutinized him. "You had yerself too much Saturday night? Appeared you were havin' a fine time with all thet free whiskey a'flowin'. Ain't nothin' like a free-spendin' Southerner around to likker us up."

Pa Bence swatted at him, but Rodwell jumped back and let out another amused, "Whooeeee! Ain't you touchy! And you spillin' more likker than most fellers drink!"

"Shut yer flappin' trap, or I'll fling you cubs right out o' my house," his father threatened.

"Yes, sir! Yes, sir!" Rodwell replied, still grinning. "One thang fer sure, this little cub o' yers don't take one bit to the idee o' sleepin' out in the cold. You know Ma would never o' had it, her little Rodwell out in the cold."

Yammering was the word for it, Kate thought as they blathered on and on at each other. Nonetheless, she was glad for the diversion and for the fact that Sarah was purposely stepping between her and Rodwell to get the food from the stove.

Sarah shot a stern glance at her in-laws. "In case you want to wash up, the food's going on the table in a minute."

"Say, ain't our Sarah got fire in her eyes?" Rodwell exclaimed, grinning again. "Her eyes ain't near as blue as Kate's, though. Not near as blue."

Pulling at his bushy mustache, Aubin looked from Kate to Sarah. "They . . . both of 'em . . . got blue eyes . . . like Ma's was." He started and stopped as if he were halt of tongue. "Sarah got light blue . . . Kate got dark blue. Ma's eyes was . . . somewheres between."

"Ain't our Aubin t-o-o smart!" Rodwell teased, back-stepping from his annoyed brother's reach. "Ought to be a politician. Why, we could send him right off to the capital in Jeff City—"

Blood rose to Aubin's face, and he doubled up his fists. "Want to fight?"

"Stop it, you two!" their father yelled, even though Rodwell was backing off, grinning. "Stop it 'fore I brain ye! Fer the life o' me, I don't know why ye cain't be more quiet like Stephen."

"Speak o' the devil!" Rodwell exclaimed as Stephen opened the back door.

With his serious, elongated face and dark blond hair, Stephen showed no resemblance to his father or to his brothers. His black suit, white shirt, and black cravat set him even farther apart.

Rodwell turned to his father with amazement. "You mean you want us to be long-faced like him?"

"Quiet!" Pa Bence snapped. "Already had some shootin' this mornin'!"

"Wasn't us!" Aubin said. "Maybe someone after Stephen. He's rilin' some folks, talkin' up fer darkies—"

"Quiet!" his father yelled louder than ever. He added, as an afterthought, "Likely someone'll be draggin' out a body or two from the woods this afternoon."

Stephen drew an unhappy breath and lined up behind them for the wash basin. His eyes met Sarah's in a long, measured look, as if for reassurance.

Kate noticed her sister give him an almost imperceptible nod, then saw Stephen's look of relief. Once again she sensed that this was a dangerous place for Sarah to live. Twelve years ago, her sister had met Stephen in grade school in Independence. It was after his mother's death, when he'd lived with his old aunt who'd refused to take in Aubin and Rodwell because of their unruliness. Sarah and Stephen had courted for years, and when he returned to Weston, he'd planned to build her a house for a wedding present. Unfortunately, the plan had gone awry. Before the wedding, the river town of Weston had been the hemp capital of the world. Just after the wedding, the muddy Missouri had shifted its course a mile westward, abandoning the town entirely. The Bences had lost their slaves, their investment in two wharf warehouses, and most of their small hemp plantation. Only the family house and the outbuildings on a few acres remained.

As they made their way to the breakfast table, Sarah said to her father-in-law, "Don't forget, we'll be eating dinner in town with the Davisons after church."

"Eatin' with the Davisons?!" he yelled. "Them northerners! You never told me you was!"

"I did yesterday," Sarah replied. "Don't you remember?"

"Don't right now," Pa admitted, "but I remember other things. I'll niver in my life forgit what them abolitionists done, part o' it right here in town last year to John Doy!"

Kate darted a questioning glance at Stephen. "I never heard about it."

"John Doy, a Kansas Free Stater, was conductin' slaves on the Underground Railroad," her brother-in-law explained. "In Kansas, they were stopped by some slavers who nabbed Doy, his son, and the slaves, then brought them here to Weston. Had them locked in our jail."

"Tell 'er about thet jury!" Pa Bence put in angrily.

"Well, at first, the jury couldn't decide if Doy had kidnapped a slave or not," Stephen continued. "Finally they gave him five years in the Missouri Pen. Right after, the Kansans came over the river and sent a note to Doy to be ready at midnight. At midnight they rousted the jailer and told him they'd caught a famous horse thief. The jailer believed it and opened the jail front door. Well, the Kansans tied up the jailer—"

"Hog-tied 'em!" Pa Bence added with a vehemence that made Kate stiffen her spine.

"That they did," Stephen agreed. "Then they took Doy back to Kansas, and even had their picture taken with him for the newspapers, rubbing salt in the wounds here."

"Worst o' all," Pa Bence interjected, "thet jailer was my kin. I ain't gonna forgit it, makin' fun o' my kin. And thet's only the beginnin' o' troubles with abolitionists. Missouri men like me ain't gonna forgit! Abolitionists—especially Kansans—bring us nothin' but strife. Let's set and eat now!"

Kate decided not to say anything as she sat down in her chair. So far, her words had brought her nothing but strife too. What's more, endless aggravations existed on both sides, and it was clearly useless to argue with someone like Pa Bence.

After a moment, Sarah said, "I promise I told you about our being invited out for dinner. I've got ham for you, and potatoes and cornbread."

"Don't like yer goin'," Pa Bence objected.

"We already accepted their invitation," Stephen said. "You want me to tell them that my pa won't let me come?" He looked at his brothers. "Wouldn't everyone in Weston have a good time with that one! They'd be saying, 'Rodwell, does your daddy allow you to do this . . . Aubin, does your daddy allow you to do that?' Why, they'd laugh us out of town!"

His father frowned. "Well . . . all right this time, since it's decided, but no more o' thet visitin'. And don't get no idees from them Davisons." He heaped his plate with eggs, sausages, and cornbread. "And don't forgit we'll be needin' supper at home."

Sarah hesitated while she poured his coffee. "Supper's all made for you, too," she said, then moved on. "Fried chicken, potato salad, and that dried peach pie you like. We'll stay on for the church box supper social tonight."

"Ye won't be here tonight either?!" Pa Bence roared.

"Whooeeee!" Rodwell interrupted. "That means we kin go to church without hearin' hell and damnation . . . just buy a box supper and box a gal in! Maybe even a right pretty gal like Kate Talbot."

Kate winced, and Pa Bence's ire was momentarily suspended.

"If you buy a girl's box supper, you'll be expected to act decently," Sarah warned Rodwell. "Like a gentleman."

"One thang's sure," Rodwell said, forking up a fried egg yolk. "I ain't nothin' at all if I ain't a gentleman."

Aubin guffawed even harder, spewing cornbread crumbs from his mouth. "Then, Brother Rodwell, you ain't nothin' at all! And by now, Sister Sarah, you sure ought to know it!"

Pressing her lips together, Sarah headed for the stove with the coffeepot. Stephen's father was hollering again, and his brothers had gone from yammering to haranguing.

Kate kept her lips clamped shut.

Two horses pulled the farm wagon down the muddy lane, and Kate bumped beside Sarah and Stephen on the hard seat. Sarah had a firm grip on her Bible, reminding Kate that she hadn't even bothered to bring hers along from Independence. In the thick woods around them, there was no shooting now, she noted as they rode along the lane toward Weston Road. No bodies, either. Maybe it had just been hunters in the woods. She did feel, though, as if someone were staring at them from the house. Turning, she made a pretense of checking the box suppers in the wagon bed, then darted a look back toward the white two-story clapboard house.

Morning sunshine reflected off the rectangular windows of the austere dwelling, making it impossible to see inside. She felt certain, though, that at least one of the Bences must be watching.

She turned forward again. "Whew, it's warm," she said as she dropped the fringed white shawl from her shoulders.

Sarah let her shawl down, too, giving her a tight smile. "Mama would be glad to see us wearing her shawls."

"She would," Kate agreed. "She worked so hard to get them finished before Christmas." Bumping along on the wagon seat, she added, "Let's hope it's not too warm to spoil the fried chicken and potato salad in the box supper."

"They'll hold," Sarah answered. "I put chunks of ice around them. We get good winter pond ice here."

Stephen looked warm in his black Sunday suit, but perhaps because it made him appear dignified, he made no complaint.

The Bence woods around them were thick with dogwood, elm, hackberry, sugar maple, basswood, and walnut; at length, the wagon drove out into a clearing. Ahead, on the drier hills, stood burr oak, black oak, white oak, and hickories. No one was about, not even fellow travelers, and Kate felt calmer as they watched the horses bobbing along before them, mud slopping onto their legs.

Once they'd passed the second wooded section, Stephen looked out with them at the farms, some with high tobacco drying barns and some with low hemp-walk buildings. In the fields, tobacco plants grew in the rich loess soil scraped loose by ancient glaciers, and the plants had reached a fine height for mid-April.

"Seems like only yesterday the slaves were walking backwards on the hemp walk, makin' us miles of rope," Stephen reminisced. He flapped the reins over the horses and darted a guilty glance at Kate. "Expect you're disappointed in Weston, like everyone else. It sure wasn't like this before the river shifted west."

"Why, no, I'm not disappointed," she assured him. "I knew some of Weston's settlers had given up and left, but I didn't entirely know what to expect."

Stephen shook his head sadly. "We were gettin' more 'n more prosperous . . . buyin' land and slaves and investin' in wharf warehouses as if the riches wouldn't ever end. Platte County grew more hemp than any county in the whole country, and the Bences grew a good bit of Platte County's hemp."

Kate drew a long breath, then tried to appease him. "Weston has made great strides since the Platte Purchase."

"And that only twenty-three years back, in '37," he answered. "By '55, we had over five thousand people, lots of churches and schools, flour mills, a brewery and distillery, four hemp warehouses, tobacco presses, meat packers. . . ."

Sarah cast a worried glance at her husband, but he took no notice of it.

"Not to mention lots of outfitters for the wagons trains west," he continued. " 'Queen of the Platte Purchase,' they called Weston."

He felt guilty for not providing better for Sarah, Kate decided. Guilty, and letting all of the aggravation about it run around and around in his head.

"Even if it's some distance off now, Weston's still a beautiful sight when you're sailing by on the river," Kate said brightly. "Green and hilly . . . and all the red brick buildings clustered together in town. I heard that riverboat captains used the gold dome on the Presbyterian church as a landmark to steer by."

He nodded. "The church bell called stevedores and draymen to the wharves when a steamboat was comin' in, and the riverboats shipped our tobacco, tallow, hemp, pork, and wheat clear to New Orleans. In turn, we were investin' in warehouses and brown sugar, and doin' fine at it too. Why, steamboats stopped at our wharf and loaded hemp bales almost to the top of their smoke-stacks."

Kate had seen the hemp shipments at Wayne's Landing near Independence. "All of Missouri was proud of Platte County hemp," she said. "Just think how our whole country depended on it for rope."

Stephen looked somewhat gratified, then his long face returned to his defeated expression. "You see how matters changed. I feel bad, especially for Sarah. I promised her our own house as soon as we were married, and now all we can do is keep hopin' against hope that somehow things will change back."

"You mean that the river will turn back towards Weston?" Kate inquired. It seemed unlikely. Every year the Missouri shifted far-ther west. She hoped he wasn't deluding himself.

He shook his head. "No sense in hopin' for that. The state's talkin' new railroads, though, and that'd be a big help with shippin' goods. Anyhow, if things don't change back, Weston will end up a ghost town . . . a ghost town half-hidden in a pinched-up valley."

"I didn't have much time to think about Weston's troubles when I left Independence," she said to change the subject. "I had troubles myself. You'll never know how much I appreciate your taking me in."

He nodded. "Glad to help. It took some doin' on Sarah's part, but I finally come around to the way you see slavery. My family didn't treat our slaves too good, back when we had 'em, except tryin' to keep up their value. Anyhow, I admire your speakin' out about it."

Kate smiled at him gratefully. There was no sense in bringing up the question of how long she might have to stay with them. Her father thought it would be a few months before people's memories of her upbraiding the visiting preacher with her view of Scripture had dimmed.

As they rode on toward town, nothing further was mentioned about her visit, nor about the morning's gunshots. In the quiet she recalled accounts that described Weston as nestling in a small valley, guarded at its portals by picturesque high bluffs, and blessed with the richest agricultural land beyond Egypt's Nile Valley. Explorers like Marquette had taken their ease at the port while exploring the Missouri River, waxing eloquent over its sweet grasses, wild game and birds, and sparkling spring water. And the settlers from Virginia, Kentucky, and Tennessee had turned the old river port into a fine town, Kate thought. If it weren't for Stephen's family and the lack of a river, she would be pleased to live in Weston herself.

The small red brick church stood at the edge of town, its white steeple pointing skyward. Golden forsythia draped over the grasses at the edge of the nearby woods. A good many saddle horses and sturdier horses for wagons and buggies had already pulled up at the hitching posts, and worshippers greeted each other as they made their way to the building.

As Stephen drove up with the wagon, Kate saw curious stares turned on her. Fortunately their attention was diverted as a fine blood bay stallion trotted up to the hitching post, though the horse was of less interest than its rider. Kate thought she'd never seen a man quite so handsome. Beneath a fine head of dark blond hair that waved just onto his broad forehead was a well-chiseled face with a straight nose and strong chin. Most intriguing, however, were his cool silvery gray eyes and the amusement playing around his thin lips. He was in his latter twenties, she guessed. Thirty at most. She watched as he swung off the blood bay with careless ease, his eyes taking in everything and stopping on her.

She dropped her gaze immediately and smoothed the soft folds of her yellow dimity. When she glanced up, he had busied himself with the reins at the hitching post, but as he finished with the horse, he looked at her again. His smile was a startling white against his sun-browned skin, and he nodded most courteously.

"Good day," Stephen said to him, climbing down from the wagon to hitch their horses to the post.

The man returned his greeting cordially.

Sarah whispered from the seat beside her, "That's Charles McCourtney from Natchez, Mississippi. His family inherited a tobacco farm here when their old Uncle Namen died . . . not that they had need of it. They already own one of the finest plantations in Natchez. He's been coming to church here for most of the month, and half of the eligible girls in Weston and their mothers have an eye on him."

"It's surely understandable," Kate whispered back. "He doesn't look the type to shout 'Whooeeee' either."

Sarah almost laughed. "I daresay not. From what I hear, he's a refined gentleman."

When Stephen and Charles McCourtney finished speaking, Charles let his eyes stray back to Kate and Sarah. He gave them another nod. "May you have an enjoyable day, ladies," he said, then headed towards the church.

Kate nudged her sister. " 'Ladies,' he called us. Too bad he didn't see I was one of 'them sassy gals under these infernal good manners.' "

"Why, Katrina Elizabeth Talbot!" Sarah exclaimed. "I'm sure you wouldn't go after a man just because he was rich and handsome. Or would you?"

"The opportunity has never presented itself," Kate retorted with amusement. She had never "gone after" any man, with one exception, and she didn't intend to do so again. "And don't you dare let it be known that my given name is Katrina Elizabeth. I wouldn't want Rodwell to get hold of that piece of information. I can just hear him letting loose with endless streams of 'Whooeeee, Katrina Elizabeth! Whooeeee!' "

Sarah did laugh this time and, for a moment, she looked as lively as a girl. "I'll keep it for bribery, so you'd better watch out."

Stephen helped them down from the wagon, looking pleased himself. "What are you two carryin' on about?"

Sarah took his arm playfully. "Woman talk. You wouldn't be interested."

He grinned, then escorted them up the red brick walk to the church. "I'm not so sure of that. Never hurts a man to know what the womenfolk are thinkin'."

Kate and Sarah exchanged amused glances, and Kate was glad to see her sister happy again. She and Stephen looked so perfectly suited to each other.

Inside, the church was also red brick, and fronted by a

polished black walnut altar. Sunshine slanted through the small stained glass windows, turning the walnut pews a golden brown. At the pump organ to the left of the pulpit, a thin woman played a familiar hymn. As they headed up the middle aisle, Sarah gave a discreet wave to a pretty blonde woman, who smiled and returned the wave with a gloved hand. Beside her, a narrow-shouldered gentleman nodded most genially. Very likely Greta Davison and her dentist husband, with whom they'd have dinner after church, Kate decided.

While Stephen waited, Kate made her way into the pew, followed by Sarah. Kate looked up front, her eyes lighting on the hymn name and number chalked on the song board to the right of the pulpit.

She was startled to see a clearly abolitionist hymn, "Once to Every Man and Nation," listed; it was not one she expected to hear in the very heart of "little Dixie," where so many settlers had come from the South. Moreover, everyone knew that James Russell Lowell, author of the words, stood strongly against slavery. No one seemed to object, though, and Kate sang out with the others,

Once to every man and nation,
Comes the moment to decide,
In the strife of truth with falsehood
For the good or evil side;
Some great cause, God's new Messiah,
Offering each the bloom or blight,
And the choice goes by forever,
'Twixt that darkness and that light.

She realized that Charles McCourtney was seated just across the aisle from her and that he watched her from the corner of his eye. Was he a Christian? If so, he surely must see the wrongs in slavery. On the other hand, pastors in the South were said to be using the Bible itself to justify the institution of slavery.

McCourtney's deep baritone filled the space between them, and Kate sang on with growing unease. Despite her outspokenness, every once in a while she had gnawing doubts. Did she have the entire truth about slavery? Here in Missouri, most farmers worked alongside their slaves in the fields. Some might call the local farms "plantations" to sound pretentious, but none she knew of in the region were entirely self-supporting like the true plantations of the deep South.

The minister stepped up to the pulpit to make the announcements, including one about the box supper at five o'clock, and Kate only hoped that Rodwell wouldn't come to "box a gal in," as he'd put it.

While the minister finished the announcements, her mind rushed on. Would Charles McCourtney deign to attend such a simple entertainment as a box supper? He was probably more accustomed to extravagant balls in Natchez and New Orleans, with hoop-skirted Southern belles in attendance.

Glancing sideways, she caught him watching her again and felt oddly pleased. Not that she'd ever be interested in a Mississippi planter—nor any other big plantation man, for that matter. It was only that he might make her visit to Weston more interesting, she told herself. Moreover, God might use her to influence Charles McCourtney against slavery, as Sarah had done with Stephen. After all, with God it was said that all things were possible.

The minister launched into a mighty sermon from the thirty-seventh psalm. "Fret not thyself because of evildoers, nor be thou envious against the workers of iniquity. For they shall soon be cut down like the grass, and wither as the green grass. . . ."

To her relief, the sermon was clearly against slavery. She half-expected Charles McCourtney to rise with indignation at the admonitions, but he did not. To her amazement, he appeared to be in total agreement.

2

After the service they made their way from the church, and Sarah introduced Kate to the departing worshippers in the churchyard. Everyone was kindly and welcoming, but several of the women eyed Sarah with concern, making Kate wonder again if something in the Bence household were even more amiss than she thought.

The onlookers had also noted her introduction to Dr. Davison and his wife, Greta, and Greta's cheerful "We'll see you at our house shortly." But the Davisons had been cordial to the Southerner, Charles McCourtney, too.

Now a little grandmotherly woman with gray hair and rosy cheeks spoke to Sarah. "Why don't you ever come into town to our Ladies' Church Circle, Miz Bence? It'd be a pure pleasure for us to get to know you better."

Sarah appeared flustered. "I'd truly like to, Mrs. Minton, but I've been so busy."

"Now that your sister's visiting, might be you can come tomorrow," Mrs. Minton added. She eyed Sarah as if her words held a hidden meaning, then added, "We sew and, when we're able, we like to . . . encourage each other the best we can."

Sarah cast a nervous glance at Stephen, who gave her a

surreptitious nod. "Kate and I—" Sarah's voice came out too loudly and she modulated it. "We'll surely try to come. Thank you."

"Tomorrow at two, then," Mrs. Minton said with another significant look. "We're meeting for tea at my house this week, instead of at the church."

What lurked under the polite invitation? Kate wondered. What was little Mrs. Minton saying to Sarah? Or was it only her imagination running away with her?

Strangely, Kate recalled an appeal made by the famous abolitionist, Angela Grimke, to "all Christian women of the Southern states." She had beseeched them to persuade every man of their acquaintance that slavery was a crime against God and man, and she urged immediate action. Women who owned slaves should free them at once, begin to pay them for their work, and educate them, whether it was against the law or not. Even Sarah had converted her husband from his pro-slavery bent, Kate reflected. She herself had made no converts yet with her reckless talk.

As she turned, she overheard the worried voices of the menfolk. "What about last night's shootin's over in Kansas?" one was asking. "You hear about that?"

"Burned down a barn, too, they say," another man replied. He was small in stature and appeared to be Mrs. Minton's husband, for she took his arm and he patted her hand.

"Don't like it," he added. "Missourians striking back fer last week's rampage on our side, I expect. Kansas newspapers will be calling us 'Missouri fiends' again, and ours will be blastin' them as 'Kansas redlegs' and 'jayhawkers.' "

"If you ask me, the newspapers only inflame border ruffians into more fightin'," a puffy-eyed man said, "and some of them ruffians got no more convictions than a hog. They just like ridin' around shootin' . . . and worse."

The Bences came to mind, and a shiver passed up Kate's back. Stephen must have thought of them too, for he glanced at Sarah with dismay. "It's the same now in Independence," Kate assured them. "Only there, merchants are trying to dampen the newspaper's fervor."

"Why's that?" Mr. Minton inquired.

"They hope to avoid secession," she explained.

"Your father has a mercantile in Independence, doesn't he?" Mr. Minton asked. "The big mercantile."

Kate nodded. "He does."

"Well, can't blame him for trying to quiet the newspapers," someone else said. "It's more than lives lost in a war. Store goods, houses, animals, everything. I hear the insurance companies are even checking merchants' political leanings. Matters would be a lot worse if Missouri didn't have hard currency."

Their words drifted away as Kate noticed Charles McCourtney riding toward them on his fine blood bay. It struck her that the slave-owning opposition was in their very midst. Yet he seemed perfectly guileless, even honorable and innocent. Perhaps he was one of the slave owners who was kind to his slaves and treated them with dignity, she thought. After all, not all slave owners were evil.

"Good day, ladies," he said in his deep southern voice. "Good day, gentlemen."

"Good day," several replied.

Kate merely nodded pleasantly.

After he'd ridden on, one of the men remarked, "Blamed plantation owner's son, even if he does come to church and have fine manners."

Was it possible that this church in "little Dixie" was a pocket of abolitionists? Kate wondered. First the abolitionist sermon, now all of this talk.

"McCourtney's selling off his uncle's slaves," the puffy-eyed man said, "but some say he's got other reasons to be here too. He's been askin' a powerful lot of questions—"

Mr. Minton interrupted. "We heard there was shooting this morning over your way, Stephen. In your front woods."

"Probably hunters," Stephen replied uneasily. "More rabbits than usual this spring. We do a lot of huntin' ourselves."

"Awful lot of huntin' going on nowadays on other folks's property," another man put in. "Expect it's got more to do with huntin' rebels and abolitionists than with cookin' up rabbit stew."

Stephen took a firm hold on Sarah's elbow. "If you'll excuse us," he said, "we'd best be goin' along now. Friends are waitin' dinner for us."

"Careful you don't get blown to kingdom come during the main course at the Davisons'," one man half-joked.

Others gave thin laughs, making Kate feel even more uneasy. There had been a strange undertone to the entire exchange. What was going on?

As Stephen helped her and Sarah into the wagon, he muttered, "I'd be a sight happier if people would talk about anything else. Bad enough to live in a divided family without gettin' hammered on after church, too."

"It'll be a fine dinner," Sarah promised, setting her Bible on her lap. "You just wait and see. Greta does things so well, and her husband seems very pleasant. It will be nice for Kate to meet them too."

"Maybe we shouldn't be goin'," Stephen countered. "Pa doesn't like it at all."

"We told them we'd come," Sarah protested. "We accepted their invitation, and they're expecting us."

"I just hope we won't be sorry about it in the end," Stephen answered, then headed for the hitching post.

Kate asked her sister, "Are you good friends with Mrs. Davison? You've never mentioned her in your letters."

"New friends," Sarah answered with hesitation. "I visited her for tea last week."

She darted a nervous glance at Stephen, who was unhitching the horses and conversing with another man. "Stephen thinks it's good for me to get out of the house now and again so I won't be so lonely for womenfolk."

"It's surely a good idea," Kate answered, uneasy for her sister. After a while she remarked, "It was nice of the Davisons to invite me, especially since I arrived here so suddenly. How did Mrs. Davison happen to know I was here?"

"I suppose Stephen's father let it out when he went drinking," Sarah said. "Remember, he rode into town the night you arrived? It—it's hard to predict what he'll say when he's been drinking. Nothing would surprise me."

Stephen climbed up on the wagon seat with them, and Sarah quieted immediately.

Moments later, they were riding along. Kate looked about with interest at the town, since she'd arrived at the Parkville River Landing some distance away. Years ago she'd seen Weston from a riverboat, back when it was the second-most important port west of the Mississippi. Even then, most of the frontier log buildings had been replaced by red brick structures, giving it a civilized appearance. Now the warehouses and the livery stable— once near the wharf—stood over a mile away from the river, as did Heileiman Blacksmith and Harness on Thomas Street. The small hotels, saloons, and mercantiles also looked forsaken.

"It's a fine town," she remarked to fill the silence, "a town worth saving."

"That's what the Davisons say, too," Sarah replied. "They're bent on staying here to raise their children, no matter what happens."

As they passed the large three-story International Hotel, a few saddle horses and a horse and buggy waited at the front door. Several fashionable visitors stood out on its top balcony.

"Built by our famous Ben Holiday," Stephen told her. "You know, the man who started the Pony Express. Hotel used to be the biggest on the Missouri River west of St. Louis. Now it's barely gettin' by. Beyond it, that three-story brick building is the high school, which has lost a good many students."

"Sad," Kate said. "It's so sad to see things go downhill."

"Sad, all right," he allowed.

No one replied, and he said, almost to himself, "I'm torn in both directions—sometimes toward leavin' like so many of the others, and sometimes toward stayin'."

Before long they approached a residential section, and Stephen whoa'ed the horses in front of a charming red brick bungalow. It was larger than most of the nearby houses and surrounded by sloping lawns and fine trees. In back, by the outbuildings, stood a smaller brick house.

"Slave quarters?" Kate asked Sarah.

Her sister shook her head. "No, they hire free blacks. You'll like the Davisons. Dr. Davison was the army dentist for the soldiers over at Fort Leavenworth for a few years and admired Weston so much that he bought tracts of land and built this house here."

"An army dentist? A Yankee?"

Stephen helped them down from the buggy, and Sarah uttered with humor, "A Yankee."

"He must be heartily disliked," Kate remarked.

"No, everyone seems to like Dr. Davison," her sister answered. "I've never heard a bad word said against him."

Stephen turned a wry smile on them. "Probably folks are scared to speak out against him in case they need their teeth pulled."

Kate gave a laugh.

As they started up the red brick walkway, Dr. Davison opened the front door. "Welcome!" he called out to them heartily. "Come in! Come in!"

He was a fine-looking man of medium height, with lively brown eyes, a patrician nose, and dark wavy hair. He was likely part Welsh, judging by his name, and possibly some French, judging by his appearance.

In the large foyer, Dr. Davison greeted each of them with genuine interest. Then he turned toward the sound of footsteps hurrying down the stairs. "Ah, here comes my Greta," he said as his lovely blonde wife arrived. "She was seeing to the children."

Greta Davison was as fair as her husband was dark. Her blonde hair was fashioned into a stylish French twist, and her blue eyes sparkled. "We're so pleased you could come," she said with a slight Dutch accent. After exchanging further pleasantries, Greta hesitated, then remarked with a warning glance, "I have such interesting guests for you to meet today. Won't you come in?"

Kate caught a glimpse of the distant parlor, which was as fine a room as one could find in Independence. The dark wooden floor and dark furniture were brightened by a Persian rug on the floor and blue damask draperies hung by the windows. Lustrous blue upholstery covered the sofa, where two other guests sat—one of them Charles McCourtney!

As she stepped into the room, he rose to his feet, as did another young man with bright blond hair. The second man was not quite as striking in appearance, but was nonetheless fine-looking. They both wore black broadcloth suits and vests, and white linen shirts with high stocks around their necks.

"May I introduce you lovely ladies to Mr. Charles McCourtney and his newly-arrived stepbrother, Mr. Andrew Kendall, whose parents own the Beaumont Plantation in Natchez, Mississippi," Dr. Davison said rather formally.

Another slave owner! Kate thought, though Andrew Kendall did have a pleasant demeanor.

"They're distant cousins on my mother's side," Dr. Davison explained. "The fair-haired side of my family, I might add." He smiled wryly at his wife. "There's a streak in my family that's drawn to blonde women."

"*Und vhy not?*" Greta asked, thickening her Dutch accent playfully.

They all chuckled.

"This is Miss Kate Talbot of Independence, who is visiting her sister and brother-in-law," Dr. Davison continued.

Once the introductions were concluded, Kate seated herself on a blue parlor chair. From what she had gathered, the Davisons were abolitionists—and here they sat in the fine parlor with the sons of a plantation owner. She wondered what such different hosts and guests might discuss, and was not too surprised to hear them begin with the spring weather and the crops. As they spoke, Kate glanced again at the furnishings and noted a bouquet of purple lilacs in a crystal vase on the pianoforte, filling the parlor with their sweet perfume.

Before long a plump, middle-aged Negress came into the parlor, followed by a thin, furrow-browed Negro man of a similar age. Freed blacks, Sarah had said. There were a good many in Missouri, and abolitionists were the ones most likely to hire them.

"Here are Penelopa and Alfron," Greta said with enthusiasm. "And just in time, too. Everyone must be as famished as I feel."

The servants, nicely dressed in black uniforms, appeared hesitant, then gave polite nods. Penelopa carried a silver tray with goose liver pâté on crackers, and Alfron's tray held a stack of crystal plates and small cups of pink punch. Penelopa possessed a kindly manner, and as she approached Kate, her dark eyes brightened. "If you please, ma'am," she said, the tray shaking slightly.

"You must all try Penelopa's goose liver pâté," Greta Davison suggested. "She's the very best cook in the entire state of Missouri."

Penelopa shook her head. "Oh no, ma'am!" she protested.

"Well, we think so," Greta said.

Kate began to feel nervous herself. "Then I shall have to try some." She took a small crystal plate from the tray and helped herself to the pâté-spread crackers.

Penelopa nodded formally.

Taking a bite of the goose liver pâté and cracker, Kate noticed that both Charles McCourtney and Andrew Kendall watched her with undue interest, and wondered why. It seemed unlikely that they'd have heard about her reason for leaving Independence.

Penelopa moved on, stepping between Kate and the men to serve Sarah and Greta. Alfron stopped before Kate, offering the pink punch. As she looked up at him, his eyes filled with consternation, and she quickly helped herself to a cup of punch.

Once everyone had been served, Penelopa and Alfron made another round with the pâté and punch, then Alfron announced as stiffly as if he were a British butler, "Dinnah will be served in half an hour."

Kate felt uneasy, but the others were remarking about the excellent pâté and the pleasures of Southern cooking. She glanced at Greta Davison, who still appeared nervous. Upstairs, small children laughed merrily, and Greta quickly turned to the sound. Of course—a mother concerned about her children and the dinner, that's all it was, Kate decided.

"I hope you can tell us about what's happening in Independence, Miss Talbot," Charles McCourtney said to her.

She replied rather abruptly, "No more than one reads in the newspapers."

He gave her a broad smile, not at all rebuffed. "Perhaps I'll go by Independence on my way home to see for myself." He held Kate's gaze with his. "I wasn't aware that Missouri had such charming young ladies. I expect there's a good deal more for me to learn about your splendid state."

Kate managed a pleasant nod at him. Best to be courteous to these Southerners if she was to convert any of them. After all, they couldn't help how they'd been raised. Moreover, as much as she hated to admit it, Charles McCourtney's attention was downright pleasurable.

Greta Davison's nervous manner continued as they made their way to the dining room, though she did grow calmer once they were seated at the finely-appointed table and her husband had said grace.

When Kate opened her eyes, she caught the southern men observing her over a vase of yellow tulips. Heat rushed to her cheeks, and she looked down at her daintily flowered plate on the white cutwork linen tablecloth.

"Well, Miss Talbot," Charles McCourtney said, "it appears that Cousin Greta has chosen her centerpiece to complement your lovely yellow dimity dress."

Greta spoke quickly. "I'm afraid not. I just met Miss Talbot at church this morning, so there was no way for me to know what she might wear."

Charles turned his handsome smile on their hostess. "Ah, but you ladies seem to have an innate sense for knowing about such things. At least, our Mississippi ladies do."

"May I inquire how you happen to know about dimity?" Greta asked him, her cheeks dimpling.

"Our mother is a font of information about fabrics and clothing," he answered without hesitation, then turned to smile again at Kate. "And we have three sisters, not to mention numerous cousins and nieces."

"And seamstresses always on hand," Andrew added with a meaningful glance at his stepbrother.

"Yes, of course, seamstresses," Charles replied smoothly.

At least Charles was a welcome change from the young men of Independence and the louts in Stephen's family, Kate decided. More important, he was not too enticing for her to resist. She followed Sarah's lead, complimenting their hostess on the flowered china, hand-worked tablecloth, gleaming silver, and French crystal.

For dinner, the fish course was Spanish mackerel, followed by a saddle of lamb entree, with carrots, greens, biscuits, and roasted potatoes. As they ate, Kate remained courteous but quiet, giving Charles McCourtney's questions about life in Independence only polite responses.

Yes, Independence was a diverse place, she agreed. Yes, it was in a sense like the Far West since it was close to the Santa Fe Trail, which had brought in Mexicans, Spaniards, Indians, French Canadians, and Germans.

"I understand your Negroes in Independence own slaves themselves," he remarked easily.

"Some do," she replied. "For example, Hiram Young, who bought his own freedom by whittling ox bows. Now he buys slaves, and they work for him until they earn enough to buy their own freedom. Then Hiram takes that money and buys more slaves. It's a revolving fund, and a number of slaves attain freedom."

"Are all of your Negro slave owners like that?" he asked.

"No," she conceded. "He is an exception."

It occurred to her that if she made trouble in Weston, there was no place to flee to, except perhaps to Grandfather Talbot's in California—an appalling notion. Independence was her home, and she would return to it. The thought of her predicament was enough to curb her tongue, at least momentarily.

For dessert, cider cake and black walnut pie were served with thick cream. After Penelopa and Alfron left the dining room, Dr. Davison asked Charles McCourtney, "How have the townsmen been treating you?"

"The Southern sympathizers have been very kind, sir," Charles answered in his deep voice, then he smiled wryly at Kate. "With a few lamentable exceptions, even the others have generally treated me better than I anticipated."

Kate forked up a bit of the delicious black walnut pie and tried to ignore him.

"And you, Andrew?" Dr. Davison asked.

"I've only been here two days, not long enough for Westonians to take much note of my presence," he replied. "I've spent all of my time on Uncle Namen Ormond's farm, making final arrangements for its sale."

His voice softened and his blue eyes darted to Kate. "Not that I wouldn't like to become better . . . well, better acquainted with some . . . umm . . . people here."

Pretending not to understand, Kate sipped her coffee.

When she darted a glance at them, she noticed that Charles McCourtney was hard put to keep from laughing at his stepbrother's ineptness. Even Sarah and Stephen watched the interchange.

Once they'd finished their dessert and coffee, Greta suggested to Sarah, "Wouldn't you and Kate like to come upstairs to visit with the children before their naps?"

"Yes, I should like to see them again," Sarah responded. "And Kate loves children too."

"Then, gentlemen, if you'll excuse us, we'll leave you to your cigars and brandy," Greta told them, rising from the table. "Take your time, and we'll read to the children."

The men came to their feet, Stephen somewhat belatedly, and Kate knew the Southerners were watching her as she left the dining room. As they started up the stairs, she overheard Charles ask Stephen, "Would it be seemly for me to invite your lovely sister-in-law to go out carriage riding?"

Stephen's answer was curt. "You'd have to ask her."

She heard Dr. Davison laugh. "I thought that might be the way the wind was blowing. I saw you watching her at church this morning. A man who starts watching a young lady in church is asking for wedlock. At least, that's what happened to me."

The men chuckled and spoke on pleasantly.

At the top of the stairs, Sarah whispered to Kate, "You've certainly captured yourself a new admirer."

"Two, I'd say," Greta said as she hurried along behind them. "Not that I blame them. Kate, you're a beauty. I can't imagine why you're still unmarried."

"Kate's had her chances," Sarah explained, "but the right man hasn't appeared yet. At least, not one right enough to suit her."

Greta laughed. "Just as I suspected."

"Only once I thought she was smitten," Sarah added.

Only once, Kate remembered, and now Albert Morton was dead. Ridden off two years ago for the great Rocky Mountain gold rush because gold had lured him more than she could. Worst of all, after spending most of her school years with him, she'd been so certain he'd return for her.

She shook her head at the two women. "Why do married women always have to be such matchmakers? In any event, I'm not sure I would be interested in Southern men."

"Not even such handsome ones?" Greta teased.

Kate tried to hide her smile. "Not even such handsome ones."

Upstairs, the children's room took up half of the bungalow's second story, though it held only two beds and a crib. Lacy curtains hung over the three dormer windows to the cushioned window seats, under which were bookshelves. Other shelves held a fine collection of dolls and buggies and numerous other toys.

"What an enchanting room," Kate remarked. "It looks like an illustration from a nursery rhyme book."

"Exactly the effect we hoped for," Greta replied with pleasure, admiring it herself. She straightened a crocheted bed coverlet over a pink satin bedspread. "We want the girls to have a wonderful childhood. This world offers trouble enough when one grows older."

The three girls—dark-haired Marie-Elena, blonde Lucinda, and tiny brown-haired Olivia—were even more charming than the room. They curtsied for Kate and Sarah, then took them by the hand to show off their doll house and its miniature fixtures, furniture, and draperies.

After a while, Greta suggested, "Let's read something from *Grimm's Fairy Tales* before you girls have your naps."

"Snow White! Snow White!" Marie-Elena called out, and the others chorused it with her.

"Snow White it is," Greta agreed, fetching the book from the bookshelves. "A fine story demonstrating both good and evil. Perhaps Sarah or Kate will read it to you."

"Kate's our family's reader," Sarah told them. "Our younger sisters and brothers never get enough of her reading. She has such a dramatic bent."

"Then Kate it is," Greta said. "If she's willing."

Pleased at the accolade, Kate gave a nod and took the book. "Let's sit on the bed," she suggested.

The girls hurried onto the bed with her, their eyes sparkling with anticipation. Once they were settled, Kate looked through the book's table of contents and found "Snow White." Before long, she read, "It was the middle of winter, and snowflakes were falling like feathers from the sky. In a far-off land the Queen sat at a window of her palace. . . ."

Kate kept the girls' rapt attention. When she finished, they wanted another story, but it was time for their naps. Finally they were tucked into bed. "You sleep well," she told them. "I'll see you again."

In the hallway, Greta put a finger to her lips and led Kate and Sarah into the sewing room. Greta closed the door behind them and stood against it, then took a deep breath. "I have something to tell you. I don't know quite how to begin, except I know you both share our abolitionist sympathies. An . . . unusual situation has arisen here in Weston."

"An unusual situation?" Sarah repeated.

Greta nodded. "You'll keep this in confidence, no matter how you decide?"

"Yes, of course," Kate and Sarah agreed, almost as one.

Greta began cautiously. "You know there are people who help slaves escape to the North, some as far as Canada, to find homes where they can earn their own way and make new lives for themselves."

Kate darted a glance at Sarah, and they both nodded.

"Well-organized groups arrange such passages at the peril of their own lives," Greta continued. "When there's need, they help to guide these poor unfortunates out of slavery. In our eyes, it seems the only way we can make amends for this scourge on our country."

"Do you mean to say that you and Dr. Davison are part of the Underground Railroad?" Sarah asked with amazement.

Greta eyed them carefully, then nodded. "As you probably know, there are 'stations' along the way through much of our country where escaping slaves are fed and sheltered until another 'conductor' meets them and guides them to the next station, and eventually to freedom in Canada."

"What about the Fugitive Slave Law?" Sarah asked. "The penalties are dire if you so much as conceal slaves, let alone rescue them from their owners!"

Greta nodded. "The danger is great, not only for us but for our daughters. It takes people of strong conscience to be in such a movement . . . people who are convinced that owning another person is absolutely unacceptable."

"What brings you to such a strong conviction?" Kate asked their hostess.

Greta closed her eyes for an instant, then opened them and looked at Kate. "I ask for your complete confidence in this, too."

When they agreed, Greta pressed her lips together, then spoke with difficulty. "Several men in my family are Dutch sea captains. For two generations now, they've transported slaves from Africa to this country. As if that isn't reason enough, the fact is that I . . . have kin who are far darker than I."

They stared at her, appalled. In Kate's case, as was true of her entire family, the leaning toward abolition came from knowing both slaves and free Negroes in Independence, and simply concluding that slavery was wrong. The fact that Greta had slaver sea captains in her family—and mulatto kin!—was not only shocking, but good reason to be in the Underground Railroad movement.

"I'd like the two of you to consider being part of the movement," Greta added, tears in her eyes.

Kate's knees felt weak, and she lowered herself onto the window seat. Before her sister could speak, she asked, "If we do help, what would we be required to do?"

"We need someone to take Penelopa and Alfron to the border to a Kansas ferry that will be waiting tonight."

"Penelopa and Alfron!" Kate whispered. It was no wonder Greta and the two servants had been so nervous.

"I've kept them here for several months," Greta said, still standing against the door. "So long, in fact, that the neighbors seem to think they are free blacks in our employ, which is indeed how we treat them. Unfortunately the usual conductor who helps to move people isn't available now. We'd also like to free some of the slaves who'll be chained up at Halfway House tonight."

"What is Halfway House?" Kate inquired.

"An inn out in the country, a fiercely raucous place where they hold slaves who are being transported while the overseers or owners sleep upstairs," Greta explained. "A place of poor repute, as might be expected."

Sarah asked, "Would there be slaves who belonged to your Southern guests' uncle?"

Greta nodded. "Yes, we expect some from his hemp farm to be there."

"How many all together?" Sarah asked.

"Most nights five or six are manacled in the cave under Halfway House. We'll also be freeing those from the Namen Ormond estate, and Penelopa and Alfron," Greta replied. "Maybe twelve all together. We'd not only be freeing them, but diverting everyone's attention from Penelopa and Alfron while we're at it."

She and Sarah could be jailed for aiding fugitive slaves, Kate thought. She might have spoken out recklessly against slavery in Independence, but she'd never done anything this perilous.

Sarah sat down on the window seat with her, equally disconcerted. "I don't know, what with Stephen's father and brothers being so rabidly pro-slavery, and with so many in the North not truly wanting the blacks. . . ."

"I'm sorry to say that's true," Greta admitted.

A troubled glimmer came to Sarah's eyes. "I'm not sure what to do. I'm torn one way, then the other. How soon must you know?"

"In the next few hours," Greta replied.

"The next few hours!" Sarah echoed.

Greta nodded.

"Then I'd best discuss it with Stephen while we're still here at your house," Sarah said. "But how?"

"Perhaps you can ask him to come up here to the sewing room, to show him something you'd like to have arranged in your house," Greta suggested. "The window seat . . . or the sewing box which my husband so cleverly designed."

"I-I'll tell Stephen I'd like a window seat like this," Sarah said. "It's true. It would be handy for sewing."

Greta turned to Kate. "And you, Kate? How do you feel about it? What will you do?"

Despite all of the dangers, Kate felt a growing conviction to put her words into action. "I'd like to help if I can."

"What will we be expected to do?" Sarah inquired.

"One of our friends will unchain the slaves," Greta said. "It would be our job to get them from there to a particular ferry."

"In the middle of the night?" Sarah asked.

"Yes. Two o'clock. It's a job to be done in darkness. In the midst of it, we need a woman to send into the tavern as a decoy in case any men are still up. Then while she's distracting them, we'll get the slaves away."

"But the men hereabouts would know me," Sarah objected.

"Yes, they would," Greta replied. She turned to Kate. "That's why we're hoping you'll do it, Kate. We have a black wig and lip rouge . . . and a rather showy frock. If you decide to do this, the frock is already packaged to give to you when you leave. You wouldn't be alone in the effort, and you'd be protected as best we can."

Kate felt her mouth drop open. "I'd be a tavern decoy?"

"Yes, exactly," Greta answered. "I know it's unsavory, but it's the only way we can see to do it."

Kate's mind flew to the tavern wenches in Independence, not that there were many with the wagon trail falling into disuse. It would be an interesting drama to undertake, that much was certain. She would have to improvise on the spot.

"Our parents would be furious if I allowed her to do it!" Sarah protested. "I feel responsible for Kate. That's why our parents sent her to me."

"I'm twenty years old, Sarah," Kate said with mounting courage. "I'm responsible for myself. What's more, I'm not so certain Mama and Poppa would be furious. They're not as outspoken as I am, but they do their part."

Sarah stared at her with uncertainty and, while Kate had a chance, she turned to Greta. "My role would be merely acting a part."

"Precisely," Greta answered. "You might say we'll put you into a drama for a few minutes, then take you out as fast as we can."

"I believe I could do it," Kate decided.

Sarah still looked worried. "It's true that you've always carried off ruses well, Kate. The best in our family, for that matter, but I don't know. . . ." She turned to Greta, "What will happen if we don't do this . . . assignment?"

"Penelopa and Alfron might not escape. Some people are already suspicious about them, so suspicious they're ready to flee to Kansas on their own, which is far more dangerous. It's taken an effort to hold them here this past week."

The worst that could happen was giving up her time and comfort, Kate thought, and the best, she'd have a memorable adventure while achieving something she believed in. "I'll do it," she decided. "I've been talking like an abolitionist, now I'll act the part."

"I should warn you, there are risks," Greta said.

Kate nodded. "I'm willing to take them."

Greta looked relieved and turned to Sarah. "We'd also need you and Stephen, and your wagon. If you and Stephen decide to help, it would be judicious for you to drive over to Halfway House this afternoon to study the lay of the land."

"I'll ask him, then," Sarah replied. "Does he know of this at all?"

Greta nodded her blonde head. "He does. He was invited to take part in it yesterday."

"No wonder he's been acting so nervous," Sarah said, wide-eyed. "We've never kept secrets from each other! Who asked him?"

"It's best for everyone not to know too much about the others involved," Greta answered. "That's why Stephen didn't tell you. What we needed was for both of you to hear our plans this afternoon, and once you'd decided how you felt about it, to ask him for the final decision."

"Then we've accomplished the first part," Kate said.

"Yes, the beginning is more or less accomplished," Greta said. "It complicated matters when I had to invite Charles and Andrew, but Charles hinted so strongly for an invitation after church last week that I gave in. There was no avoiding it for today, with him leaving shortly."

"Let's go downstairs before I lose my nerve," Sarah said. "I feel so overwrought, I don't see how you can—"

"One grows accustomed to it," Greta assured her, "though I've been nervous with Charles and Andrew here for dinner. We'd better go down now or they'll wonder about us."

How often did the Davisons take part in slave escapes? Kate thought as they made their way down the stairs. Likely it was better not to ask anything further about it.

When they arrived in the parlor, the men came to their feet, Charles and Andrew from the blue damask sofa. Kate seated herself near them on a yellow parlor chair, thinking it might be a good time to create a small diversion right here in the parlor. She smiled encouragingly at the two of them, and they responded with surprised interest.

They scarcely noticed when Sarah said to Stephen, "I wonder if you'd come up to see the window seat in Greta's sewing room. She told me I might show you. It's so clever, with compartments for storage right under the seat."

Stephen raised his brows with husbandly patience and rose from his chair. "Then I'll have to see it, won't I?"

As he and Sarah started for the stairway, Kate lifted her dark lashes and smiled again at Charles and Andrew. "It is a pleasure to be in the company of such well-mannered Southern gentlemen," she said. "I do wish Northern men had your fine manners."

"It's our honor to be in the presence of such a beautiful young lady," Charles McCourtney returned smoothly.

Andrew made no reply, but watched her with surprise and renewed interest.

Charles was far too handsome, she thought again, while Andrew seemed more the sort of man who might be a fine friend.

"Did you enjoy the children, Kate?" Dr. Davison asked her.

"I did," she replied in all honesty. "They are as dear as can be." So dear it seemed a wonder the Davisons might endanger not only themselves but their daughters.

"Kate read to them ever so beautifully," Greta said. "They couldn't have been more pleased. If I hadn't tucked them in most firmly, poor Kate would still be up there reading."

"I have a good many younger brothers and sisters," Kate explained. "I do enjoy children."

Not surprisingly, both men returned her smile.

Dr. Davison turned to Charles. "Have you decided how long you'll be staying in Weston?"

"Only a few more days, until we conclude Uncle Namen's affairs. We hope to be done before a full moon."

"Before a full moon?" Kate asked. "That seems a strange way to time one's departure."

Charles gave her a wry nod. "We understand that your border ruffians like to ride by a full moon. Even at home, it's a time when our people become more riled and there's apt to be uprisings." He hesitated. "But that's an unpleasant subject for ladies. At any rate, we sold off a good many slaves yesterday. They'll be traveling downriver in the morning."

"To your plantation in Natchez?" Greta inquired.

"No. Most were a bit too long in the tooth for Beaumont," he replied regretfully. "Our need there is usually for younger, strong field hands. These were older. I fear we rejected all on that count."

Were families broken up? Kate wondered. And what would happen to them, now that they were old? She glanced at Andrew, and was glad to see even more regret in his expression.

Dr. Davison rose from his chair. "I should have gone upstairs to explain the workings of that window seat to Stephen. If you'll excuse me—"

Greta said, "Only the town dentist could be so interested in details, but I'm grateful that he is. Now, gentlemen, do tell us more about your families."

It seemed that Andrew's mother had first married Dr. Kendall, Andrew's father. When the doctor died of cholera, Charles's father, a long-time admirer of Mrs. Kendall and a widower with a small son, had proposed.

"It may sound boastful, but Mother is surely the most beautiful lady in Natchez," Andrew said.

"I wouldn't go that far," Charles protested. "There are some mighty beautiful younger women in Natchez, though none to compare with the present company."

Kate had to smile, and Greta put in, "Southern gentlemen are so gallant, but I will say that we ladies do enjoy it."

Before long, Sarah, Stephen, and Dr. Davison made their way down the steps and into the parlor. Stephen gave Kate an almost imperceptible nod, making her swallow hard. They were going to attempt it! They were going to free slaves!

"I see I have my work cut out for me," Stephen was saying, carrying the matter off very well. "It's a good sewin' room idea for Sarah, havin' a window seat with light comin' over her shoulder."

"Greta and Penelopa find it a fine arrangement," Dr. Davison replied. He laughed at Charles and Andrew's curious expressions. "It's easy to see that you gentlemen are unmarried. It's amazing, the jobs we encounter."

Charles and Andrew smiled indulgently. "We do have women-folk back at Beaumont," Charles replied in a wry tone, "and they are known to let their wants be clearly heard, often more insistently than one might hope."

Everyone chuckled, and Andrew added, "Yes, womenfolk do seem to have a special eye for convenience."

"Well, we'd best be goin'," Stephen said, "if you'll excuse us."

On the way to the front door, Kate thought Stephen must have learned his good manners from his old aunt back in Independence, for he turned to Greta and Dr. Davison with confidence. "We can't thank you enough for the fine dinner and the fine company. We don't get out often, and we appreciate your kindness."

As Sarah expressed her gratitude, Kate noticed that two developments were taking place on either side of her. By the door, Stephen was accepting a brown parcel . . . probably the showy frock Greta had mentioned, and to Kate's right, Charles McCourtney and Andrew Kendall were making their way toward the door.

She turned to the two Mississippi men with haste. "Gentlemen, I bid you farewell."

Andrew took her hand and kissed it most chivalrously. "A pleasure to have met you, Miss Talbot," he said, his blue eyes sincere. "I hope this won't be the last time we meet."

"Thank you—"

Kate was glad to hear Greta interject, "Then you'll have to

come to church next Sunday morning, won't you, Mr. Kendall? I have the impression that Miss Talbot is the kind of young lady who attends church every Sunday."

Andrew's eyes turned to Kate. "Then I most certainly shall if we're still here. I was sorry to miss the worship service this morning."

Charles McCourtney stood back, waiting until his stepbrother had finished his conversation with her. Stepping forward, Charles took her hand and bent over it. His lips brushed her fingers. "Be sure to pack a fine box supper, Miss Talbot," he murmured. "And put a spray of wildflowers on it, so I'll be certain to know which is yours."

She forced herself to say, "But the ones who make the box suppers are supposed to be a secret. Perhaps . . . perhaps farther south the traditions are somewhat different from what they are in Missouri—"

His silvery gray eyes shone with amusement and, still holding her hand, he shook his head. "We have the same tradition about box supper donors being kept confidential, my lovely Miss Talbot." He kissed her hand again, the wave in his golden hair falling forward slightly over his forehead, his warm lips lingering on her skin.

A languid sweetness invaded her body, setting her flesh tingling and blood rushing through her veins.

When he straightened, he looked her in the eye. "Wildflowers," he repeated. "It would please me greatly."

It took a moment for her mind to recover and move onward.

Here was an opportunity to do exactly what she'd hoped for! she thought. An opportunity to convert him from slavery. She ignored the unprincipled voice in her that would very much like to be keeping confidences with Charles McCourtney no matter what the purpose might be.

3

In front of the Davisons' house, Stephen helped Kate up into the wagon. Once she was settled, she glanced toward the stable some distance away. Charles McCourtney and Andrew Kendall were mounting their saddle horses.

Stephen climbed up to the wagon seat on the other side of Sarah. "I had to get out of there fast or I'd bust," he said. "I couldn't believe we were in the same house with them slavers while we were plannin' to undo them."

Kate was still watching Charles McCourtney and Andrew Kendall, and returned their waves as they rode away.

Stephen rolled his eyes. "If you ask me, that dentist and his wife have nerves of pure iron."

Sarah looked equally edgy. "Greta claims you get used to it after a while, but I don't see how I'd ever get used to living so precariously."

"I don't either," Kate had to agree.

Stephen flicked the reins over the horses' broad backs. "Let's go, boys! We'll ride toward town nice and slow until those two slavers are out of sight."

And the sooner the better, Kate thought. As for putting wild-flowers on her box supper, she'd been half-tempted when she was in Charles's company, but now the idea seemed downright outrageous.

Before long the two men disappeared from view, and Stephen let out a relieved breath himself. "We'll head for the Platte City Turnpike to look over Halfway House, since Kate's never seen it. I've sure never looked at it with somethin' like this in mind! Never in my life even thought such an idea."

Kate suspected that Sarah was growing increasingly uneasy, and she hastened to say, "Tell us about Halfway House, Stephen."

He kept his eyes straight ahead on the bobbing heads of their horses. "The place is a run-down inn and tavern halfway between Weston and Platte City. Usually it's full of travelers and drunken soldiers from over the river at Fort Leavenworth."

"But it does a busy trade, even though it's no longer by the river?" Kate asked.

Stephen nodded. "No other place around like it, I guess. It's always been for slave owners, overseers, and traders when they're takin' slaves by the river. Probably always will be. It's got that reputation."

"We heard in Independence that there are escape tunnels here under the Missouri," Kate said. "It doesn't seem possible."

"No one knows," he replied. "Expect when we've freed them tonight, people will likely think the slaves went by tunnel under the Missouri. Most ferries won't take 'em."

"Do you think there are escape tunnels?" Kate persisted.

"Doubt it," he answered. "There's more guessing than proof. Lots of talk on how slaves are freed hereabouts. Some say Judge Elijah Sorter hides slaves in his basement and gets them over to Kansas on their way to Canada, but I doubt that, too."

They lapsed into silence as he turned the horses left at one corner, then right, and headed them toward the outskirts of town. Glancing back, Kate was glad to see that no one had followed them.

Stephen looked back, too. "Appears we got rid of 'em. Let's hope our luck holds."

At length Kate asked, "How do the slaves actually get to Halfway House?"

Stephen raised his brows. "When abolitionists—Kansans or otherwise—get too troublesome over on the river, the slaves are unloaded at the Rialto Landing. They put 'em into wagon beds and cover 'em with hay or straw, and bring 'em to Halfway House. There, they chain 'em to rings in the stone walls down in the cave, then the slavers go upstairs to regale themselves with drinkin' and gamblin'."

"And the next day?" Kate prompted.

"The next day, they ride back to the river and travel south by riverboat. Or sometimes the darkies are auctioned off at Halfway House's front door. Of course, that's chancy, bein' so close to the Kansas border."

"I'm not clear on what we're to do," Sarah said. "Do all of us go into the place?"

He hesitated, his long face turning even more somber. "Not all of us."

"What do you mean, not all of us?" Kate asked.

He replied with reluctance, "Only you go in, to start."

"Only Kate goes in!" Sarah echoed before Kate could speak. "You can't mean it! Greta told us she wouldn't be alone, that she'd be protected. I thought someone would be in there with her!"

Stephen turned to look at the horses. "Only a little later, if necessary. Kate's supposed to keep their interest at the bar. We'll be nearby and stop everything if there's more trouble than she can handle, though it doesn't seem likely that time of night."

"Stop everything?" Kate asked. "You mean we'd stop the entire attempt?"

He nodded. "I don't like it, either, but you're the only unknown woman around, and we figure they'd find that interestin'. The idea is for you to sit down at a table, say you're dyin' of thirst, drink some cider, and not talk much unless you have to. At that time of night, if men are still up and about, we figure they'll amble over to you of their own accord."

"It's too dangerous, Stephen," Sarah objected. "And now that I think the entire matter over—"

Kate interrupted, "It's going to work." She added with more bravado than she felt, "If there's one thing I can do, it's create a diversion. I can take care of myself, Sarah."

"I don't know," her sister argued. "I don't believe you've ever warded off men in a tavern."

"I'll do it," Kate assured her, looking at the horses herself. "Don't worry. It'll be fine."

"Well, I don't like it," Sarah answered. "For one thing, some of the so-called abolitionists aren't always so lily white themselves. Some are no more than ruffians using abolition as an excuse to go shooting and robbing across the border. Look at Poppa in Independence, having to sell our trading post . . . just keeping the mercantile in town where it's safer."

"I know," Kate answered. "I know all about it."

"They say over in the town of Lawrence, Kansas, you can see women wearing the very dresses that were stolen here in Missouri . . . that Lawrence is the auction place for Missouri's stolen goods. Probably they even sold the very goods they stole from Poppa's mercantile last year."

"Not that Missouri ruffians haven't raided Kansas," Stephen put in. "Some Missourians are just as bad."

For years, Kate had heard absurd excuses for the fighting. One was that Kansans envied Missouri's prosperity, which came from being founded long before Kansas had a chance to grow and prosper. Since Missourians had such a head start, Kansasans felt they could steal what they pleased. It was almost as if neither side had ever heard "Thou shalt not steal" and "Thou shalt not kill."

"There's cause for anger on both sides," Stephen said. "I've thought it over, and we're freein' Weston slaves, not stealin' goods or other deviltry. This is separate from the border ruffians on either side. It's nothin' more than freein' a few Weston Negroes from slavery."

Kate knew his reasoning, but understood her sister's doubts too. She gazed out at the redbud trees that blossomed at the edge of the woods. Tangles of vines grew between the stands of oaks, mulberries, and black walnuts. It struck her that sometimes the border ruffians were like those vines, tangling up the entire slavery question so much that it was impossible to understand who was in the right or who was in the wrong.

Sarah must have accepted her husband's line of reasoning, for she finally drew a deep breath and said, "All right, then. What do they want me to do?"

He gave her an uneasy smile. "They, uh . . . they want you to dirty up your face and dress like a man so you can act as a lookout for Kate in the tavern."

"Dirty up my face and pose as a man!" Sarah repeated. "Why, Stephen Bence, that's—"

"I know, Sarah. I know it's dreadful, but it can't be helped. Believe me, we discussed it plenty, and it plain can't be helped."

"Why don't you go in there with Kate?" Sarah asked him. "Or one of the other men?"

He sounded all too sensible. "Everyone has duties they're best suited for. I'll be busy unchainin' the darkies and gettin' them to the wagons. There's no one else to keep an eye on Kate."

Sarah scowled at him. "And just how am I supposed to look like a man?"

"Now, Sarah . . . I'm not sayin' it'll be easy," he countered, "but

I've been thinkin' about it. You can wear some of my old clothes and tie your hair up in one of my caps. Maybe wear a pillow so you look like you have a paunch."

"Stephen!"

He hastened to add, "You always look so thin and pretty, no one would ever guess it's you."

Her scowl faded slightly. "Well, you did say the right thing there."

"Come on, Sarah," Stephen implored. He chucked her under the chin with his fingers and gave her a contrite smile.

Finally Sarah allowed him a small smile in return.

Before they could forget her entirely, Kate asked, "How many others will be with us?"

"Three wagons comin' from Weston," Stephen answered. "I'm not sayin' whose, so no one lets things slip. While the diversion's going on upstairs, we unchain the slaves in the cave and get them into the wagons. When that's done, it's my job to run upstairs to ease you and Kate out. Others will put the slaves on a ferry waitin' to take them across to Kansas."

"So Kate just creates a diversion, and I keep an eye on her. That's all?" Sarah asked.

Stephen nodded, then glanced at his wife. "You don't have to do this if you don't want, Sarah. I just remember how you always told me *we* have to do something. You were clear about the *we*."

Sarah rolled her eyes skyward. "I asked for that, didn't I?"

"We'll do it," Kate assured her, "though I'm afraid I'll feel like Rahab the Harlot all the while I'm diverting the men."

"I'd just as soon forget that part of it," her sister answered. She turned to Stephen. "How do we get home when it's over?"

"I'll drive you in the wagon. All you'll have to do is hide under the hay in back."

Glancing out at the road, Kate reminded herself that she'd

claimed to be against slavery. No matter how this plan struck her, now if ever was the time for action.

After a while, they saw Halfway House standing in the gently rolling countryside some distance away. It was a three-story dilapidated place, its yard overgrown with tall weeds. Only a few horses and wagons were hitched out front, likely because it was Sunday. Even from here, Kate saw under the inn to the roof of the cave where the slaves were kept manacled to the walls. According to Stephen, the main floor was for drinking and eating, and the upstairs for sleeping.

She drew a resigned breath. "What are we looking for?"

"We need to know the lay of the land," Stephen answered. "Places to hide if need be, like those copses of trees to the back and to the sides. Better to know 'em now than try and find 'em at night. Besides, at two in the morning, we might not be as alert as we should be."

"It's an all-night tavern?" Kate inquired.

"It's always open," Stephen replied. "And Sunday nights they do more business because the taverns in town close for the Sabbath."

"Won't it look peculiar if a woman shows up out of nowhere in the middle of the night?" she asked.

"Should make it all the more interestin' for them," he answered. "If they've been drinkin' 'til that time of night, they probably won't have the sense to consider if it's peculiar or not."

They were quiet as Kate considered the situation.

Stephen observed, "If trouble comes and we have a choice, it'd probably be best to take that copse of trees behind us, the one closest to home. It looks big enough to hide a wagon."

At length, he called out to the horses and slowly turned them around on the road. "Don't think we should go any closer. We've seen everything we need to anyhow. The place is a lot busier at night."

Kate could imagine the drunken louts, having seen the same type stumble out of the Independence taverns. Diverting them seemed an unsavory prospect.

"Expect it's time to head for the box social," Stephen remarked. "Don't tell any of this."

Sarah let out a deep breath. "The only good I can see in this whole scheme so far is it's turned you into a talker. I haven't heard you talk so much in fifteen years as you have lately."

He chuckled, and Kate smiled inwardly. Perilous as the plan might be, she guessed that for Stephen it must be an exciting adventure.

When they arrived at the churchyard, buggies and wagons were tied at the hitching posts, making the scene as cheerful as a country painting. Tables stood covered with white cloths, and women in their bright frocks fussed with preparations. The men in their shirtsleeves carried over wooden benches for seating, and small children played lively games on the north side of the church building. The only unoccupied space, Kate noted, was the graveyard.

Among those just arriving was the Davison family in their fine black carriage. Greta's blonde hair shone in the sunshine, and she smiled and waved at Kate, Sarah, and Stephen as if nothing mattered as much as the box social. Kate returned the wave with as much confidence as she could muster. They'd already agreed to be openly friendly, since people would know they'd had dinner together.

As Stephen tied their horses to the hitching post, Charles McCourtney rode into the churchyard on his blood bay. It seemed that every young woman there gazed at him with interest, while the menfolk eyed him with distrust and a shade of resentment.

He slowed his horse to a trot as he approached the Bence wagon. "Good afternoon, ladies," he said, nodding to Kate and Sarah.

"Good afternoon, Stephen. It's a pleasure to see all of you again."

"Good afternoon, Mr. McCourtney," Kate replied.

She saw him take note of the box supper Sarah brought out from the wooden carton under the wagon seat. Luckily it was Sarah's own and in a plain picnic basket—since only unmarried girls' box suppers would be auctioned. Her own box, more obvious in wrapping of leftover yellow calico and yellow ribbon, was still hidden.

"Ready for the box supper auction?" he inquired.

"I hope so," Kate answered, trying to hide her excitement.

Stephen came to her rescue. "I'm sure hungry."

"You're always hungry," Sarah put in with humor, and they all chuckled.

In the midst of it, Charles mouthed to Kate: *Wildflowers*. He gave a polite nod to all of them, then urged his horse forward toward the hitching post.

"What was that all about?" Sarah asked.

Kate shrugged. Moments later, she was glad to see Charles was dismounting and speaking to a man at the hitching post.

"That's Fred Barnes, a lawyer," Sarah remarked. "Probably the one helping with Namen Ormond's legal matters."

Kate watched them going toward the refreshment table, not far from the box supper table.

Horses pounded into the churchyard behind them, and the unmistakable voice of Rodwell Bence filled the air. "Whooeeee, Kate Talbot! I aim to be havin' supper with you!"

Kate cringed. Judging by the wide grin on his face, he was most confident. It occurred to her that he might already know which box was hers—maybe he'd even seen it at home. And if he hadn't, he would surely recognize the yellow calico, since it was leftover goods from their kitchen curtains!

Everyone around heard Rodwell's announcement, and Kate felt

distressed as Stephen helped her down from the wagon. She reminded herself that if she was expected to create a diversion at a tavern, she could surely endure whatever might take place at a sedate church social. Fortunately the fiddlers began to play lively music, and people turned their attention to them.

"You want me to carry your box supper up to the front table?" Stephen offered.

"Yes, thank you. Try to mix it in with the others."

His eyes filled with both concern and amusement. "I doubt that would confuse interested fellows with any brain at all."

Kate smoothed out the skirt of her yellow dimity and regretted again that she'd worn such a bright dress. Between it and her bright yellow calico box supper, the men would likely think she yearned for attention.

Sarah took her by the arm. "You don't have to look quite so disinclined to have a good time."

Kate attempted a smile. "It might be better than appearing too eager."

"Could be," Sarah acknowledged, then raised her brows. "Some women like courting . . . the truth is, I did myself. But I don't envy you this afternoon, Kate. I don't envy you one little bit, with Rodwell eyeing you."

Rodwell had hitched up his horse and was starting toward them with his broad grin.

"Hold him off, Sarah," Kate begged, "for a while anyhow."

"What'll you do?"

An idea flew to mind. "I'll go into the church."

"That, if anything, should hold him off," Sarah predicted. "I swear those Bence men are downright scared of churches. Go ahead, hurry!"

As Kate rushed across the yard, she caught a glimpse of Rodwell watching her departure, his grin quickly fading. Nearby, the Davison girls called out, "Where are you going, Miss Kate?"

"I'll be back shortly!" she answered.

She nearly ran to the church door, and from the corner of her eye, noticed clusters of color at the graveyard's edge.

Wildflowers!

Inside the church door, she finally caught her breath. Looking for an escape route, she saw the open side door to the graveyard and headed down the aisle for it. A breeze wafted through the open door, ruffling the grasses and flowers around the graveyard. No one had followed her yet, and she sat down on a nearby walnut pew, ready to flee.

Still no one came in.

After a while, she settled back in the pew and absent-mindedly rubbed the smooth warm wood near her skirt. Now that her box supper was at the auction table, it seemed she had no choice. The question was: would she rather take tonight's supper with Charles McCourtney or with Rodwell Bence? Both men needed converting to an abolitionist viewpoint, so her decision amounted to a purely personal preference. That was simple! She got to her feet and peered out the side door. No one there, either. She made her way through the grasses to the nearest cluster of white buttercups and began to pluck them, then moved to the yellow borage and prairie violets.

After she'd gathered a nice bouquet, she carried them through the empty church to the front door. As she stepped outside, the flowers were fairly easy to hide at the side of her full-skirted frock.

Spotting a freckle-faced, redheaded girl of about ten, Kate beckoned her. "I'd like to have flowers on my box supper," she told the child. "Would you slip up there and put them under the bow on the yellow calico box?"

The girl's eyes sparkled. "Yes, ma'am, be glad to. You want to pretty up the box some, I guess."

"That's part of it," Kate replied, and sent her off toward the front table.

She was glad to see she'd chosen a clever girl who peered about calmly and waited for the right moment. People were still arriving on horseback, in wagons, and in carriages, and with the endless commotion and the fiddlers playing, no one seemed to notice the girl at her errand.

Kate started for the table where Sarah and Stephen had settled with the Davisons. She was glad to see the girls waiting for her to join them; perhaps their presence would also help to deter Rodwell.

"Miss Kate!" they called out. "Come read to us!"

"I can't think of anything I'd rather do," she answered, hurrying to them.

As she sat down on their bench, they excitedly thrust their *Grimm's Fairy Tales* at her. "Well, then," she said with relief, "what shall we read?"

At five o'clock the fiddlers put up their instruments, and the auctioneer stepped up to the box social table. "Ladies and gentlemen, if you'll just gather around up here now for our box supper auction. You know the money we make on auctioning off these suppers is a help to our church budget, so let's bid 'em up as high as you can go."

He waited for the crowd to come forward, and Kate noticed the younger men taking a special interest in the proceedings. Rodwell stood out like a hellion in the crowd of young men who looked for the most part like churchgoers. "Just look at these beautiful box suppers!" the auctioneer called out. "Don't know where our young ladies get such good ideas on dressin' up plain old boxes. Ladies do beautify things, don't they?"

Not waiting for an answer, he held up a white box with a big spray of lilacs tied under the ribbons, then inhaled the purple flowers' perfume. "There's nothin' like lilacs!"

Setting it down, he showed a box wrapped in red gingham with three red tulips tucked under the bow. "Tulips, one of the cheeriest flowers in all creation."

"And here," he said, picking up Kate's box supper, "we even have a bouquet of wildflowers. Don't God make 'em beautiful in Missoura!"

Kate watched the auctioneer put her box down, and from the corner of her eye, she saw Rodwell. For an instant, he scrutinized her yellow calico box with a baffled expression, then his grin reappeared. When she glanced at Charles McCourtney, he'd just finished talking with his lawyer companion as if nothing of importance were underway.

The auctioneer held up two more boxes, extolling their virtues, then the auction began in earnest. "What do I hear offered for this fine white box with the perfume of lilacs about it? Do I hear fifty cents? Will someone give me fifty cents to begin the bidding?"

A slight tension filled the air, and faces turned to the plump blonde girl who sat at the next table with her family.

After a moment, an equally plump young man at another table called out, "Fifty cents!"

The girl blushed, and her family looked delighted.

"Do I hear more?" asked the auctioneer.

"Sixty cents!" one of the girl's brothers shouted. "Sixty cents!"

"Seventy cents!" the suitor countered, prevailing. Flushed with success, he went forward to claim his box supper.

"Who donated this supper?" the auctioneer inquired.

"Here!" her father answered. "Gretchen Schmal!"

The crowd applauded, and the girl and her suitor turned redder and redder, especially when he came to claim her.

Kate cringed, watching the couple make their way through the crowd and start for the road. What would happen to her? She wouldn't feel safe with either Charles McCourtney or Rodwell Bence if they wished to sit out of sight of others. If only Sarah hadn't been so set on coming!

"Next let's take up this box with the tulips!" the auctioneer decided.

This time faces turned to a pretty dark-haired girl at a nearby table. She raised her chin a little and gazed ahead with pretended innocence.

The auctioneer waited for silence. "Who will offer fifty cents for this tulip box supper?"

"One dollar!" a young man shouted.

Even Charles and Rodwell turned, scanning the crowd to see who could start the bidding at such a high level.

From the other side of the crowd came, "Two dollars!"

"Two-fifty!" the first bidder returned.

"Two dollars and fifty cents!" the auctioneer called out. "Do I hear any more offers?"

"Two dollars and sixty cents!" the second bidder answered.

"Two-seventy."

"Three dollars!" the second bidder shouted, and won the bidding, to the girl's consternation.

After the box supper and its donor were brought together, the auctioneer turned for another box supper. "Now, staying with the flowers . . ." He picked up Kate's yellow calico box. "What am I bid for this calico box with Missoura wildflowers?"

"Fifty cents!" Rodwell yelled, raising a hand. "I bid fifty cents!" He glanced over the crowd at Kate, grinning.

Across from her on the bench, she saw Sarah and Stephen stiffen with dismay.

"Fifty cents, I hear fifty cents," the auctioneer sang out. "Do I hear—"

"Five dollars," Charles McCourtney interrupted.

Nearby someone whispered a stunned, "Five dollars?"

"Five dollars," the auctioneer continued. "Do I hear another bid?"

"Five-fifty," Rodwell replied, then glanced at Kate, his grin growing uncertain.

Beside her, Sarah whispered to Stephen, "Where would he ever get so much money?"

"Five-fifty," the auctioneer called out. He looked toward Rodwell. "Do I hear another bid?"

"Ten dollars," Charles McCourtney answered, shocking the crowd into a tense silence.

"Ten-fifty!" Rodwell shouted.

"Twenty dollars!" Charles countered.

Rodwell's shoulders drooped, and his face turned red with anger.

"Twenty dollars!" the auctioneer exclaimed. "Twenty dollars! Do I hear another bid?"

No one spoke, and Rodwell turned on his heel and stalked away angrily.

The auctioneer announced, "This fine yellow calico basket with the wildflowers is going, going, gone for twenty dollars to a gentleman I believe is from Mississippi!"

Charles McCourtney stepped forward with his money in hand, and the auctioneer asked, "And who is the fair donor of this fine supper?"

Kate raised her hand with trepidation. With everyone turning toward her and murmuring about the high price for her favor, she would not remain unknown for tonight's Halfway House assignment!

Beside her, Sarah whispered, "Just be pleasant and, whatever you do, don't give away anything about tonight."

Kate nodded, then managed a smile as Charles McCourtney arrived at her side with the box supper.

"Thought I should help with the church budget," he remarked

with mock seriousness. He turned to Sarah and Stephen and added, "Part of the Lord's work, you know. . . ."

She hoped he might want to stay at the table, but he added, "I thought we might eat supper by the graveyard, where these wildflowers would feel right at home."

Well . . . so he'd seen her go back to pick them!

She excused herself, got up from the table, and nodded at him again. She supposed she should appreciate his rescuing her from Rodwell, but instead, she felt resentful.

He must have read her thoughts, for when they were out of everyone's hearing, he remarked, "Considering the looks of that lout, I thought it best to rescue you."

"Thank you," she managed. "Thank you very—"

A shot rent the air, and she turned.

Rodwell sat on his horse and shot his gun wildly into the air again. "I'll get you yet fer this, you blamed Mississippian!" he yelled. "I'll get you!" Apparently satisfied with the crowd's attention, he spurred his horse through the churchyard and rode off down the road.

The crowd had quieted, but now they buzzed. "What's that Rodwell Bence doing here anyhow?" asked one.

"Wouldn't want him threatening me!" another exclaimed.

Someone else was saying, "Ain't even safe in the churchyard nowadays!"

As they walked away, Charles remarked dryly, "It appears that fellow had his mind set on winning this supper. I can't help but think that with such a show of temper on his part, it must be at least as good as Mississippi cooking."

Kate drew a breath. "Sarah made every last bit of it . . . and since our mother taught us to cook, I expect you'll find it's a mixture of German and Missouri cooking."

He looked at her and laughed, the sun gleaming on his dark

blond hair. "Miss Kate Talbot, I think you are going to be a most interesting companion."

"I don't know about that."

He laughed again, but she ignored it. Now that she walked alongside him, she found him taller than she'd remembered, and broader in the shoulders. In the sunshine, he was even more attractive— surely the most handsome man in the churchyard.

"I took you for Irish," he said, still amused. "Let's see . . . if you're German, your name must be Katrina."

"Never mind!" she returned, smiling herself.

He shook his head. "You're feisty for a Katrina!"

"I'm a Missouri girl, and Talbot is English!"

"Is that so?" he inquired.

"That's so."

He loosened his cravat and looked even more appealing as he stood there studying her. "English . . . no wonder you have such a lovely skin on that beautiful face . . . and neck . . . and likely—"

"*Mr. McCourtney!*"

"Are you sure you're not Dutch like Greta? You have a Dutch girl's friendly face. You'd make a lovely rosy-cheeked Dutch girl with wooden shoes."

She ignored him and trudged on into the graveyard, walking just to the side of the crosses and tombstones. After a while she inquired, "Pray tell, where did you plan to sit? Perhaps on someone's grave?"

Chuckling again, he gestured toward a bench that was half-hidden at the edge of the nearby woods. "While you were plundering the church's wildflowers, I noticed that yon stone bench was placed here just for us."

Hmmmmph! she thought. As it was, she felt uncertain about sitting in a secluded place with him—even if she was meant to change his views on slavery.

When they arrived at the bench, she used her hand to brush the dirt and leaves from the old wooden bench. "It must have been placed here for us some years ago."

"Could be," he laughed. He whisked a white linen handkerchief from his pocket. "Here, let me." Handing the yellow calico box to her, he wiped the bench clean with a flourish. "Now, shall we be seated?"

She eyed him, then sat down and smoothed her yellow dimity demurely.

He set the box supper between them on the bench and untied it. Removing the lid, he said, "Well, well . . . what have we here?"

Instead of answering, she was still trying to decide whether to stay. If only he hadn't paid so much for her box supper. Everyone would notice if she walked out on him, and they'd talk even more about her.

"Looks like that long-forgotten dish, Southern-fried chicken," he observed. "And here are potato salad and pickles . . . and forks and knives. Very civilized."

At least the box was between them, she thought, and despite everything, she was famished. She picked up a fried chicken drumstick with her fingers and bit into it.

"Ah, well," he said, picking up the other drumstick, "it appears we're not going to be too civilized after all. Suits me. There's a good deal to be said for being barbaric at a church picnic."

She made no reply, only hoping that greasy fingers were not conducive to more hand kissing. All afternoon she had tried to forget the unsettling moments with him in the Davisons' foyer, but something in her was drawn to him, something far beyond altering his ideas on slavery.

By the time they began to eat their dried peach tart, Kate felt less concerned, possibly because he'd grown quiet. When she'd finished, she sat back and listened to the birds twittering in the woods.

"A fine place, this graveyard," he remarked.

"Yes, it's nice and peaceful."

He offered his handkerchief, and she wiped the food from her fingers.

He peered into the box. "No brandy for a gentleman?"

"No brandy," she answered. "Not even for such an expensive box supper."

"That it was," he agreed, smiling broadly.

Watching her, he removed the box supper from between them. "Miss Talbot, are you afraid of me?"

"Of course not!"

"Then why are you twisting my handkerchief?"

Noting the gleam in his eyes, she folded up the handkerchief and returned it to him with care.

"Don't you like me?"

She wanted to rise from the bench, but he caught her hand in his, and at his touch, she once more grew weak.

His voice turned husky. "Come here, Miss Katrina. It was a delicious supper, and a kiss from your lovely lips would be sweeter than brandy."

"It isn't proper—"

"Come here," he persevered, slowly gathering her to him. "You look as if you'd fit perfectly in my arms. I do believe that's why God planned men to have bigger arms than women, don't you?"

For an instant, she tried to pull away, but not as strongly as she should, and then she was fully in his arms and his breath was warm in her hair.

Behind them, someone coughed loudly—once, then again— and the two of them quickly moved apart.

When Kate turned around, no one was there. "Just a minute," she said, "I want to see—"

Seizing the moment, she hurried into the church and shut the side door, latching it behind her. Outside in the graveyard, there were voices, one sounding like the minister. She heard Charles say, "She's gone into the church. Yes, sir, a fine church social, but I'm afraid my duties call. I have to ride back to my uncle's farm now. Miss Talbot will know."

At long last, she ventured out the front door, only to see him ride away through the churchyard. Suddenly she knew who he reminded her of, albeit slightly: Albert Morton, who'd ridden off on her for the '58 Rocky Mountain gold rush, and, instead of coming back with gold in his pockets, had in no time at all been killed.

When she saw Charles McCourtney didn't so much as turn back, she felt a surge of indignation, followed by a penetrating pang of regret.

It was early evening when they returned to the Bence house. Pa Bence, Aubin, and Rodwell were sprawled in the parlor, drowsing on the parlor sofa and chairs, a bottle of whisky and glasses near at hand. Likely resting up for the night's carousing, Kate thought unhappily. She recalled what Stephen had said—Halfway House was the only drinking place open on Sunday nights.

Stephen was out in the barn with the horses, and Sarah put a warning finger to her lips. She and Kate closed the kitchen door and began to clean up the mess the men had left. When the kitchen was finally tidied, they headed quietly for the stairwell to go upstairs. It was an ideal time to ready their clothes for the night's undertaking, and Kate carried the low-cut red taffeta frock. The frock looked far too large around the middle; they'd have to take in the waist seams considerably.

"What?" Aubin asked, rousing from a chair. "Who's there?"

Kate hid the red taffeta dress behind her, and Sarah put a cautioning finger to her lips.

Aubin sat up. "What ye doin'?"

"We have some sewing to do," Sarah whispered, and Kate thought her sister must feel as she did, glued to the floorboards by Aubin's gaze.

Even worse, Rodwell and Pa Bence were rousing themselves.

Rodwell, looking bleary-eyed, saw Kate and gave her a slow grin. "I bin waitin' fer ye, Kate Talbot! McCourtney might'a put up twenty dollars fer yer box supper, but I git to sit with ye free o' charge right here in the house."

"What're ye jawin' about?" Pa Bence demanded groggily.

"Whooeeee, Kate Talbot!" Rodwell called out, jumping to his feet. "I git to be with ye free o' charge! Ain't thet the truth, Aubin? We doan' have to spend no twenty dollars to be with this sweet sassy gal who lives right in our house."

"And I thought you'd be interested in Kansas girls!" Kate said hastily to deflect his thinking.

"Kansas girls?" Rodwell exclaimed. "I doan like nothin' about 'em! Why, the whole state ain't worth spit. All they got there is tornadoes, blizzards, an' clouds of grasshoppers eatin' up their prairies!"

"How 'bout prairie fires?" Pa Bence put in as he came to his feet. "Kansas ain't even got a decent river."

"How about the Kaw?" Kate suggested to keep them off balance.

"Most times you can't even run a steamboat in it!" Rodwell countered. "Why you so interested in Kansas anyhow?"

"Not me! I thought you were! You're always talking about it."

If Sarah wasn't going to move up the staircase, she'd have to herself, Kate thought. "If you'll excuse us," she said, and started up the steps.

"What's that yer hidin'?" Rodwell asked, his long legs closing the distance between them. He grabbed the dress and held it up for all of them to examine. "Whooeeee, Kate Talbot! Whooeeee! I'm sure lookin' forward to seein' you in this! And here we thought—"

"It's not mine," Kate interrupted, grabbing it back. She started up the stairs, and fortunately Sarah was right behind her. "Sarah and I just have to mend it. We'll be downstairs later."

"Must be thet Davison woman's dress," Pa was saying behind them. "Some o' them high-falutin' ladies wear 'em jist like saloon gals. Sets a man's mind to wonderin' if there's a difference between 'em."

Kate gave an audible sigh of relief as she let Sarah into her room and locked the door behind them. She leaned back against the white-painted door. "I don't like to speak badly about Stephen's family," she said, "but I'm nervous about them. To put it plainly, I don't feel safe here with his brothers, maybe not even with his father."

Tears welled in Sarah's blue eyes, and she pressed her lips together.

"Sarah?" Kate asked with suspicion, "Do they treat you right?" Her sister let out a sob and turned away, clenching her fists.

"Oh, Sarah."

Sarah choked out, "I don't want to talk about it!"

Shocked, Kate finally said, "Just tell me one thing. Does Stephen know?"

"Most of it!" Sarah returned. "That's why Aubin has to live out in the old log house by the barn. Stephen walked in when Aubin was tryin' to drag me. . . . Aubin's not very bright. . . ." She stopped, unable to go on.

"And then?"

When Sarah caught her breath, she managed, "Stephen warned that we'd leave if they ever tried anything again, and they don't want us to go. You can probably see already that Stephen does most of the work, and I keep the house and cook. Besides, they'll listen to him."

Kate had noticed little of that, but then she hadn't been here long. She caught her sister in her arms. "I'm so sorry, Sarah. Sorrier than words can say. I didn't dream you had such difficulties. Why don't you and Stephen come home to Independence?"

Sarah pulled away and backhanded the tears from her cheeks. "Believe me, we've talked of it, but I think he feels bound to build me our own house as he promised. And there's something more that holds him . . . something he won't say. And he still hopes things will get better in Weston. My troubles with Aubin and Rodwell . . . it's nightmarish to him, too."

Kate turned away and lay the red dress across her bed. "Are matters better now?"

Sarah nodded. "Most of the time Aubin and Rodwell leave me alone. I just have to be careful when they're drinking. That's when there's trouble."

It struck Kate that the whole time she'd been there, she'd never seen them sober. "Let's take in that red dress. Now that I've heard this, doing our assignment tonight seems almost like revenge."

"I've thought that, too," Sarah said. She blew her nose on her pocket handkerchief, then took a deep breath. "I'll get the sewing kit from my room while you try on the dress."

Kate unlocked the door and stepped out above the stairs with her sister to be sure she'd be safe.

Down below, Stephen stood by the staircase, listening to his father with reluctance.

"Ye stay away from them Davisons!" Pa Bence was shouting. "I don't want ye consortin' with no abolitionists!"

"Just wait till thet moon's full a few days from now," Rodwell added. "We're gonna ride out an' kill us some!"

Kate backed into her room, but still heard his words.

"Gonna ride out an' kill us some abolitionists!"

4

Kate rolled over in the warm bed, blinking at the candlelight. Who was shaking her? Sarah . . . it was Sarah, and they were in Weston. But why would her sister awaken her in the middle of the night?

"One o'clock, time to get ready," Sarah whispered. "It's raining . . . wear your winter cloak. I'll light your candle."

Heart pounding, Kate sat up in bed and swung her feet to the cool plank floor. This was the night she'd truly fight the institution of slavery.

Blinking again, she saw that Sarah was already gone, the door closed behind her. Kate hurried across the floor to the wash pitcher and basin, and dashed cold water over her face. Rain pattered on the window, muffling her sounds. Hurry, hurry, hurry.

In no time she washed, pinned her hair up tightly, and buttoned the low-cut red taffeta frock. By the flickering candlelight her reflection shimmered in the mirror, and she was astonished at her appearance in the tight frock. She was appealing as a sordid woman! Actually appealing! Perhaps if she'd dressed like this two years ago, Albert would have remained in Independence and married her instead of being lured off to the gold rush. This was no time for wild imaginings, she told herself. Still, it was a wonder to see herself in such a frock. Hurrying again, she pulled on the black curly wig and was transformed into a stranger . . . a tavern wench.

Sarah opened the door, looking entirely different herself in Stephen's black hat, old clothes, and a pillow-stuffed midsection. "Oh my, Kate!" she whispered. "A good thing Mama can't see you! Well . . . hurry! Stephen's getting the wagon. One candle is enough."

Kate snatched her gray wool cloak from the hook behind the door and slipped into it quickly. After blowing out her candle, she tiptoed from the room. In the hallway, loud snores rose and fell from Rodwell's and Pa Bence's bedrooms.

Numbly she followed Sarah down the stairs and to the kitchen, where Sarah took a loaf of bread from the bread box. "I feel queasy," she whispered.

Kate's voice remained hushed. "Queasy?"

Sarah nodded. "Only in the mornings."

"Oh, Sarah, you shouldn't be going with us! What if . . . what if . . . ?"

Sarah shook her head. "It's likely just nerves about tonight and from living in this house. Grab that umbrella."

Kate took the umbrella from its hook, then followed her sister out the kitchen door. Sarah closed the door behind them carefully, but it still banged against the wood.

"What if they awaken?" Kate whispered as she put up the umbrella against the rain.

"They won't," Sarah answered. "Stephen slipped laudanum into their whiskey bottle. He just hopes it was enough." She hesitated. "The one to be concerned about is Aubin, sleeping out there by the barn. The horses are noisy, and the wagon is, too, but the rain should muffle it."

"You think the rain is God's provision for us?"

"Hush!" Sarah said, putting her arm around Kate's waist as they stood under the umbrella. "There's the wagon. Stephen put up the old hickory bows and the canvas cover over them. You'd think we were traveling to California or Oregon."

Kate held her cloak shut as Stephen helped them silently into the wagon bed under the white canvas cover. She and Sarah settled on the blankets, then took hold of the wagon sideboards.

The wagon seat creaked as Stephen sat down on it. Moments later, they started off. As they bumped along down the lane, the light rain stopped, and when they reached Weston Road, the moon and stars glimmered through veils of black clouds.

"Any chance Aubin heard you?" Sarah called softly through the front puckered canvas hole to Stephen.

"Don't know," he replied. "The blamed horses were noisy. Probably shoulda put more laudanum in the whisky, but I didn't want to kill 'em. Seems like enough to drug 'em a while, though."

"Is there any more whisky in the house?" Sarah asked.

"No," Stephen replied. "It was their last bottle."

Kate sat back against the wagon's front planks. Now that they were safely away from the house, she felt better. She tugged a blanket out from beneath her and spread it over Sarah's and her lap, then down to their feet.

Sarah tore off a bit of bread and offered the loaf to Kate, who pulled off a twist of it herself. Even the bread was damp and cold.

"You know what to do?" Sarah asked.

Kate nodded. "I go into the tavern, sit at a table, and ask for cider. If there are men about, I keep their interest while Stephen and the others free the slaves and hide them in the other wagons. After a few minutes, you come in and stand by the bar near the door. If anything goes wrong, you create a diversion and I get out fast."

"Right," her sister answered. "You have money to pay for the cider?"

"I do."

"What if you have to keep the men's interest a long time?"

"I'll decide then and there what to do. I've decided to play dumb with them. As dumb as can be."

They rode for what seemed hours, then the wagon slowed and Stephen whoa'ed the horses quietly.

He whispered back through the puckering hole in the canvas. "Sarah! Kate! Get out here and walk the rest of the way. Careful where you step. And don't talk to the darkies chained up, when you pass 'em."

They climbed onto the wagon seat by Stephen, who pointed out the lighted windows of Halfway House, then helped them down in the dim moonlight. "God help you!" he said. "God help you!"

They started off, Kate holding up her frock from the mud, and Sarah holding up her husband's baggy trouser legs. The ground was uneven, and it was slow going as they slogged along.

When they finally neared the lighted windows, Kate saw the cave under the inn and the outlines of men and women chained to the rock walls. Several moaned, and she longed to reassure them. In the moonlight their eyes were huge and white, and one of the women called out, "Mercy, Lord! Hab mercy on us!"

"Shhh!" Kate warned.

To her relief, they quieted.

When they reached the tavern door, Sarah whispered, "I'll wait here. Don't worry, I'll be in as soon as it seems right. Can't have them think we came together, or they'll be suspicious."

Kate nodded, then grabbed a deep breath and opened the tavern door. Immediately, the reek of whisky and unwashed bodies assailed her. She swallowed, then headed through the rustic room for an empty table not too far from the door. Besides the barman and one man at the bar, the other tables held six or seven men who were gambling, drinking, or sleeping with their heads on their arms. For an instant the cause of slavery dimmed in her mind, and she reminded herself again of their plan. Its success hinged on her playing her role well. Gathering her courage, she chose a chair from which she could see both the door and the bar.

The barman's sleepy eyes opened wide to see her. "Well, well," he said hazily, "who we got here? Ain't niver seen you afore, have we?"

Kate seated herself, aware that the other men were turning and looking at her. "Cider, if ye please," she said more loudly than she'd intended.

The barman inquired with a hint of contempt, "Would that be hard cider or just plain cider?"

"Plain cider, if ye please," she replied. She hoped they didn't hear her voice tremble.

"Cider comin' up," he announced and began to pour it from a tin pitcher into a cup. "How'd you git way out here? It's three mile to town an' two mile to the river."

She gave him a stupid smile, as if she didn't quite understand. Sitting back, she felt the other men's scrutiny, and ever so slowly, slipped her gray wool cloak off her shoulders and onto the back of the chair.

"Well, now," intoned a tall spindly man who got up slowly from the bar. "Look who we got here, an' look at that there red dress. Ain't she a purdy thang? Ain't she jist as purdy as kin be?"

Kate made herself smile. "Thank ye, kindly," she replied. "I do thank ye kindly, sir."

By the time the barman arrived with her mug of cider, other men were rising to their feet and ambling toward her.

"You lookin' fer company?" the barman inquired.

Not trusting herself to speak, Kate shrugged as if it didn't matter. She took a coin from her cloak pocket and paid him in case she had to leave fast.

From the corner of her eye, she saw Sarah enter the tavern in her manly attire. The others glanced at the new patron, then apparently deciding he was either harmless or uninteresting, they turned their attention back to Kate.

She sipped cider from the dirty tin cup, wondering how Stephen and the others were faring outside with the slaves. Surely there'd be noises in their efforts to free them of manacles and leg irons. But she heard no noises at all.

The memory of their moans gave her courage, and she smiled again at the men as they approached.

"Well, if you ain't a beauty," a genial red-nosed old fellow remarked to her. "You come from these parts? Can't say I recall meeting you hereabouts."

"Thank ye. I do thank ye kindly," she answered. "It's kind o' ye to say so, sir."

After a moment, one remarked, "She's simple." He tapped a finger to his forehead in slow motion. "Simple-minded."

"Why, thank ye!" Kate told him. "I do thank ye kindly, sir."

They rolled their eyes at each other.

"Say, Mick," one said, "what if yer old woman hears 'bout you talkin' to this beauty?"

Mick ignored them, his green eyes on her. "What's a gal like you doin' in here?"

Trying to decide how to create a noisy diversion, she thought, and hoped she looked calm. She had to do something to keep their attention—and now . . . right now! A wildly improbable idea flew to mind, and she said, "Why, I hoped to hear ye men sing. I heerd ye do singin' in here."

"Singin'? You want to hear us singin'?" one echoed.

"I heerd ye sing somethin' wonderful," she said sweetly.

"Can't say I been asked much o' late," put in Mick, suddenly reeling. He hiccuped. "I favor somethin' sprightly. How 'bout you?"

"Oh, so do I, sir!" she exclaimed. "I do like sprightly music! Nothin' nasty, ye hear?" She darted a quick glance at the other men in the tavern. Most sat about grinning or eyeing her with suspicion.

A dark, whiskery man ambled up. "Reckon you'd be givin' us each a kiss if we sing?"

Appalled at the thought, Kate managed an indifferent shrug. If she refused, she'd ruin the camaraderie they were establishing. "Ye want kissin'?" she asked, thinking fast. "Why, I'll jist have to wait'n see if ye be good singers, won't I?"

"Ohhhhhh! Hear that?" one yelled. "She'll kiss us fer singin'. I niver heard the like of it!"

Kate didn't dare glance at Sarah. Instead, she smiled at the men with encouragement.

" 'Oh, Suzannah!' " Mick decided. "We'll start the singin' with 'Oh, Suzannah!' Ain't any too nasty fer our little lady." His hiccups gone, he raised a hand to direct the other men, then started in his low voice, "Oh, I come from Alabama with my banjo on my knee, and I'm goin' to Louisiana, my true love for to see. . . ."

Others joined in, and by the time they got to "Oh, Suzannah, don't you cry for me!" every man around her sang along with him, most with amusement.

When they finished, Kate applauded. "Ye sing wonderful . . . jist wonderful like I heerd. Why, ye should be singing with one o' them travelin' shows. Ye sure ye ain't some o' them paid singers that travel 'round the country?"

"Travelin' singers! She thinks we're travelin' singers!" one exclaimed, and they all laughed uproariously.

Their laughter faded as the tavern door opened and they watched three men staggering in: Pa Bence, Aubin, and Rodwell!

Kate felt her face go white as they stared at her, and she quickly pulled her cloak back over the red dress, hoping they hadn't already recognized it—or her for that matter.

Staring at her, Rodwell raised a feeble, "Whooeeee!"

His father slammed an arm across his chest. "Shet up thet yellin', ye heah me?"

"I hear ye," Rodwell replied groggily.

"Git to the bar!" Pa Bence roared.

They might be drugged and drunk, Kate reflected, but it hadn't stopped them from searching for more drink.

"We're a'singin'," one of the singers told them.

But the Bence men now appeared to be more interested in whiskey, with the exception of Aubin, who halted in the midst of his staggering to gaze at her.

"Come on, Aubin," Pa Bence commanded angrily, "you ain't no singer. Think on what happened the last time ye took to a bar girl. Ye still got the scars on yer face to prove it."

"Need a drink!" Rodwell said, his words slurred. "We kin see to that gal later. Yeah . . . we'll see to 'er later."

It seemed to take forever, but the three of them headed for the bar and were finally settled on the stools.

Mick ignored them. "Don't know when I had such a good time. Let's give 'Yankee Doodle' a try."

"Sounds Northern-like ter me," objected the tall, spindly one who'd been half-asleep at the bar.

"'My Old Kentucky Home' then," another suggested. "Wouldn't want to start no war over singin' to a gal."

"When we gettin' them kisses?" the whiskery man inquired.

Kate shrunk back against her chair, and inspiration struck. "I only heerd one song, an' there be . . . um . . . ," She counted slowly, pointing a finger at each of them, "five of ye a'singin'. Seems like I need to hear five good songs to be a'givin' out five good kisses."

She watched them roll their eyes at each other. The three

Bences were watching her now from the bar too. In fact, Rodwell was eyeing her with a hint of recognition, and she took another drink of the cold cider from her mug to hide her face.

"I do believe I know thet gal from somewheres," he remarked.

Kate drank from the tin mug again.

"A black-haired gal like some I knew in Kentuck," Pa Bence remarked, then hiccuped so hard he slopped whisky from his cup onto his shirt. "Ain't nothin' like them black-haired Kentuck gals, I'll say that fer sure. Shoulda married me one."

At long last, the men began to sing "Old Dan Tucker."

As they sang, Kate strained to hear sounds of progress outside. She saw Sarah glancing at the door as if she also were unsure of what to do.

Suddenly someone outside yelled, and shots rent the night. Across the room, Sarah hurried to the door. Turning, she beckoned to Kate and disappeared into the darkness.

Kate stood up, thinking quickly. She raised her hands to direct the men's singing, backing to the door. "Jist wanna see what they's a'yellin' about!" she explained. "I do like thet song! Now that's what I call singin'!" She turned and sashayed out like an Independence bar girl. "I'll be right back, you heah?"

The instant she was outside around the corner, she lifted her skirt and ran wildly into the night. And not any too soon either, for she heard the men pounding out after her.

"A raid!" one yelled. "A raid to get them slaves from below!"

Men came racing from the tavern.

"Git to thet cave!" someone yelled.

In the moonlight, she was glad to see Sarah running ahead of her and a wagon coming toward them. Amidst shouts, wagons took off in all directions. Everything transpiring around her—shouts, shooting, horses whinnying—happened quickly, yet seemed frozen in time.

Run! she told her feet. *Faster!*

Looking at the wagon, Kate stumbled on a rock, and her cloak fell from her shoulders.

Run! No time to get it now!

Little Mr. Minton from church drove up smartly in his hay-filled wagon and shouted, "Get in the back fast!"

Kate and Sarah let down the tailgate and climbed on as shouts and shooting filled the night.

"Hide under the hay!" Mr. Minton called back. "There's a wire frame to keep it up over you."

They pulled up the tailgate, and burrowing under the hay, Kate called out, "Go!"

As the wagon jolted forward, they lay on the hard boards, burrowing deeper and deeper under a frame that held most of the rank-smelling hay above them.

Kate put a hand to her mouth to keep from choking on the dust. "What happened?"

"Don't know exactly," Sarah replied.

Shots rang out from all around, and Mr. Minton urged the horses to greater speed.

Sarah gasped, "When I looked out from the bar, people were running and wagons racing about. Someone waved a lantern, then there was a shot and the lantern fell. Whoever it was got shot, that's sure."

"Let's hope it's no one from our side," Kate choked out. Her nostrils were filled with damp dust, and she held her nose to stifle a sneeze.

The wagon's bumping and sliding in the mud was bad enough, but the night's cold dampness made it even worse. What she wouldn't give to be in her cloak . . . or even in men's clothes like Sarah, instead of the low-cut red taffeta. "The wages of sin" flew to mind. This time, though, it wasn't her sin. These wages included being chilled, scratched raw, and thoroughly miserable.

After a long time, the night grew quiet, and Mr. Minton pulled the wagon into a copse of trees—stopping beside the Bence covered wagon. "Get in that wagon and make a run for it," he said. "Octavius from Ormonds' plantation is driving. Says he doesn't want to escape with the rest."

In the dim moonlight, Kate saw an African with gray hair and a grizzled beard holding the reins. A slave who actually didn't wish to escape?

"Quick!" he urged, helping them up. "Mistuh Stephen's in back . . . shot bad. Got to get out o' heah."

Sarah let out a strangled cry, and Kate let her sister climb into the wagon bed first.

"Where to?" Kate asked.

"Not to yo' home, no ma'am," Octavius answered. "Dem Bences be aftah you when dey heah you be in dis. Eben drunk, dey shootin' straight. Seems de best place tonight be de closest . . . my cabin at Ormand Plantation. No one 'spect you dere . . . or me, neither! Not when dey thinks we all done up'n escaped! You be decidin'."

"Fine," Kate replied. "Let's go there then." It seemed they had no other choice. The sounds of pounding hoof beats and shooting grew nearer again.

Sarah was already in the wagon bed. "Stephen!" she whispered. "Oh, Stephen!"

"Hurry . . . hurry!" Octavius told Kate, and she climbed in under the canvas top. He slapped the reins across the horses. "Gid up, boys! Gid up! He'p us, Jesus!"

The wagon jerked forward, and Kate almost fell. Faint moonlight streamed through the puckering holes of the white canvas, and as she caught her balance, she saw Sarah bent over her husband. He lay on a horse blanket, clutching his leg in agony.

Appalled, Kate asked, "How did it happen?"

He gave a muffled moan as they jolted along. "Didn't put enough laudanum in the whisky," he managed. "Didn't want to kill 'em! Wish I had some of that laudanum now myself."

"Rest," Sarah told him. "Rest."

But Stephen couldn't rest. "My own pa shot me," he said in pain. "Maybe he didn't know it was me in the dark, but I heard him say, "Got one!" It was him."

Kate swallowed hard.

"He's bleeding badly," Sarah whispered, her voice trembling. "You can see it from under his trousers. It's the calf of his leg. Stephen, hold still!"

Kate pulled down her petticoat and ripped off a narrow strip. "Here," she said, thrusting it at her sister.

Sarah took it and quickly wrapped his leg. "Octavius is right. We can't go to the Bence house. We can't ever go there again."

Shivering, Kate reached for a rough blanket to wrap around her shoulders. How could matters have gone so badly? she wondered as the wagon pitched and swayed onward. She prayed, *Heavenly Father, Thou knowest how we wished to fight against slavery! Why did this happen?*

No answer came.

At the Ormand plantation, Octavius drove through the dimly-lit night to the slave quarters. A dog barked at the main house, then at long last quieted.

Octavius spoke urgently. "Soon as I stop, drop de tailgate an' git in mah cabin. No one expect whites dere."

"Think you can walk?" Kate asked Stephen.

"One leg maybe," he managed. "Other's shot . . . bad."

They rode along through the dilapidated slave quarters, and Octavius stopped the wagon in front of a pine-board cabin that leaned heavily to one side. "Here. Go on in an' put out de lantern. Got plenty o' pallets in back. I aim to hide dis wagon an' horses, and be back quick wid yo' blankets."

Kate pulled down the tailgate and scrambled out of the wagon, then helped Sarah to ease Stephen down. He moaned fiercely as his good foot hit the mud, then grabbed for Kate and Sarah's shoulders as if he'd faint.

"Hold on a little longer!" Kate pleaded, strengthening her grip on him.

Once they'd staggered clear of the wagon, Octavius slapped the reins across the horses' backs, and they took off, the wagon tailgate flapping.

Kate and Sarah struggled under Stephen's weight as they helped him to the shanty's wooden porch. Kate darted a glance around the slave quarters. Quiet . . . though here and there lights flickered. Maybe the slaves ran off so fast, they'd left lanterns burning. Either that or they wanted to make the cabins look occupied while they escaped.

Maneuvering Stephen through the cabin door, Kate eyed the room in the lantern light. Plank table, two benches . . . cracked glass windows . . . raised sleeping pallet . . . rocking chair by the fireplace . . .

"Let's get Stephen to the back room," Sarah gasped as they strained to hold him.

They staggered through the front room, then down a step into a back room with three raised pallets. When they stopped, Stephen groaned and pitched toward a pallet in a dead faint.

Sarah swayed, stumbling toward the pallet and landing on her knees. "Help me get his legs up on it."

Finally Stephen lay on the corn shuck filled mattress, and Sarah sat on the unpainted floor beside him, softly sobbing. Kate flung off the tight black wig and ran back into the front room for the lantern, stopping in the cooking space to get a long sharp knife. The knife would serve for cutting away Stephen's trouser, cleaning the wound, and—if worse came to worse—for their protection.

"Kate, please cut away his trouser leg," Sarah sobbed. "I swear I can't."

"I'll do it, Sarah. You hush."

She placed the lantern on the nearby table. With a houseful of brothers, she'd seen many a male limb and helped Mama dress many a wound. Clenching her teeth, she grabbed Stephen's woolen trouser leg with one hand and carefully pierced the fabric just above his knee. Next, she sawed the knife around the fabric, then cautiously pulled the bottom down. His leg was bleeding badly, but the bullet had passed through, which is good news.

She swallowed the bile in her throat and took off her already torn petticoat. "Tear me two more strips, Sarah—"

Outside, shouts and gunshots rang out.

Kate grabbed the first strip and wound it quickly around Stephen's calf. "Douse the lantern!"

The light flickered, then the room was pitch dark.

They listened to the shouts in the darkness, Kate's heart pounding wildly.

At long last, the cabin door creaked opened, and Octavius whispered, "Jist me. Keep quiet."

He crept to the back room, carrying their blankets. "It's dem Bences. Dey takin' de oppo'tunity to scout out de place. Mistuh Namen never made 'em welcome. Said dey trash, all 'cept Mistuh Stephen and you, Miss Sarah."

Kate felt Sarah's body tense. "We have to get out—"

"Hush, now," Octavius said. "We only gots to outsmart 'em. Why, when dey see me comin' from de barn, dat no-good Rodwell was hopin' to shoot. I jist puts my hands up an' say, 'I ain't no runway slave, suh. I aim to stay right heah in Missoura where I gots it good! You wants me to show you 'round?' " He sighed, as if such predicaments were usual for him. "Yas'm," he said, "we gots to outsmart 'em."

"Did Penelopa and Alfron get away?" Kate asked.

"Yas'm. Got clean to the river. Dey's headed fer Kansas, den up to de promised land, dey reckon."

"What about our horses and wagons?"

"Left 'em hitched in de barn in case we need 'em fast. Brought yo' blankets in f'om de wagon fo' tonight."

"Thank you, Octavius."

Before long, horses pounded through the slave quarters. "Any of ye niggers here?" Pa Bence yelled. "Any of ye niggers still about?"

Octavius got up. "He know I be about, so's I'd best repo't fo' duty fo' dey start lookin'." He hurried through the cabin and out the door. "Heah Ah be, suh! Heah be Octavius at yo' service! Ah was jist gittin' my coat, suh!"

"Well, come along," Pa Bence yelled. "There's a wounded man needin' to be carried into the house! Ye niggers don't know the meanin' of the word hurry. Don't know the meanin' of it!"

Who could the wounded man be? Kate wondered. Andrew Kendall? Charles McCourtney? As far as she knew, no one else was staying at the Ormond house.

"Ah's a'comin', suh! Ah's a'comin'!"

"Whooeeee! Let's chase him in! See how fast he kin run!" Rodwell yelled. "If we catch 'im, we'll carry his skin home to Miss Kate Talbot. Whooeeee! Maybe she'd take to me then!"

Kate drew a disgusted breath.

On the encouraging side, however, it sounded as if the Bences had ridden off thinking that she and Sarah and Stephen were still at home.

In the distance, she heard Octavius call out, "Ah's runnin', suh! Running as fast as my old bones kin go!"

At length the night quieted, and Kate felt her way across the cabin to another corn-shuck pallet on the floor. "Here, Sarah, lie down until Octavius returns. When everything's quiet, we'll clean up Stephen's leg."

"And then what?" Sarah asked. "Even if his family doesn't suspect we were in the raid, they'll soon see we're missing . . . and the wagon, too. They'll know—"

"We'll just take one day at a time for now, the way Mama says. One day at a time . . . and one night."

She guided Sarah along to the pallet. Had the Bences been so drunk and drugged they hadn't noticed the wagon and horses were missing when they left? Was it possible? Considering their usual condition, it wouldn't be altogether surprising.

After some time Kate heard Sarah and Stephen breathing deeply with sleep, and she made her way to the other pallet. Best to rest, she decided as the corn shucks rustled under her in the rough mattress. She must have slept, then awakened to a distant racket, then slept again. It seemed hours later that the cabin door creaked open.

"Jist me, Octavius," he whispered in the darkness.

Kate whispered back, "I thought I heard another ruckus a while ago."

"Yas'm, it was dem Kansans," Octavius replied. "I tolds dem dey's no trouble heah at Mastuh Namen's. No trouble heah, no suh. Expect dey believe me. You try to sleep now, Miss Kate—"

"Who was it you had to carry in?"

"Mistuh Charles, ma'am."

Charles McCourtney shot too! she thought, her emotions in a turmoil.

"He gots shot right 'longside his head. Ain't much blood, but he sho' be knocked out. Yas'm, clean knocked out. Reckon he seein' plenty o' stars now."

"What was he doing at the raid?" she asked.

"Someone let out 'bout a raid at Halfway House, an' he knew his uncle's slaves be dere. Got himself slavers like him to stop it."

"Men on each side of the slavery question wounded," she thought aloud.

"Yas'm. Dat's it, fo' sure."

She shook her head. All they'd accomplished for their trouble was to help a few slaves escape—and probably inflamed more tempers on each side. They hadn't made much of a dent in the institution of slavery thus far.

As the sun rose the next morning, rays of light pierced the cabin windows, and Kate slowly opened her eyes. The floor creaked in the cabin's front room, and she eased her aching body into a sitting position. At least Stephen still slept and Sarah, though awake, was resting.

Kate got to her feet and tugged her red taffeta frock into place. "Shhh," she whispered to Sarah, then headed for the open doorway between the two rooms.

Octavius sat on a worn bench by the plank table. "Mornin', Miz Kate," he said quietly.

"Good morning."

He gave her a nod. In the light of day, his hair and beard were grayer than she had expected. He must have noticed her gaze, for he said, "I be old, Miss Kate. Old . . . but still fast in de head. Always was fast, my mammy said. Fast thinkin' boy, though it weren't always good thoughts, that be sho'. Weren't always good thoughts."

She kept her voice low. "Well, I'm glad for your fast thinking last night. And I'd appreciate your ideas on what we should do next."

He raised his grizzled brows. "If was me, Miss Kate, Ah'd get out o' Weston fast. The slavers, they be comin' at us f'om one side, an' the abolitionists f'om t'other. Ain't no peace near de river. Get away f'om dis Kansas-Missouri borduh. Yas'm, git out o' heah entirely."

She glanced at Stephen sleeping in the dilapidated room behind her. "We have to clean his wound."

"Ah gots some laudanum f'om de house last night." He headed for the cooking area and reached into a metal box. "Ah gots bread from yo' wagon too. Figured best to bring it heah in de cabin, or de barn rats eat it."

He took a large brown sweater from the back of a rickety ladder-back chair. "Gots a sweatuh fo' you f'om de house. It raggedy, but ain't no mo' o' Miz Ormand's clothes left. Her family clean everythin' out right after her funeral."

"Thank you, Octavius," Kate said, truly grateful. "I'm glad to have it." She pulled on the rough sweater and buttoned it up, and slowly began to feel warmer.

Behind her, Stephen let out a cry of pain, and Sarah hurried from her pallet to soothe him. She rested a hand on his forehead, then turned to Kate and Octavius. "He's burning with fever!"

"I be gettin' watuh," Octavius said. "I knows somethin 'bout bringin' down a feber."

Kate tore off more of her petticoat for wet compresses, and at length Octavius returned with a bucket of water.

They all set to work, trying to bring down Stephen's fever. After nearly an hour, he drifted off into an uneasy drowsing, and they treated the wound the best they could. Considering his fever, it seemed impossible to leave Weston at the moment.

"I'd appreciate it if you'd unhitch the horses from our wagon for now," Kate told Octavius.

"Thought so," he said. "Ah thought so mahself. Ah do it fo' Ah go to de house to he'p wid Mistuh Charles."

As the morning passed, Kate and Sarah brought Stephen's fever down somewhat, and the laudanum kept him quiet. That afternoon,

Kate stepped to the slave cabin door to get a breath of fresh air. The shabby slave quarters were deserted, except for a clucking hen and her chicks pecking along the muddy lane. The air was so warm, Kate unbuttoned the brown sweater and began to take it off.

Quite suddenly she heard someone coming to the cabin. She turned, ready to take flight, then decided it was likely only Octavius bringing food. To her amazement, Andrew Kendall appeared around the corner carrying a wicker hamper, his flaxen hair even lighter in the sunshine. She gasped, then quickly pulled the sweater on again and began to rebutton it.

He studiously averted his eyes. "Good-day, Miss Talbot."

"Good-day," she responded uneasily. "I didn't expect you. How . . . did you happen to know I was here?"

Andrew grinned. "Octavius was hustling about, trying to get a dinner together in this basket, and I finally wrested the truth from him. He's a good fellow, but has some difficulty with dissembling."

"And you . . . you're not . . . angry?"

He shook his head. "I expect I'm more surprised than anything, though I knew there were border troubles before I arrived. In fact, that's why my stepfather sent me—to see if Charles were still among the living, since he'd stayed so long without sending word home about himself or his charge."

"His charge?" Kate inquired.

"His responsibility to sell Uncle Namen's farm, or 'plantation' as Charles and Octavius are wont to call it. We didn't expect it to take quite so long, and Mother was concerned."

"Is Charles all right?"

Andrew frowned. "We don't know. He's still unconscious. The bullet grazed his head. The wound is minor, but apparently he fell off his horse, too, and that compounded the injury. Dr. Harby came this morning. He tells us it's difficult to predict the recovery time in such cases."

Kate recalled Charles's paying the exorbitant price for her box supper and his ardent embrace in the church graveyard. She still felt uncertain about her feelings for him, though she hadn't abandoned her hope of reforming his views on slavery.

Andrew handed the wicker hamper to her. "I'm afraid it's simple fare. The housekeeper was among those decamping, but the house is well provisioned."

"I . . . we thank you so much," Kate said. "As you might guess, I have different sentiments about slavery than you Southerners might. . . ."

"It's not necessary to convert me to your thinking," Andrew replied, his gaze meeting hers.

Neither did she wish to discuss it with him under these circumstances, she decided. Still, what did he mean? That he was disinterested in her abolitionist stance? Or in agreement with it? Perhaps he was as confused about it as she sometimes felt.

Now that she held the hamper, Andrew stepped back. "If I'd known Stephen was injured, I'd have sent the doctor here this morning. He's coming again tomorrow. I'll send him over if you'd like."

"It's probably a wise idea. I think we can pay him."

He hesitated. "I assume you don't wish for Stephen's family to know of his whereabouts?"

"No . . . no, please don't tell anyone."

He nodded. "I give you my word."

"I'm most grateful."

He raised his flaxen brows. "The Bences have been asking around. Apparently they didn't realize you were all missing until this morning."

"Stephen's father doesn't know he shot his own son?"

Andrew's blue eyes widened. "I didn't know either. I presume they don't." He hesitated, then said with reluctance, "His father and brothers can't be pleasant for a decent man like Stephen to live with."

"I guess not. Fortunately for him, he was brought up by an old aunt in Independence. That's where he met Sarah when they were children."

Andrew nodded thoughtfully. "I see. Well, I'd best leave you to eating dinner."

"Thank you for your kindness, Mr. Kendall."

She thought he might ask her to call him Andrew, but he seemed to be considering something else. When he spoke, it was to say, "I don't like to see your family living out here in the slave quarters. Would you like to move into the house?"

It was tempting to do so, but Charles could emerge from unconsciousness . . . or visitors see them . . . possibly even Stephen's family. Another problem came to mind too, prompted by her role in the tavern: despite Andrew Kendall's kindness and apparent good manners, he might have designs on her. "I think it's best to stay here," she answered, "but I'm grateful for your offer."

He gave another nod. "I'll send Dr. Harby here tomorrow," he said upon leaving.

What a peculiar situation, Kate thought as she reentered the cabin. Slavers in the main house and abolitionists in the slave quarters. Still, she was grateful for the food basket and for Andrew Kendall's unspoken permission to remain on the land. She only wished she knew what had happened to Greta and her family, and to little Mr. Minton from church, who'd ridden up in his wagon like a knight in shining armor.

Kate set the wicker hamper on the plank table, removed the white linen cloth, and gazed with gratefulness at the bounty: ham, cheeses, bread, nuts, and a jar of cold apple cider.

In the back room, she heard someone stirring. Looking in, she saw Sarah getting up from her pallet and Stephen sleeping.

"Andrew Kendall brought us a basket of food," Kate whispered. "Somehow he inveigled the fact of our presence from Octavius."

Sarah stared at the foodstuffs. "I can't quite believe it. Whyever would Andrew Kendall bring this?"

"Perhaps our family is praying for us," Kate said.

Sarah nodded. "I think we should be praying as well." Closing her eyes, she raised up her head and folded her hands. "We thank Thee, Heavenly Father, for these provisions when we truly need them . . . and for sending them through a most unlikely person. We are encouraged, Father, by Thy care in this, and we pray now for Thy leading out of this dreadful plight. In Christ's name we pray. Amen."

"Amen," Kate added.

In the afternoon countless riders arrived at the big house. Some even rode through the muddy lane past the cabin. At sunset, a knock sounded at the slave cabin door.

Kate darted a worried glance at Sarah, then went forward cautiously. Whoever was knocking expected slaves, so she'd pretend to be one . . . one who was unable to open the door at the moment. Gathering her courage, she inquired, "Who be dere?"

After some hesitation, a man's voice answered with amusement, "I be heah. I be Andrew Kendall a'bringin' you some suppuh, Miss Kate."

Kate put a hand to her mouth. Surely he'd think she'd lost her wits! But then, he'd answered with humor himself. Despite everything, she almost laughed. "I'm sorry," she said, coming out onto the porch. "There've been so many people about today, I didn't know who might be here."

His blue eyes held a hint of amusement. "With that accent, I didn't know who was inside, either."

She thought they might have had a good laugh if it weren't for

Stephen's and Charles's serious conditions. Uncertain whether she should invite him into the cabin, she remained standing on the porch.

"How is Stephen faring?" Andrew inquired.

"No better, I fear. And Charles?"

"Still unconscious."

After a moment, she said, "If it weren't for your kindness, I don't know what would be happening to us. Sarah and I have endlessly discussed what to do, but we've reached no resolution."

"It's understandable," he replied. "Worst of all, the countryside is full of men looking for partisans on both sides—slaves and abolitionists. I'm afraid it won't be safe for you to stay much longer. In fact, I've come with a proposal. If you'll allow me to come in for a moment. . . ."

She opened the door for him and eyed him cautiously. "A proposal?"

He hastened inside, and closed the door quickly. "You may have heard the activity at the house this afternoon."

"Yes, we heard horses and voices. Loud voices."

"It seems that we both have difficulties," he continued. "For your part, the Bence men saw a black-haired woman wearing a red dress at Halfway House last night, and they say she greatly resembled you. In addition, they've found a cloak they think is yours." He hesitated, "To put it nicely, they've sworn revenge."

Kate swallowed.

"They're watching the roads and riverboat landings for all three of you. Worse, their kin and drinking friends have been informed of your abolitionist leanings and are on alert. I understand your views are generally out of favor here in 'little Dixie.' "

"They are . . . and I tend to be reckless. My father says I don't stop to weigh the consequences."

Poppa's words came ringing back. "You're full of boldness,

Kate, but you don't pray before you act. Boldness—failure—shame, that's your way. And it will be until you put God's will before your own."

Familiar sensations began to creep into her heart as she stood facing Andrew Kendall, and she recognized them all too well—failure and shame.

"My side of the problem is only slightly different," Andrew was saying. "The abolitionists—Kansas jayhawkers in particular—have Charles on their 'wanted' list. Apparently they think he's asked too many questions with regard to the Underground Railroad."

Kate recalled Pa Bence mentioning a Southerner likkering them up, and it began to make sense.

"Here's my reasoning," Andrew continued. "First, Charles has to return to Natchez before the jayhawkers find him. Secondly, you and your family will benefit by leaving Weston for the time being. Since I have to remain here while legal matters are concluded, I propose to provide provisions and two more horses for the wagon so Octavius can drive all of you to Independence as soon as our patients can be moved. Even sooner, if worse comes to worse."

Kate's heart sank. "It's impossible for me to stay in Independence for any length of time. I had to leave, as it was."

"I thought that might be the case," Andrew replied. He thought it over. "Actually, it makes my alternate proposal more feasible."

"What might that be?" she asked.

"For all three of you to accompany Charles to the Beaumont Plantation in Natchez, where you would be welcome to stay with our family until conditions improve."

Kate was incredulous. "Go to Natchez, Mississippi?"

"I see no alternative," Andrew replied. "I promise my mother will see to your safety."

It was an utterly preposterous idea. It made no sense at all for abolitionists to travel to Mississippi. On the other hand, it could be quite sensible if they valued their lives.

"Can we stop in Independence to see my family?" she asked. "We might not see them again for a long time, and Sarah hasn't seen them since Christmas." Her mind raced on. "We wouldn't have to go to the house, but to an old cabin some distance out in the fields."

He began to shake his head, but he must have seen the pain in her expression, for he relented. "Only if it seems safe. And only if you're very cautious."

5

Long before daybreak, they set out through the dim moonlight in the covered wagon. The air was redolent of damp greenery, and owls hooted as Octavius drove toward the eastern edge of town. In the wagon bed, Stephen lay drugged on pillows and quilts, and Charles McCourtney lay close beside him.

Kate adjusted the blanket under Charles's head as the wagon jolted along, then wrapped her own blanket around herself more closely and struggled to her feet. Shivering, she peered out through the canvas puckering hole at the moonlit countryside.

'Cold?" Sarah murmured, just behind her.

"Cold and nothing to see out there except shadows," Kate answered quietly. "Should have picked up my cloak when it fell in the mud, but everything was so frenzied when we fled Halfway House."

"Frenzied scarcely describes it," Sarah replied. "At least I'm warm in Stephen's clothes."

"You look warm, albeit a bit manly."

"Never mind!" Sarah replied.

Kate almost smiled. Sarah's appearance in men's clothing was all the more unseemly since she was usually so ladylike.

As they bumped along, Kate considered the more serious

DICKINSON AR
PUBLIC LIBRARY

aspects of their predicament. Last night, Andrew had heard reports of Stephen's family staking out the nearby river landings. As for Charles, the abolitionists had grown more than suspicious of his free-spending in Weston to loosen townsfolk's tongues. Surely there must be a reasonable explanation for his actions, she decided. Unconscious, he'd looked so vulnerable.

She decided not to think about it, and, instead, thought back to Andrew.

This morning they'd found their way to the covered wagon by lantern light. Before she'd climbed onto the wagon, he'd remarked, "What's taking place here on the border is a sad commentary on mankind."

"Not everyone is bad," Kate had answered. "You've been more than generous to us."

He had given her a small smile in the lantern light. "I'm far from perfect . . . which brings up another unpleasant matter." He'd removed a small gun from his pocket. "Can you ladies use this?"

Sarah drew back so quickly he might have been offering her a snake. "I can't abide firearms!"

"Our father taught me how," Kate replied.

Andrew handed the gun to her. "Be careful, it's loaded."

She nodded, the cold gun in her hand. It was heavy, like those she'd sold at the mercantile.

Stephen moaned, and Sarah quickly expressed her gratitude to Andrew for helping them, then climbed up into the covered wagon to see to her husband.

Andrew's blue eyes met Kate's. "I'll see you soon, at the cabin in Independence, or in Jefferson City, or Natchez."

"I hope so."

"Be cautious, Miss Talbot."

"Thank you for helping and for treating us so well."

"I wish circumstances might have been different," he said, then added with concern, "and that I were going with you."

"I wish so myself, Mr. Kendall."

"Andrew," he said. "Just Andrew."

The name suited him well, she thought, for it meant brave and manly.

She'd stuck the gun in the top of her boot and, climbing up onto the wagon, hoped the Bences never learned that Andrew had sheltered them and provided food for the journey.

At the last moment he'd removed an envelope from his frock coat pocket. "If you arrive in Natchez first, would you deliver this to Paul Thompson, the minister at my family's church?"

"Yes, of course," she'd replied.

With so much border fighting, it very likely held his last will and testament.

Now they drove on quietly in the covered wagon. Andrew had given the old slave a traveling pass, and the plan was for him to deliver them to Independence by way of the less-used roads.

On the far side of town, Octavius called back to them in a hushed voice, "A carriage be waitin'."

Kate rose to her feet and peered out the front puckering hole again. In the dim light, a carriage stood on the road facing them. "If it's trouble, we'll have to outrun them."

"Yas'm!" he replied, slapping the reins over the horses' backs. "Giddup, boys! Giddup!"

Kate took the gun from her boot with trepidation.

As they neared the carriage, the driver held up a lantern, and a woman stepped out to wave them to a halt.

"It's Greta!" Sarah whispered. "Stop the wagon!"

Kate let out a relieved breath and stuck the gun back into her boot. Yesterday she'd sent Octavius with a message to Greta saying she and Sarah were leaving and needed clothing. Knowing Greta's sympathies, Octavius had likely divulged the details.

They halted beside the carriage, and Greta hurried to their wagon, her lantern flickering. "Octavius, we've brought parcels for your wagon."

He scrambled down, making room for Kate and Sarah to climb out onto the driver's seat.

Greta's lovely face was pained. "I feel responsible for your having to leave. You have no idea how dreadful I feel about it. Perhaps there was another way—"

"We made the decision," Sarah told her, her voice strained too.

"I appreciate your taking it like that," Greta answered. "As it is, I feel heartsick about how matters turned out."

"What was Mrs. Minton's invitation to tea about?" Kate inquired.

Greta drew a breath. "If you hadn't been willing to take part in the plan Sunday, we were going to try again. An alternate scheme."

Remembering Charles, Kate put a finger to her lips, then pointed to the wagon.

"Who . . . ?" Greta asked.

Kate climbed down and said quietly, "Charles McCourtney is in there unconscious. We don't know when he'll regain his senses."

Greta's eyes widened. She quickly turned to her driver, who was taking parcels and clothing from their carriage. "Ask Octavius where he wants them in their wagon."

She took two cloaks from him and checked the colors in the lantern light. "Brown for you, and gray for Sarah. They're old but warm."

"And welcome," Kate said. She passed Sarah's cloak up and put the other on herself, and at once felt warmer.

"I've brought food, too," Greta told them. "Some of our friends have contributed." She hesitated. "I haven't known you long, but I know your hearts, and I shall miss you. If I need to write you at

Beaumont, I'll be circumspect."

Tears filled Kate's eyes. "Is your family well?"

Greta shook her head. "My dear husband is hurt, or he'd be here with his good wishes. Penelopa and Alfron left, but she drowned in the river, as did another woman."

Stricken, Kate said, "I'm sorry, truly sorry."

"As am I," Greta replied, "but I feel a peacefulness about what lies ahead, no matter what happens."

"How I wish I did," Kate replied.

Octavius stood ready to climb onto the driver's seat, and Sarah called down to Greta, "It was a pleasure to meet you."

"On my part, as well," Greta answered. "Let me pray for you before you go." She placed a hand on Kate's shoulder and raised the other toward Sarah. "Heavenly Father, keep these precious souls under Thy watchful care. Guide their steps. See them safely on their journey, and give them strength to overcome obstacles. Forgive us all our sins and keep us in the way everlasting. In Thy Son's name, we pray. Amen."

Peacefulness . . . Kate felt it now. A wondrous peacefulness.

They gazed at each other, likely for the last time, then Kate climbed up on the wagon with Octavius behind her. Once she was settled, he urged the horses forward, and Kate and Sarah waved at Greta as they drove off.

"Stephen and I started off so bravely in Weston, and now see how it's ended," Sarah said. "If it hadn't been for the river changing course, we'd have had our own house. It might not have come to this."

"Perhaps not," Kate agreed, her peacefulness already dissipating. The attempt at Halfway House had been less than successful, which made fleeing Weston all the more painful too.

They rode on through the woods, heading southeast and paralleling the river toward Independence, but staying well inland. As the pink rays of dawn streaked the sky, they were already some distance from Weston.

Just before they reached the Missouri River, Octavius whoa'ed the horses by the dense woods bordering the road. "Best give yo' husband some laudanum now, Miz Sarah," he called into the wagon. "Gots to keep 'im quiet on de ferryboat crossin' de river. Gots to close up de puckerin' holes too. Gonna hab'ta ask God to keep de men quiet, so we doan do no lyin'."

Kate was in agreement. She might be rash, but she did not intend to be a liar. Stephen often moaned and this was no time for it; fortunately, Charles rarely made a sound in his unconsciousness. To their relief, Stephen took the painkiller from Sarah without complaint. If worse came to worse on the ferryboat, they might appear to be common drunks who had passed out.

"I think Sarah and I had better change clothes here, too," Kate told Octavius.

"Yas'm!"

She and Sarah climbed from the wagon and made their way into the woods, then quickly changed into the frocks Greta had brought them. Kate wadded up the red taffeta dress and stuffed it under a rock to give it a proper burial.

Returning to the wagon, Sarah wore a light gray cotton frock under the gray cloak, and Kate wore a frayed dark blue, at least one size too large, under her brown cloak. Kate tucked the gun back into her boot before they climbed into the wagon. They looked sufficiently nondescript, Kate decided.

They drove on through the countryside until, at long last, they saw the Missouri River and the ferry. Octavius halted the horses behind six other wagons waiting to cross.

Beside Kate, her sister pressed her lips together, looking nervous. Kate darted a glance behind them. "Likely we're overly anxious about Stephen's family following us."

"They don't give up easily," Sarah answered. "If they can't find us, they're apt to hire bounty hunters."

"Do you really think so?"

"I do," Sarah answered. "They might not seem smart, but they're clever and vindictive."

Kate felt uneasy as Octavius drove the horses onto the ferry, and she eyed the scrawny boy who waved their wagon toward the far railing. He was likely too young to be a bounty hunter. Moreover, it seemed impossible that anyone might have preceded them unless they'd come by river.

She climbed down from the wagon behind Sarah, and they stood by the wagon while Octavius positioned himself between the horses.

Two squalid men in dirty buckskins stood nearby, gawking at them. "Wahl, lookit by thet wagon!" one said. He called over to Kate and Sarah, "You two beauties ridin' on this here ferry alone?"

"Ignore them," Kate whispered.

"Just so Stephen doesn't wake up," Sarah whispered back.

Octavius shot the two oglers a warning glance, and Kate murmured, "Let's look out at the river."

She was all too aware of the gun in her boot and her reluctance to use it. Once the ferryboat cast off, they stood watching the river traffic, which ranged from the whitest and the grimiest of steamboats to keelboats, flatboats, and Indian canoes. Some of the larger craft carried loads of lumber downstream to the delta country, then returned upstream with sugar, molasses, cotton, and whiskey. When she glanced back, the men ogling them had moved on.

Kate's mind wandered to the old log cabin in Independence where she'd told Andrew they would go. It had been the first house on Talbot land at the edge of Independence, the place where

Grandfather and Grandmother Talbot lived while they built the big log house. Later the cabin had housed other pioneers, and even a few of the family's honeymooners.

As the ferryboat neared land, Kate and Sarah climbed back onto the covered wagon seat. Fortunately Stephen and Charles were still quiet.

Once the ferry was tied up, Kate surveyed the wharfside crowd. No familiar faces. No one paying inordinate attention to them, either.

Saddle horses rode off the ferry first, then the wagons. Finally it was their turn, and Octavius called out a lively, "Giddup, boys! Giddup!" As the horses and wagon jolted forward, Kate and Sarah watched the busy wharf: disembarking and oncoming passengers, stevedores bustling about with cargo. No one was overly interested in them.

"I feel safer this side of the river," Sarah said when the wharf was behind them.

"I'm not sure I do," Kate replied. "We'll have to drive straight to the cabin. Octavius can go to the house to tell them we've arrived. We'd best get inside the wagon now, so no one recognizes us."

Octavius halted the horses, and the two of them climbed under the canvas covering, careful not to awaken the men.

They drove on again.

When Kate peeked out of the front puckering hole, the scenery grew more and more familiar, even in the gathering darkness. After some time, she told Octavius, "There . . . pull into the lane between the fields."

As they rode in the lane, she was glad the crabapple trees and bushes on either side had leafed out, hiding the wagon from the house. It was regrettable to miss the welcoming view of the big oaks and black walnuts that led to the sprawling log house, especially now at sunset, but coming to the cabin was far more prudent.

"Expect the cabin's in disrepair," Sarah remarked.

"I think not. Remember Thomas Warrick, the widower who married Cousin Callie's friend? He lived in it almost two years. Last month he went back to New York. He didn't know much about country living when he arrived, but he learned."

"I'd forgotten about him," Sarah admitted. "In Weston, it seemed as if I lived a thousand miles away." She hesitated. "Even when Stephen and I came to visit, everything felt different. I guess I changed, too."

You lost your courage, Kate thought. *Instead of being the self-assured elder sister, you lost your courage.* And considering her life at the Bence house, the loss was understandable.

One of the men moaned.

"Stephen?" Kate asked.

"I'm sorry to say 'I hope so,' " Sarah replied. "As far as I'm concerned, Charles McCourtney can stay unconscious for a good long time. I don't trust him."

Kate made no reply, but memories flashed to mind: Charles riding up to church in Weston . . . gazing at her from his pew . . . buying her box supper at such a high price . . . his arms around her in the graveyard. . . . Almost as quickly, she again recalled Angela Grimke, the famous abolitionist, saying that women should persuade every man they knew against slavery. Surely she was the one who would show Charles the truth, Kate thought. Perhaps that was why she and Charles had met, even why he'd had to leave Weston when she did. Surely he'd come to understand the dignity of human beings, regardless of color. Her cheeks warmed with enthusiasm. She'd make a difference, but this time not with reckless words and actions. This time she'd be influencing a man, just as Sarah had done with Stephen.

Darkness was falling when Kate saw the familiar old log cabin. Its glass windows gleamed in the last rays of light, and only a few twigs lay about. Even the nearby oak tree's branches were trimmed from the roof, and Mama's old homespun curtains hung neatly at the windows.

Octavius brought the horses to a halt at the cabin's hitching post. "Here we is," he announced, then opened the canvas puckering hole. He looked in at the men. Stephen was still drugged, and Charles's condition was unchanged. "What we do wid dem?"

Kate climbed down from the wagon. "I don't know."

"Maybe leave them in the wagon until we've talked with Poppa," Sarah decided. "He'll know what to do."

"It might be best for you to go to the house and tell Poppa we're here," Kate told Octavius. "Just ask for Mr. Talbot and tell him you have to speak with him alone. Watch for who might be about."

"Yas'm," Octavius replied, nodding his grizzled head. "Yas'm, I do dat. Exactly how you says."

He tied the horses to the hitching post, then opened the cabin door to check inside. "Look fine. I'll head fo' de house." With a nod of conviction, he set out toward the windbreak of trees that lay between them and the field near the house.

Kate made her way into the cabin and, despite their predicament, felt joy at being home. Weston had been interesting, and Natchez was supposed to be the most beautiful place in the South, but what could be more heartwarming than Independence, Missouri, even in an old log cabin?

Sarah lit a lantern. "Wonder if Mama made *rolladen* and *apfel strudel* for supper? Now that I mention it, I can almost smell them."

"Me too," Kate answered. She looked around the cabin, noting again the stone fireplace, two pole-and-rope bed frames, the plank table with two benches, and an old rocking chair. "Nothing that a little sweeping and dusting won't fix."

"I'll sweep the floor," Sarah said. "It's light enough to see. Poppa and the boys can help us carry the men in. They can sleep on the beds, and we'll sleep on bedrolls. For safety's sake, we might want Octavius to sleep by the door."

"Fine," Kate answered, though the plan sounded overly optimistic to her. "Go ahead and sweep. I'll wait out by the wagon in case we have to make a run for it."

Outside again, the quiet reassured her. The clouds over the moon had moved on, giving them moonlight to see by. It was reassuring too, to have the wagon. If trouble came now, she could drive the horses herself. At long last, hoof beats sounded from the direction of the house. One horse.

Sarah came out with the lantern. "Who is it?"

"Don't know," Kate answered, peering at the trees in the moonlight. A rider pounded around the tree windbreak, and at the last moment, she recognized him and his old horse, Brownie. "It's Poppa! Poppa!"

Moonlight glinted on a rifle on his saddle and a gun in his belt, entirely at odds with his character. In moments he was reining in Brownie, dismounting, and holding her in his strong arms. "Oh, Kate, you firebrand, you're safe!"

"Oh, Poppa!"

Mama called him a gentle giant, and he looked it in the bright moonlight. The silvery light turned his reddish-brown hair grayer, and he resembled the daguerreotype of Grandfather Benjamin Talbot.

Her father shook his head at her fondly, then quickly gathered up Sarah. "Sarah . . . I should never have sent Kate to you. Octavius told me—"

"It wasn't her fault," Sarah protested. "We would have been in the conspiracy even if she hadn't come, but she made such a perfect decoy—"

"A decoy!" Poppa echoed. "Kate was a decoy? What are you talking about?"

"We'll tell you later," Kate hastened to say. She was glad to be wearing the frayed blue frock instead of the red taffeta. "Is it safe for us to be here?"

"Exactly what I'm coming to," her father answered. "Stephen's father and brothers came at midday in an uproar. We invited them to dinner, and then right at our table, they claimed you'd been part of an abolitionist conspiracy, shaming them in Weston. They calmed down long enough to devour hearty portions, then rode off, likely to find a tavern and strong drink. We told them we hadn't heard from you, but it's plain they expect you to come here."

"It's just as I feared," Sarah lamented, "Stephen so sick and we can't stay!"

"Maybe here at the cabin for a few hours . . . or maybe all night," their father said hesitantly. "Your mother is gathering up food and clothing for Octavius to bring. He explained about Stephen and Charles McCourtney in the wagon. What were McCourtney and his stepbrother doing here in Missouri?"

"Concluding their uncle's legal matters," Kate answered.

"I see," Poppa said. He hesitated only an instant. "Do you have a plan?"

Kate briefly explained Andrew's idea, trying to sound confident.

"Go to Natchez, Mississippi?" their father exclaimed, his eyes wide with disbelief.

"We thought it was absurd at first, too," Kate replied, "but it's the only idea that's at all feasible."

"Mississippi feasible?" he asked.

"Think about it a minute, Poppa," she said.

He drew a breath. "It's impossible for you to stay here, that's a fact. And I can't think where else to send you nearby." He hesitated. "Going to Mississippi is such an outrageous notion, it might be the only real possibility. But I can't bear to think of you two going! I should have listened to your grandfather and left

Missouri long before matters came to this pass."

"We'll only be gone for a while," Kate assured him and herself. "And Andrew tells us his mother is very gracious and kind, and we'll be well cared for."

"I've heard of the Beaumont Plantation." He shook his head. "I don't know. . . . I don't even know that we should take the men out of the wagon for a rest in the cabin. Here, hand me the lantern. I'd better have a look at them."

Taking the lantern from Sarah, he climbed up on the wagon and peered in. Finally he got down again, his face sorrowful. "It's a sad sight, but they appear to be out of pain."

He cast a curious glance at Kate. "Charles McCourtney is a handsome man, even lying there unconscious."

She felt warmth rising to her cheeks. "He's a slave owner," she countered as if that should end any speculation.

"So he is," her father replied.

Sarah put in, "He paid twenty dollars for Kate's box supper last Sunday at church."

"Twenty dollars!"

Kate snapped, "It only bought the box supper!"

"I'm glad to hear it," her father replied, studying her again. "What does his stepbrother look like?"

"Poppa!" Kate objected. "You think I don't have any sense at all!"

"It's plain that women are apt to judge men by their looks, not by their characters—"

"You taught us better," she interrupted.

"I hope so. I surely hope so. But I also thought I'd warned you not to be bold."

He turned to Sarah. "Whatever possessed you to attempt such a risky venture? You might have been killed!"

"I'm sorry, Poppa." She cast a glance at the wagon where her husband lay. "Believe me, I am as sorry as can be."

"It seemed so right to do something to help fight slavery!" Kate told him. "I thought God would approve."

Poppa's voice grew gentle. "Did you ask Him? Did you pray?"

Ashamed, Kate looked away at the moonlit sky. "I guess I didn't."

"Hereafter, stay away from wild escapades. Both of you!"

Kate pressed her lips together, reminded of her usual course of behavior—boldness and rash talk or action, then failure . . . followed by shame and misery.

"Andrew Kendall is a fine gentleman," Sarah said into the silence. "He strikes me as trustworthy."

"Thus far I'm not impressed with the judgment either of you has shown in this matter," Poppa replied. He looked at Kate. "How did you come to be a decoy?"

Kate swallowed hard. "Sarah, you tell it."

As Poppa stood listening, Kate was glad her sister used only sketchy details to explain the debacle.

When the entire tale had been told, Poppa shook his head with dismay. "I dislike your getting caught up in such exploits. I repeat, hereafter, stay away from wild escapades."

"We intend to," Sarah promised. "We'll remember this all of our days. We've had more than enough of adventure."

He nodded, somewhat mollified, and Kate looked away. It seemed that she was all too often in escapades.

"If this plan goes forward, how will you travel to Natchez?" Poppa asked. "You surely can't go the entire way in that wagon, and it isn't safe to leave here by riverboat."

Kate drew a breath. "Andrew thought if that were the case, Octavius should drive us away from the border until we could board a train."

"At least that's a good plan," Poppa replied. "Where does this

Andrew stand on slavery?"

Kate shrugged. "He lives on the Beaumont Plantation."

"I see," Poppa said unhappily.

Mosquitoes started buzzing around as thickly as her troubles, and Kate slapped one on her arm. "Maybe we should go inside. Even after sitting on the wagon seat so long, I prefer to sit down."

"Likely tired of being questioned," Poppa said.

Fortunately, just then they heard someone approaching the cabin on foot, and Octavius called out, "Jist me . . . it be jist me, Octavius, an' yo' mama. Doan shoot! Doan shoot!"

Kate hurried out into the moonlight, Sarah right behind her.

Octavius carried an array of baskets and bundles as well as a pack on his back. Behind him, Mama rushed to them with an armful of blankets and a small lantern. Her graying blond hair shone like a halo in the golden lantern glow as she approached.

"Oh, Mama!" Kate cried. "I'm so sorry to worry you."

"*Ach,* you girls . . . you girls!"

As usual, when Mama was excited or nervous, her German accent thickened. "You girls are past worry. It rests in God's hands . . . in God's hands. I've asked Him to make some good of all of this yet." She thrust the lantern and blankets at Poppa. "Here, I want to hold my girls."

Held against her mother's soft bosom, Kate wished she were a little girl being comforted for a minor misdeed. When at length she drew away, she asked, "Do the rest of them know we're here?"

"Not yet," Mama answered. "They only know something's happening and to be quiet. First we'll see what to do. Come, into the cabin. Adam, please light a fire so I can heat up food for our girls."

He shook his head at her. "Not with the Bences about! For all we know, they're watching the house. As it is, it's chancy to be at this cabin. I pretended to be taking a leisurely perusal of the property when I rode here."

"And did you see them?" Mama asked.

"No, but that doesn't mean they won't ride by any moment."

"Those monsters!" Mama's outburst sounded as bad as a curse, coming from her. She threw an embarrassed glance at Sarah. *"Ach,* I'm sorry, Sarah! I know Stephen is different."

"It's all right, Mama," Sarah assured her.

"Anyhow, I brought a medicine kit," Mama rushed on. "Octavius said Stephen is hurt."

"Let's talk in the cabin," Poppa said.

Inside the cabin Mama quizzed them, all the while directing the unpacking of the baskets, parcels, and the backpack on the plank table. Finally everyone settled on the benches, and Octavius was sent out to tie Brownie to the hitching post.

"The roast and potatoes are still warm," Mama said, "but the *apfel strudel* is stone cold by now."

"Oh, Mama!" Kate said. "We're hungry, but we're more glad to see you."

"And I am glad to see you." She stopped fussing with the food and turned to them again. "What have you eaten today?"

"Ham and bread," Kate replied in all honesty.

"A wonder you haven't fainted," Mama said. "And Stephen! Where is he?"

"In the covered wagon, full of laudanum," Sarah explained. "We decided it's best to leave him alone 'til he wakes up by himself."

"When he does, I see to him," Mama decided. She sat down at the table with them. "Eat, girls. Please eat. Sarah, you look so peaked. Does everything go good with you?"

Sarah shook her head slightly, and something intensely private passed between them.

Mama asked, "Is it . . . ?"

Sarah gave a small shrug. "I'm not sure."

"Oh, Sarah!" Mama said softly, then leapt up to hold her in her arms. "Oh, my dear Sarah!"

They gazed at each other for a long moment, then Mama must have remembered the rest of them, for she backed away. She turned to Kate and noted her overly-large and frayed dark blue frock. "*Ach,* what a dress!"

"It's someone else's, Mama. It's a long story."

"Everything is a long story with you girls—"

"Let's have a blessing," Poppa interrupted. "Despite everything, we have much for which to be thankful."

After the prayer, Mama said to him, "Adam, what should we do now? Tell us what!"

"You know it's not safe for them here," he answered, "but they have a . . . remarkable plan."

Mama listened to his explanation, then understanding the gist of it, cried, "Impossible! Impossible for them to go to Mississippi! No, Adam—Weston was too far away to suit me. They can't go farther from us yet!"

Kate speared a piece of carrot, feeling even guiltier for setting the entire drama into motion. The gun stuck into her boot had rubbed her leg raw, but this was no time to mention that detail. Instead, she ate her carrot.

After a moment, Poppa remarked to her and Sarah, "Your Grandfather Talbot thinks we'll have a war between the states."

"Do you?" Kate inquired.

"I don't know."

"And if there is?" Sarah asked.

He drew a thoughtful breath. "The North always seems to have more of everything—railroads, factories, large cities—and the South is always striving to catch up. But the South would fight harder than one might think. Their elite likes to live by the code of chivalry . . . honor . . . boldness. But if war comes, there will be little honor for either side in the end. Nor for us, for that matter."

"Do you think the North would win?" Sarah asked.

He shook his head. "No one would win. A war would divide the country for generations." He paused. "Unless the Lord intervenes in men's hearts, the rift could last forever, as do so many in Europe. The only good that might come of it is to turn people to God."

Poppa was in church every Sunday, but it was surprising to hear him speak quite like that, Kate thought.

"Adam, maybe we should go to California to your family," Mama said, surprising Kate even more. "We can start again, make a new life."

He shook his head. "I've considered it more and more lately." His voice turned firmer. "We live on Talbot land. Talbots have never been known to give up their land to ruffians, nor to run from trouble."

"You sent me from trouble, and I merely spoke out against slavery," Kate reminded him. "And I didn't ride about in the night like the border ruffians, shooting people from pure cussedness."

"Enough!" Mama protested, her eyes shining. "I like healing words, godly words. If only slavery had been stopped slowly."

"There's no time for 'if onlys'," Poppa said. "It's not safe here with the Bences about. I'm struggling with where else to send you girls and Stephen, but the only safe place would be California."

"It's too far," Kate objected immediately.

"We'd never see our girls again!" Mama said, appalled.

Poppa nodded. "I know it. At least Natchez is closer."

He turned to Kate and Sarah. "When people come back to their senses, you can return from Natchez by riverboat. The only question is how to make the journey. You need food and medicine—"

Mama leapt up from the bench. "*Ach,* poor Stephen! How could we forget him?"

CHAPTER FIVE

She started for the cabin door, where Octavius was finishing his meal. "Did you get enough to eat?" she asked him.

"Yas'm," Octavius replied. "I sho' do thank you, ma'am."

Mama nodded, and her voice became strained. "We must get the others here to see Kate and Sarah. Octavius, *schnell* to the house and tell Jocie and Madeleine to come. Then the others to come in turns. Say only that their mama wants them here and to come quietly. No more lanterns."

"What if dey doan believe me?"

"Tell them . . . tell them I said to *mach schnell* . . . hurry! They'll know. I say it a hundred times a day. Now, Octavius, *mach schnell!*"

"Yas'm!" he replied and rushed out into the moonlight.

Before long, Kate carried the lantern to the wagon for Mama to see Stephen and Charles McCourtney.

"Likely that Andrew is right," Poppa allowed from behind them. "With two wounded men, you have to travel by wagon. They'd be too noticeable on a riverboat. Worse, they can't run. But if they recover quickly, it's a different matter."

They climbed up into the wagon and, when Mama looked in, she let out an unhappy "Ach!" followed by a determined, "We help. Somehow we help."

They were still in the wagon seeing to the men when Jocie and Madeleine came to bid Kate and Sarah farewell.

Their younger sisters' moonlit faces brimmed with concern. "Where are you going?" Jocie asked plaintively. The gold cross around her neck gleamed in the moonlight.

"We can't say," Sarah replied.

"Why are you leaving?" Madeleine wanted to know.

"We can't say that either," Kate answered. "Poppa made us promise not to tell, so it can't slip out. You can't even tell anyone you saw us. We'll return as soon as we can, believe me!"

119

They embraced twice, and tears spilled down Kate's cheeks as her sisters made their way back through the windbreak trees. Behind Kate, Mama was in the wagon arranging the things she'd brought, aided by the moonlight, and Poppa helped to feed the horses. The moonlight usually seemed a blessing, but tonight it struck Kate as sinister.

The moon seemed even brighter as their other sisters and brothers arrived two by two, mystified as they emerged from the darkness: Jonathan and Willie, Kurt and Efrem, Eva and Willie. Talbots . . . Talbot faces with blue eyes and mostly red hair. A stream of dearly-loved ones who now resembled white-faced specters.

"We'll return," Kate told each of them as they embraced. "We'll see you soon, I promise."

In the end, she was glad Mama had deemed little Alicia and Alex too young to come out, and sorely wished Sarah didn't have to make excuses for Stephen's absence.

Finally the farewells ended, and only Kate's promise hung in the moonlight: *We'll return.*

Would they? she wondered.

Their father's final plan was for them to be ready to leave any moment; to this end, the wagon was packed and the horses still hitched. Despite the preparations, he hoped they could stay for some time, at least for a good night's sleep—and if, by some miracle, they went undetected until the men were mobile, they could take a riverboat from farther down river. He'd already sent Jonathan and Kurt into town to spy out how matters stood.

The boys had been gone for a long time when hoof beats pounded down the lane toward the cabin, and Kurt shouted, "Ride! Ride! Jonathan's trying to head them off! There's abolitionists after the Bences, and they think it's our doing!"

"Go now!" Poppa shouted to Kate, Sarah, and Octavius.

They raced for the wagon.

"I'll say I heard a disturbance at the cabin," Poppa said. "Inga, run for home!"

"*Ach, Gott . . . Gott!*" Mama cried softly, then called to them, "I love you, Kate and Sarah . . . I always love you!"

"I love you, Mama!" the girls called back.

While they scrambled onto the wagon with Octavius, Poppa unhitched the horses and smacked the nearest horse's rump. "Ride to the back road!" he called out. "The back road!"

"Tell Andrew we're heading for Natchez!" Kate yelled as the wagon took off. "Say we'll meet in Jeff City as we said! And if not there, in Natchez!"

They were bumping down the lane and Poppa called out, "Take the railroad at Tipton! Godspeed . . . Godspeed!"

His words faded behind them as they headed for the overgrown back road, and Kate's heart sunk with a dread feeling that she'd never see her family again. Already their dear faces were only remembered blurs in the moonlight.

Octavius slapped the reins across the horses' backs again and again. "He'p us, sweet Jesus. He'p us!"

Beside her, Sarah gripped the seat and cried, "What if the men fall out?"

"Hush," Kate answered, bumping along wildly with her. "Mama tied them down to the wagon."

"Tied them down?!" Sarah repeated.

"Hush, Sarah, hush! Yes, just in case. They might get a little bruised, but they won't fly out!"

On the main road, shouts and gunshots filled the moonlit night, and dogs barked from the farms around them. Suddenly Kate knew why the full moon seemed so sinister tonight: evil usually favored darkness, but the Kansas and Missouri border ruffians relished riding in the moonlight.

The covered wagon jounced onward until finally the shouts and gunshots could no longer be heard. At last Octavius slowed the horses, and they heard Charles McCourtney call out from behind them, "Who tied me in this wagon?"

Kate had a sinking sensation that their troubles were far from over. A conscious Charles would likely add to them.

6

The next morning they drove eastward in the covered wagon, paralleling the Missouri River as closely as possible on the muddy road. Charles McCourtney, conscious but still dazed, sat up in the wagon, clutching the wooden side planks on his side and occasionally shaking his head as if to clear his thinking. The way he looked at them gave Kate the distinct impression that he was not only confused about their identity, but about their surroundings and situation.

When he finally spoke, he said, "As much as I admire you ladies, and regret this gentleman's pain, I do not intend to ride in this infernal wagon much longer. Man was made to ride a horse, not to bounce on hard wood."

"Perhaps we could take a riverboat when we're farther from the border," Kate suggested. "In St. Louis no one would recognize us."

"St. Louis?" he repeated, his gray eyes still glazed.

After she'd explained their whereabouts, he proclaimed,"St. Louis is too far." Frowning, he shook his head again. "May I ask what taking a riverboat has to do with anyone recognizing us?"

"The Kansas jayhawkers have you on their 'wanted' list," Sarah told him.

He stared at her. "I beg your pardon?"

Kate put it baldly. "Your stepbrother Andrew said the Kansas jayhawkers mean to kill you."

Charles stared at her, his silvery gray eyes mirroring his confusion. Finally he asked, "What's the next river landing?"

"Matthew's Tavern," Kate replied.

"I mean to get out of this infernal wagon at Matthew's Tavern Landing and book a first-class passage on the best riverboat that comes by."

"The Bences could be waiting there for us, or even at the next town," Kate told him, alarmed.

He appeared even more confused, and Sarah explained, "They're apt to shoot you, too, for being with us."

He squared his broad shoulders. "I fear no man. I may not have any duels scheduled just now, but I have never in my life run from a fight. You're likely misinformed by my stepmother, who does not hold with dueling and the fact that I try to appease her . . . somewhat."

Kate turned to Sarah, who rolled her eyes.

"We shall proceed by riverboat, ladies," he announced. "I see that I am required to take charge of this expedition."

He called out to Octavius on the wagon seat, "To the Matthew's Tavern Landing!"

Octavius called back into the wagon to him, "Beg yo' pardon, suh?"

"I said quite clearly that we are to ride to the Matthew's Tavern Landing, Randall—"

Randall?!

Kate glanced at Sarah, who rolled her eyes again.

". . . and make haste about it," Charles continued. "It's unlike you to question my instructions!"

Octavius made no reply, and Charles McCourtney added, "You should be aware after all of these years, Randall, that I carry a gun."

The gun in Kate's boot seemed to press harder against her leg, but now was no time to brandish it.

Charles took a small pearl-handled gun from a coat pocket. "I am an expert shot. Anyone in Natchez can vouch for that."

Octavius had just glanced back, and his eyes lit on the gun. "Yas, suh . . . yas, suh!" He slapped the reins over the horses' backs again. "To Matthew's Tabern Landin' we be goin', suh! Dat be 'zactly where we goin'!"

Charles eased the gun back into his pocket, and the tension in the wagon eased somewhat too. They bumped along faster, making Stephen moan fiercely. Sarah tried to soothe him, and Kate wished she could help instead of merely clinging to the wagon's splintery sideboard with all of her might. A good thing that Stephen was still tied down, she thought. One untied man who'd lost much of his memory—and had a gun—was plenty to deal with now.

"One must let our people know who has the upper hand," Charles explained, plainly referring to Octavius. "You've likely been giving Randall too much slack. I did for years myself, but I'm in no mood for it now."

Kate decided not to argue, not with Charles in such a peculiar state of mind. Moreover, he was likely one of the typical plantation sons who'd gone off to Charleston or New Orleans to read for the law, and could out-argue Beelzebub in a courtroom.

It began to rain, and they rode along in comparative silence, punctuated only by Stephen's heartrending moans. Despite everything, Charles McCourtney remained an extremely handsome man, Kate decided again. Did he remember having been with her in Weston? And the raid at Halfway House? Between dozing, he turned speculative glances at her as if glimmerings of remembrance were returning.

At noon Octavius called into the wagon, "Road sign ahead.

'Spect it be Matthew's Tabern Landin'! But you gots to do de readin'."

Clutching the jouncing wagon's sideboard, Kate got to her knees and then to her feet. True, the Wayne City and Blue Mills landings were behind them, but surely this was still too close to Independence.

She glanced out the front puckering hole, past Octavius's back. "The sign says, 'Matthew's Tavern Landing,' " she told them.

All around them, the roadsides were wooded, and the land sloped down to where the river must be. Turning, she spoke to Charles. "At the landing, why don't you go ahead to see how long it will take to obtain a first-class passage? It would be a kindness, since it's so difficult to move Stephen, and hard on him too."

"Of course," Charles McCourtney answered most courteously. He smoothed his dark blond hair, then brushed off his suit before he looked up at her with a lifted brow. "I do enjoy having beautiful ladies in my charge."

"You do?" she inquired uneasily.

He nodded, and Kate decided, for a change, to curb her tongue. Surely she could handle him. After all, he was a sick man. It would be inhumane not to be kind to him, and perhaps his mental powers would return in full force soon.

He smiled broadly at her, and she smiled in return.

She settled herself on the blankets again, and after a while, wished he wouldn't study her quite so thoroughly. A good thing she wore the dark blue frock and brown cloak instead of her infamous red taffeta.

Despite their close quarters in the wagon, Sarah was pretending not to watch them, but it was impossible for her not to take notice. She looked as relieved as Kate felt when Charles leaned back against the wagon and closed his eyes. He seemed listless and drowsy, not at all like the man they'd met in Weston.

At length, Octavius called back, "Missouri Ribuh ahead." Charles opened his eyes and straightened up like a general. "Halt the wagon!"

When the wagon had bumped to a stop, Kate got out, glad the rain had ceased. Nearby, birds warbled in the trees, and some distance below, a riverboat came around the bend in the river. Its twin smokestacks spewed black smoke against the clouded sky, and its white paint was stained brown from the muddy water, but it was a beautiful sight. Nonetheless she felt ill at ease about catching a riverboat this close to Independence. Surely someone would recognize them.

Charles had climbed down from the back of the wagon. "An ill-kempt ship," he remarked with repugnance. He came forward and looked out at the river with her and Octavius. "Not up to our usual standards for the Mississippi River, either."

The Mississippi River!

Kate deliberated about how to reply, then kept her tone gracious. "I feel I should tell you, Mr. McCourtney, this is the *Missouri* River."

He looked at her, then glanced back at the river. After a lengthy surveillance, he said with a degree of certainty, "I daresay you're right. The water's not up to the Mississippi's standards, either."

Kate thought she might have laughed if their situation weren't so dire.

She glanced at Sarah, who was still in the wagon with her and Stephen. Her sister, more white-faced than Kate had ever seen her, shrugged with hopelessness.

"We shall go by riverboat in any event," he announced. "Randall, if you please, see about obtaining first-class tickets to Natchez."

Octavius straightened his spine and looked determined to carry out the instructions, no matter how peculiar. "Yas suh, I be doin' dat right away, but I needs some money fo' tickets, suh."

Kate broke in, addressing Charles. "I thought you said you would get the tickets."

"Changed my mind," he explained. He took out his wallet, peeled off several large bills, and handed them to the old slave. "That should be more than enough. Don't run off with it!"

"No, suh. I ain't run off yet, suh. Only trouble is if dem Bences be down dere a'lookin' fo' us, dey reco'nize me. By now, dey likely know I'm wid dese ladies an' Mistuh Stephen. Or might be Kansas jayhawkers on dat boat a'lookin' fo' you, suh. Might even be an abolitionist ships like de *Arabia* smuggling mo' Sharp's rifles to Kansas."

Charles frowned. "The *Arabia?* That's the *Arabia?*"

"No, suh. De *Arabia* went down in de ribuh two years back. Ah jist sayin' it could be an abolitionist boat."

Charles glared at him, uncomprehending. "Book first-class suites straight to Natchez, if you please."

"If you say so, suh. But I 'spect we can't go straight to Natchez. Gots to change to 'nother boat in St. Louis—"

"First-class cabins to Natchez, Randall!" Charles ordered fiercely.

"Yas, suh!" Octavius answered. "Yas, suh!" With that, the old slave took off running down the hill to the landing.

Charles rubbed his forehead. "I do believe Randall's not up to his old standards, either."

Kate pressed her lips together, appalled at their plight. They stood watching Octavius and the scene below. At length she stepped back to the wagon and quietly asked Sarah, "What shall we do?"

Her sister shrugged. "We'd have been far better off if Charles hadn't regained consciousness."

Finally, when the old slave reached the distant wharf, Kate could no longer desist. She turned to the dazed man. "Mr.

McCourtney, you've had a severe blow to the head. I suspect it's caused you to confuse this slave with another. This man is Octavius from your Uncle Namen's farm in Weston, Missouri . . . the only slave who didn't run away with the others."

To Kate's relief, a glint of comprehension came to his gray eyes. He looked toward the approaching riverboat and Octavius, who, at this distance, was a small figure hurrying to the ticket window line. "That man is from Uncle Namen's plantation, you say?"

Kate nodded. "He is."

"And Kansas Jayhawkers are looking for me?"

"That's what your stepbrother Andrew told us," she replied. "Andrew claims you're on their wanted list."

Apprehension filled his eyes. "I have a ferocious headache. Please run fetch Randall, miss!"

Miss? Didn't he remember her either?

"We'll ride on in the wagon for a while as I deliberate this," he added. "I'll see if the nurse in the wagon has something for headaches."

Kate set off running down the hill. He might not recognize them, but he was beginning to be somewhat more sensible. Halfway to the wharf, she saw Octavius glance toward them, and she beckoned him back. Behind her, she saw Charles McCourtney calling out and waving him back, as well. Octavius immediately left his place in line and started back to them. Behind him, the riverboat neared the dock and passengers waited to disembark.

Lord, don't let the Bences be on there! Kate found herself praying. Nor the men chasing after Charles McCourtney!

Ahead on the hill by their wagon, she saw Sarah had gotten out and gone to the edge of the nearby bushes, clutching her mouth. Nausea! That and the confidential exchange she'd had with Mama . . . it was likely what Kate had suspected, for some of her married friends had displayed the same symptoms before having children.

By the time Kate reached her, Sarah seemed better. "Are you ill?"

Sarah smiled a little, her light blue eyes shining. "I know it's inconvenient here and now, Kate, but I believe I'm with child."

"Oh, Sarah—it's wonderful news!"

Kate would have embraced her, but Sarah held back. "Not now, please. I'm still feeling unsettled."

"Have you told Stephen?"

"Not yet," Sarah answered. "I'm not sure he'd understand in the state he's in. Oh, Kate, how is it that we are stuck here together with two dazed men? It seems impossible."

"They'll recover," Kate assured her. "They will!"

"I hope so!"

Octavius was hurrying toward them, and Kate helped Sarah into the wagon and climbed in herself. Down below, by the river, the gangplank was being put down.

"Drive on!" Charles told Octavius as he reached the wagon. "There's a change of plans. And if no one's after us, stop somewhere so I can buy a horse."

"Yas, suh!" Octavius replied, climbing up onto the driver's seat. "Yas, suh! Where you wants me to head fo'?"

Charles glanced at Kate for assistance.

"It seems best to get away from the river until we're out of little Dixie," she told him. "We'd better ride on toward Sedalia and Jefferson City."

Surprisingly, Charles asked, "Is the railroad through?"

She was grateful to hear logical thinking from him. "The tracks are through to Sedalia, but the trains only come as far as Tipton."

"Then Tipton it is," Charles decided. He called out to Octavius. "Head for Tipton!"

"Yas, suh!"

As they started off, Kate glanced down at the distant wharf. Passengers spilled off now, tending to their hand baggage and trunks, and stevedores bustled about with barrels and wooden cases of goods. Only a few looked at the hillsides, no doubt seeing them in the wagon. At this distance, however, pursuers might not recognize them.

The wagon jounced onward, first in a southerly direction and some time later, eastward. Charles hadn't asked, and she saw no need to inform him about the distance. Tipton must be a hundred miles from Independence, at best a four-day journey.

Even in California, all one heard about lately was slavery, Benjamin Talbot thought as he made his way to the parlor behind his young guests. Worse, with such strongly held convictions on each side, it seemed impossible to resolve the snarled dilemma. If only there were a middle ground.

This morning their new housekeeper's husband, Runnell, a rough and scrawny Tennessean, had made reprehensible pro-slavery remarks in front of their very noses. If only he hadn't been struck speechless at the man's nerve, Benjamin thought. As it was, he had only responded with a mild, "We tend to be on the side of abolishing slavery, sir. And we do not appreciate such rough talk, particularly not in front of our womenfolk."

"Ye don't?" Runnell had asked. "Well, jist because me wife works for ye don't give ye no right to tell us what to say. And jist 'cause ye were in Californy earlier than most, an' hate Southerners—"

"It's true that I arrived here before most newcomers," Benjamin had replied, "but I hate no man or woman. Nor is it reason to—"

"I say ye do," Runnell had retorted.

"God knows I do not!"

The man had spun away, likely to save his wife's position, and likely with an even wider smirk on his face. If only Jessica weren't too old to keep up the place. . . and if only good housekeepers weren't so difficult to find.

Now seated in the parlor, Benjamin still felt uneasy about Runnell. This past week the man had been idling around the place, and he'd be delivering and picking up his wife, Ada, daily.

He forced them out of mind, only to have his thoughts fill with the quagmire of slavery. Best not to mention it straight-away to their guests, especially not with the taste of Ada's apple pie still in their mouths.

He turned to Callie, his auburn-haired niece. "A fine Sunday dinner, wasn't it?"

"Yes, an exceptionally fine dinner," she agreed, seating herself on the horsehair sofa. She smiled at Matthew, her husband of two years. Matthew sat down beside her on the sofa, returning her smile fondly.

He'd been the guest preacher at their small country church this morning and had done a fine job on the subject of love, so fine a job that the elders had prevailed upon him to once again be their preacher this summer. Benjamin hoped Matthew would take the position. With his teaching theology at the college up at Oakland, they seldom had time with him and Callie.

Jessica bustled in and seated herself in the parlor chair near the hearth. "I've asked Ada to clean up," she said. "I fear I'll miss something, and Benjamin never remembers to tell me what's transpiring."

Benjamin gave a guilty nod and sank back into his horsehair chair. For an instant he thought he saw the top of a head outside the parlor window. He craned his neck to be certain. The bushes near the window were still. Moreover, the window was open, and they'd have heard someone out there. Likely it was only his imagination, and it surely would be senseless to bother their guests with the notion.

To break the silence, he nodded toward the *Alta California,* which lay refolded on the dark oak coffee table before them. "I don't like the tenor of yesterday's paper."

"Crime is down," Matthew replied. "Between that and church attendance being up all over the state, it seems an auspicious beginning for the 1860s. An auspicious beginning for any decade."

Benjamin shook his head. "It's slavery that disturbs me endlessly. We must stop the strife now, but it seems hopeless. The radicals in the abolitionist camp are fighting gradual emancipation, even though some of the Southerners are emancipating their slaves as quickly as they can."

"I've heard of planters freeing them in their wills," Matthew replied. "Manumitting, they call it."

"Indeed," Benjamin said. "There was even an American Colonization Society repatriating them to Liberia. A settlement there was established by a Judge James' former slaves and called 'Mississippi in Africa,' but then Mississippi's legislature prohibited repatriation. If only the Constitutional Convention had accepted Jefferson's measure for gradual emancipation, we might have abandoned slavery before it became so entrenched."

"A missed opportunity if ever there was one," Matthew agreed. "What's worse, I'm sure Jefferson knew it all too well."

Benjamin nodded. "And now firebrands on both sides cause endless turmoil. Look at the Kansas-Missouri border shootings and lynchings—and Adam and his family living right in the midst of it."

Matthew drew a breath. "I think cooler heads might prevail yet. Matters weren't as bad as the newspapers claimed when we passed through in '58. And Missourians love old Jefferson's memory. Gradualism could yet prevail."

Benjamin wished it might be the case, but he no longer held much hope for a sensible solution. "I often visualize the turmoil over slavery as water in a cauldron over a fire. The cauldron is our country. At first as the flames lick at the cauldron, the water warms. After a time, it gives off errant bubbles like this Kansas-Missouri border strife."

"And then?" Matthew prompted.

"It comes to a roiling boil," Benjamin replied. He narrowed his eyes with regret. "I fear we've only seen the warming and errant bubbles thus far, and the roiling looms ahead of us. In the end, it could split the cauldron."

"Can you persuade your Missouri family to come here?" Callie asked.

"Adam's stubborn," Benjamin admitted about his eldest son. "I've mentioned it in letters time and again, but he clings to Independence and matters improving there like an old Missouri mule. As for coming here . . . if there's a war between the states, there's bound to be trouble in California, too."

"Slavery trouble here?" Matthew asked with some surprise.

"Whenever there are problems back East, there's an influx of newcomers to California," Benjamin replied. "I've seen it happen for the past fourteen years. This will be no different."

"Surely the people who come to flee war won't be troublemakers," Callie said.

"True, there'll be those who fear war or see no sense to it," Benjamin said, "and probably some men who run from soldiering and, at worst, consider themselves cowards. But there are bound to be firebrands among them, adding more fuel to the fire."

Exactly the kind of hot-headed newcomers like Runnell, he thought. It struck him again that no matter how fine a job Ada did, nor how difficult it might be to find a good housekeeper, they would have to find a replacement for her soon because of her husband. He'd discuss it with Jessica later.

"It's hard to believe," Callie replied.

"It won't be only the newcomers," he told her. "It's thought that a third of California's population has come from the South, or like us, from the border states. And look at our state legislature, with a pro-slavery majority!"

He felt like a prophet of doom, yet having said this much, pressed on. "Already we have pro- and anti-slavery factions in San Francisco . . . and now even here in the countryside. Each faction wants California to stand with them to justify their side and—more importantly—to get our gold. Unless it's stopped, I predict brother against brother here and across the nation . . . a fierce carnage."

Matthew said with reluctance, "It's no secret about the Northern and Southern societies in town. Still, it's only talk. If it would please you, I'll look into what's transpiring around the northern part of the city."

"I'd appreciate that, Matthew," Benjamin replied. Best not to belabor the subject, he decided. As it was, Jessica and Callie looked alarmed. "Likely it will be safer here," he added. "I'll write Adam again tomorrow and try to reason him out of Missouri. With the railroad through Panama, the journey is easier now than it was by covered wagon."

"Far easier," Matthew agreed. "It behooves us to be as sensible as possible about our safety, but in the end, God will prevail. Even if matters seem impossible here on earth, God will prevail."

Benjamin managed a small smile. "Thank you, Matthew, I sorely needed reminding. I suppose what grieves me most is watching a country founded on godly principles brought down by God's arch enemy. Old Lucifer would dearly love to see this country and its witness destroyed."

Again he had an uneasy feeling, but it went well beyond someone merely lurking under the window. Now it had everything to do with evil. Closing his eyes, he prayed, Heavenly Father, forgive us our endless transgressions . . . give us Thy wisdom and deliver this family and this nation from evil!

Two days after avoiding the river landing, Charles McCourtney stopped the wagon to investigate a "Stallion for Sale" sign posted by a small farm that fronted the road. After talking to the travelers, a passel of young children ran off to search for their father, yelling, "Papa, a man wants to buy the horse!"

Once the farmer had been found in the barn, he brought out a gray stallion. In no time, the horse was saddled and Charles cantered him about the farmyard, then raced him for some distance on the road.

"Be a good strong horse," Octavius observed as Charles rode back to the farmyard. "Maybe a mite mulish. Jist so he doan take it in his head to run on his own."

Once the agreement had been struck, Charles paid the farmer and looked extraordinarily pleased. The hapless farmer, surrounded by his small children, looked glum, though he doubtless needed the funds.

Finally Charles rode the gray toward the wagon. "In case you want to buy him back, I'll sell him in Tipton when we catch the train," he shouted back to the farmer. "I expect the price will be about the same."

The farmer shook his head. "Ain't no chance o' that, but I thank ye anyhow."

It was a kind gesture, Kate thought as Octavius urged their own horses onward. Despite her suspicions about Charles, he did possess a sense of gallantry. In fact, she'd been quite impressed with it as they'd forded the swollen creeks. Once he had even carried Stephen, when the wagon snagged on sycamore roots under the rushing spring runoff.

Now he cantered the gray stallion alongside them. "At least I'm out of that confounded bouncing wagon," he remarked to her.

"Not that I lacked appreciation for such charming company."

Kate avoided his gaze, glancing at the surrounding woods instead. Flattery would get him nowhere—not that she didn't enjoy it a little.

"Once I have a sure feel for this stallion, you'll be welcome to ride along with me," he offered.

"No, thank you!"

"Miss Talbot, you surely are a northern girl, even coming from as far south as Missouri," he said with amusement.

"You mean southern girls go about riding on horses with men?" she was tempted to ask, but curbed her tongue. Perhaps she was getting over talking reckless, she thought. Mama and Poppa would never believe it.

Charles McCourtney rode alongside the wagon so amiably that one would think she had encouraged his presence. For an instant, she thought how tempting it would be to be held in his strong arms and ride with him instead of bouncing along on the hard wagon seat.

He shot another dazzling look at her. "Haven't changed your mind about riding with me, have you?"

"No. No, I have not."

"I hope you'll reconsider, Miss Kate Talbot."

Once again, she turned to the trees that bordered the road. Was her interest in him that obvious? At any rate, she was glad he'd bought the horse. Perhaps he'd tire of teasing and watching her, and occupy himself with finding their way and seeing to their safety. In truth, he had grown more attractive to her, likely because his mind had improved. He was being restored to the Charles McCourtney she'd admired in Weston.

One difficulty while he'd been in the wagon had been the intimacy between Sarah and Stephen. Restrained though it was, it had been impossible not to notice the tenderness between them and the way their eyes met. Kate yearned for such fondness and devotion, and even Charles appeared to have been affected, causing him to cast speculative glances at her. Perhaps now that would end, she thought, though she had mixed sentiments about it. Perhaps there'd be a perfect opportunity to talk to him about her views on slavery once his mind was completely restored. In any case, they would be making camp at night and, barring rain, she would sleep outside again, Charles McCourtney not too far from her. Thus far, he had been the perfect gentleman. Still, she felt uneasy about their proximity in the flickering firelight, even with Sarah and Stephen nearby in the covered wagon.

Charles hadn't given up on her, riding his gray stallion alongside the wagon. "I've named the horse Arthur from *La Morte d'Arthur.*" He smiled at her engagingly. "Like most Southerners, I admire the days of chivalry."

It occurred to Kate that Charles McCourtney was beginning to look more and more like a Sir Lancelot to her. She admired his broad shoulders and strong arms, the squareness of his face and chin, his silvery gray eyes, the wave in his dark blond hair, even the narrowness of his expressive lips.

"I, too, admire the days when knighthood was in flower," she replied.

"How do you happen to know of King Arthur?"

"My father attended Harvard. Not that it's a prerequisite for reading the classics, but we do read in our family." At Charles's raised brow, she added, "I come from a well-educated family."

"Yet your father stays in Independence, running a mercantile?"

"He does," she replied. "It's our family home, and I suppose he rather enjoys being a pillar of the community. Moreover, with one of the major rivers in the country nearby, he's involved with the family's shipping concerns."

"I see. Is he connected with Wainwright and Talbot Shipping?"

"He is."

Charles raised his brows. "An old and esteemed international firm."

"Yes."

He was rightly impressed, she thought. No matter how he might feel about shopkeepers in general, her father's Harvard education and shipping connections had elevated her and her family in Charles McCourtney's mind. Perhaps he assumed that only Easterners and Southerners had fine educations.

As an afterthought, she told him, "Even if Poppa hadn't attended Harvard, he would have been a gentleman."

"Whatever is that supposed to mean, Miss Talbot?" Charles inquired with a wry smile.

"Whatever you take it to mean," she retorted, unable to stop a smile in return.

His voice turned as smooth as honey. "Why, Miss Talbot, I do believe I had a mistaken impression about you. There's a smattering of impudence in your disposition."

"Certainly not!"

He gave a laugh. "What's more, you're especially beautiful when you're vexed. Wouldn't you say Miss Talbot is a beautiful young woman, Octavius?"

"Yas, suh," Octavius replied. He had been effecting an air of invisibility, his eyes on the horses' bobbing backs. "Yas, suh. Whatever you say, suh, I bound to agree."

Kate stifled a laugh at Octavius's inevitable reply. On the other hand, it was heartening to know that Charles finally realized Octavius was not "Randall." It was thought that when one lost one's memory, the past returned first, and then the present. Charles's mental state appeared to be returning to the present.

He bestowed another admiring glance on her. "I'd go so far as to say that Miss Kate Talbot is the most beautiful young woman in the state of Missouri. What do you think, Octavius?"

"Yas, suh! Yas, suh, I be bound to agree!"

Charles bantered on, but Kate closed her eyes as if she were drowsy. In truth, she was far from it. Instead, his interest and compliments carried her from growing pleasure to outright consternation.

It was a relief when he finally said to his horse, "Well, Arthur, it appears we're not wanted," and nudged the gray stallion forward.

Late in the afternoon it began to rain lightly, and Kate climbed back into the wagon. It occurred to her that Charles's absence, especially the lack of his scrutiny, would make a vast difference in the wagon's atmosphere. She nodded toward Stephen, who lay asleep in the blankets. "How is he?" she whispered.

"Improved, I think," Sarah whispered back. "He's quieter, though the wound isn't healing as fast as I hoped."

"We'll have to find a doctor in Sedalia."

"We need one as soon as possible."

"Have you told him about . . . about the babe?"

Her sister blushed, but her pale blue eyes shone with happiness. "I will tomorrow if he's improving. It would give him something to look forward to. I hoped you'd ride out on the seat again so I could tell him privately. If it's not raining, of course."

"Is that a hint?" Kate asked wryly.

Sarah gave a laugh, the first one in a long time.

The light rain stopped late in the afternoon, and Kate was relieved to ride outside with Octavius instead of being confined in the wagon. The rain-freshened air smelled wonderful, and it was a joy to be out among the birds and trees and rolling green countryside.

That night they made camp under a grove of elm, oak, and walnut trees, staying near a small creek. Above them, dark clouds still hid the moon and stars.

"Too dark fo' fishin' tonight," Octavius said. "Ah gots to find dry firewood, start de campfire, an' tend to dem horses."

"I'll see if I can't shoot us some game," Charles replied.

"You needs you a rifle, suh."

"Maybe not," Charles said, and rode off into the night.

How could he find game in the darkness, and with only a handgun? Kate wondered. She headed for the wagon with her lantern. Opening the grub box, she sorted through the foodstuffs Mama had given them. Flour, sugar, cornmeal, carrots, onions, cabbage, potatoes, and . . . ah! . . . a bag of dried lentils to use with the ham scraps. Soup would taste good on such a damp night.

While Sarah tended to Stephen's needs, Kate cooked lentil and ham soup in the black pot over the fire. Standing at the smoky campfire, she couldn't help but reflect upon Grandfather Talbot's covered wagon trek to California. Cooking out for a few nights like this might be difficult, but it was nothing compared to cooking every morning, noon, and night on campfires for five months.

At length Charles returned, riding Arthur through the darkness. "No luck finding game."

"I'm not surprised," Kate told him.

He dismounted from the stallion and tied him to a nearby tree. "Not surprised?"

"As Octavius pointed out, you'd need a rifle."

Charles eyed her with glimmerings of understanding.

Was he still confused? she wondered.

"Where is Octavius?" he inquired and surveyed their location. The wagon stood under the trees a short distance away, and the four horses grazed silently nearby.

"Getting water at the creek so Sarah can wash Stephen," she said.

Kate suddenly felt uneasy, seeing how Charles looked at her. It was hot by the fire, and she'd unbuttoned the top buttons of her dark blue frock.

"I smell something good cooking," he said, smiling at her in the firelight. "In fact, I feel rather like the hunter returning empty-handed from the hunt and finding his dear wife cooking a hearty soup to cheer him. Seeing you here at the cook pot is rather like watching the tender scenes between Sarah and Stephen in the wagon."

She turned quickly toward the cook pot.

Suddenly Charles was behind her, covering her arms at her sides with his and kissing the nape of her neck.

She tried to twist away. "Please . . . Mr. McCourtney!"

"Please what, my dear Miss Talbot?" he murmured. "You're not afraid of me, are you?"

"I'm not afraid of anyone," she declared. "Please stop!"

He laughed softly, and her knees turned weak. He didn't intend to stop, and her willpower was melting away. How could a man affect her like this? It seemed impossible, she thought as he turned her to face him.

"Dinner ready?" Sarah asked, climbing down from the wagon with a lighted lantern.

Charles stepped back immediately, and Kate staggered slightly as she withdrew.

"Later," he murmured. "Later, Kate Talbot."

"The lentil soup smells wonderful," Sarah said, bustling toward them. "Even Stephen remarked about it."

"It should be about done," Kate replied. Fortunately, in the firelight her humiliation wouldn't be so obvious, and Charles, the picture of innocence, was fetching tin plates for Sarah.

Later, while they sat about the campfire eating the lentil soup and cornbread from their tins, her gaze often found his in the firelight.

After dinner, Sarah whispered to her, "Perhaps you'd like to sleep in the wagon with us tonight."

"There's no room. We'd crowd Stephen."

"I know what's happening," Sarah said. "Charles is very appealing, but he's a powerful man, Kate. Be careful."

"I've had the same instructions from our parents as you have! I'll be fine."

"Then at least sleep under the wagon."

"Perhaps I shall," Kate decided.

Octavius brought out his dulcimer and began to strum a hymn on it. The steady hopeful twang on the strings filled the air so sweetly it seemed as if angels played their harps in the heavens. Dark clouds moved across the sky, and the moon dusted the forested countryside with luminous light. It struck Kate that the slave's faith was the source of his contentment.

At length, she spread her blankets under the wagon. She took the gun from her boot and hid it under the remnant of torn petticoat that served as her pillow. The soft strains of "Amazing Grace" filled the night air. Kate wondered: could she really shoot Charles McCourtney?

She thought not. After all, hadn't God commanded, *Thou shalt not kill?* She was supposed to be a Christian, even if she wasn't overly pious. Moreover, she wanted to help Charles see slavery in a new light when the opportunity presented itself.

The dulcimer music ended, and the night sounds returned. Owls hooted, night birds chirped, and animals rustled through the dark woods. Finally she said her nightly prayer and slowly drifted off to sleep. When she awakened hours later, she rose up on her elbows and looked about in the moonlight. No sign of Charles McCourtney. Perhaps in his confused state of mind, he'd forgotten her. She fervently wished that she could forget him.

The next morning they drove on quite amiably, Charles riding in front of the wagon horses as if nothing had transpired between them. Had Octavius's hymns changed matters? Had her prayers?

They forded one swollen creek after another, and were glad to find dilapidated ferries at the rivers. The next two evenings when they made camp, Octavius caught huge catfish, and Kate was careful to keep Sarah in her presence when she cooked dinner.

Only once, when Sarah was caring for Stephen, did Charles refer to their encounter by the cook fire. "I regret if I offended you," he said to Kate, then smiled appealingly. "I hope you'll forgive me."

"Of course."

She didn't know what to make of him. Was he truly contrite or only softening her for his next attempt?

On the outskirts of Sedalia, they were glad to find a doctor's shingle out in front of a house. Looking about the sparsely settled neighborhood, they decided it would be safe to stop. They pulled up the wagon in front of the house, got Stephen out, and helped him into the examining room.

After examining him and redressing the wound, the doctor said, "I don't like the looks of it."

Stephen stared at him with terror. "Do you have to amputate?"

"Now, now, we can't have our patient thinking such dire thoughts," the doctor replied soothingly. "You need to rest in a decent bed. There's a rooming house here in town—"

"No," Stephen cut in. "No, I can't hold us up."

Kate was surprised to see that he had a wallet packed with bills and paid for the doctor's visit himself. Perhaps Father had given Sarah money in Independence. If so, no mention had been made of it.

"We'll soon be on a train," Charles McCourtney assured them. "Back in civilization, matters will be better. Come along. Octavius can help Stephen back to the wagon. You'll see, things will improve."

Charles turned to Octavius, who strained under Stephen's weight. "I'll help the ladies back into the wagon."

"Yas, suh," Octavius replied. "Yas, suh."

The next day in Tipton, they were overjoyed to see gleaming railroad tracks leading to a train station. More important, there appeared to be no one in pursuit of them. Perhaps the Bences had given up.

The men sold the horses and wagon at the livery, and Octavius went down the street to search for a wheelchair for Stephen. Before long, the slave returned victorious, pushing a caned wheelchair on the boardwalk. Once Stephen was in it, they made their way to the mercantile, Octavius maneuvering Stephen along.

"Count your blessings," Sarah said softly to her husband.

He smiled up at her warmly. "I am." His smiles at Sarah clearly showed his pleasure at their expecting a child.

"We'll need new clothing and portmanteaus for the rest of the journey," Charles said. "I wonder what they might have in such a small town. If we don't find things soon, we'll have to wait until St. Louis."

Kate wanted to ask if there'd be good shops in Jefferson City, but Stephen spoke first and firmly. "I shall buy the necessities for my family."

"Of course," Charles replied.

The Tipton mercantile was small, but the prices were comparable to those in the Talbot Mercantile in Independence—a dollar for a straw hat, ten cents for a box of pins. The foodstuffs included many of the same regional specialties, such as pickled black walnuts and black walnut sauce and, for cooking, there was the same factory-made tinware.

The apparel corner held only a small selection of ready-made clothing, but Kate and Sarah found suitable cotton frocks—for Kate, a pale green and a dark russet with narrow waists, and for

Sarah, a gray and a pale rose, commodious around the middle. They took the frocks to a back storage room and dressed among the barrels and wooden crates. Kate decided to wear the dark russet under her brown cloak for train travel, and Sarah chose the light gray for under her dark gray cloak. Once dressed, Kate wadded up the soiled dark blue frock, which was now not only frayed but irreparably ripped, and jammed it into an empty barrel.

Sarah smiled. "Your wearing that frock didn't make you any less appealing to Charles that night at the cook fire."

"I'd rather not speak of it."

Sarah hesitated. "You sound sorely smitten. One hears of women who are irrationally drawn to a man—"

"Please, Sarah . . ."

It seemed impossible to her, too, that sensible Kate Talbot had somehow become so interested in Charles, and that the entire journey to Natchez lay ahead. She fervently hoped that Andrew Kendall was on his way to Jefferson City; perhaps his presence would dampen her fascination with his stepbrother.

When she and Sarah stepped out of the storage room, Charles and Stephen were waiting, and the men's eyes lit up to see them in the new frocks.

"Well, don't you two look lovely!" Charles remarked.

Kate said brashly, "As do you two."

The men wore new white shirts and black suits, and even with their growing beards, looked quite presentable.

Charles smiled and said, "It's not the finest of tailoring."

"Indeed!" Kate agreed. Ready-made clothes might save work, but there was nothing like having a well-fitted frock.

"You'd never think we'd been traveling through the wilderness," Charles said, causing the shopkeeper to eye them with speculation. Noting the man's interest, he added, "Now, if you'll show us what you carry in portmanteaus, please. We'll need one for the ladies and another for the gentlemen."

Once their purchases were completed, they pushed Stephen in his wheelchair to the City Hotel, where they ate a fine roasted chicken dinner. The wheelchair, though cumbersome, simplified matters, and eating dinner in real chairs and at a real table was a relief.

"Have you ever ridden in a train?" Charles asked Kate.

"Never," she admitted over a forkful of chicken. "Missouri has so many rivers, we haven't needed railroads for transportation." Lest he think her too provincial, she raised her chin and added, "I did see trains upriver in St. Joseph. I believe Sarah has, too. Do you have a railroad in Natchez?"

Charles's silvery eyes shone with humor. "We do. And I rode the train to Weston, so it will not be my first train ride, if that's what you're wondering."

She smiled with him, then sipped her steaming coffee. It struck her that his short light brown beard, growing since they'd left Weston, made him more sensual. She dabbed the white cloth napkin to her lips. Being with him this last week, and now sitting beside him, kept her nerves on edge. For his part, he still seemed thoroughly aware of her presence, but no longer seemed ardent in his pursuit. She wondered if he might have a fiancée or several female admirers at home in Natchez. Was he beginning to remember them? And if so, was he comparing her unfavorably?

After dinner, they pushed Stephen to the railroad station in time to find their train huffing and chuffing toward them down the tracks. The black locomotive had brilliant red trimmings, and it spewed dusky smoke through its smokestack. Behind the locomotive came the coal, baggage, passenger, Negro, and freight cars.

Hanging back behind Charles, Kate surveyed the passengers in the train's windows and then, before long, those detraining. No sign of Bences or other pursuers. Indeed, the disembarking passengers were more interested in claiming their baggage than they were in her, Sarah, or Stephen.

If Octavius expected to return to Weston, he was mistaken, for Charles said, "We shall expect you to accompany us and tend to Mr. Stephen's needs on our way to Natchez."

"Yas, suh," Octavius answered. He looked down, trying valiantly to hide his disappointment. "Yas, suh."

Kate felt a pang of sorrow for the old slave, then a surge of anger about their own situation. Standing here at the Tipton train station, it was exceedingly clear they were leaving Independence behind and, in spite of her rash promises to her family, perhaps leaving the state of Missouri forever.

7

Kate waited on the railroad platform while Charles handed their tickets to the splendidly uniformed conductor. At the man's nod, she climbed up onto the stool and looked warily into the half-filled railroad car.

"Go ahead," Charles urged from behind her.

As she started down the aisle, every passenger seemed to be watching; some even lowered their newspapers and gawked at her. Perhaps they guessed it was her first train ride.

"We'll take the seats in the rear," Charles directed. "Less chance of people jostling Stephen back there." He carried the folded wheelchair, which drew even more attention. Occasionally Charles's mind still seemed somewhat unsettled, but he appeared to be in perfect command of their situation now.

Once behind the black stove in the middle of the railroad car, there'd be less chance of being seen by any pursuers, Kate thought. She raised her chin and ignored the other passengers as she passed through the car. Fortunately—or unfortunately—with Charles in her wake, every woman on the train seemed interested, mainly in him.

Behind them, Sarah and Octavius helped Stephen along.

"Poor fellow cain't walk," a gray-haired woman remarked

about Stephen. "Wonder why he's out travelin'."

Why did people have to notice them? Kate thought. As it was, the Weston doctor who'd treated Charles and Stephen might let out the fact that they had a gun-shot man in their party, as might the doctor here in Tipton. If only they could get to Jefferson City and meet Andrew quickly.

At long last she settled on a brown leather bench by the window, and Charles seated himself beside her. Across the aisle, Octavius helped Stephen to the window seat, where he moaned as he sank into it. Sarah quickly sat down beside him and patted his arm.

Moments later, the locomotive blasted another warning, and Octavius ran for the door. His having to ride in the Negro car struck Kate as a sad state of affairs, and she called behind him, "Do you have your traveling papers, Octavius?"

"Yas, ma'am!" the old slave replied. "Yas, ma'am!"

The conductor bellowed, "All abooaarrd! All aboard for Jefferson City!" The locomotive's blast drowned out his recital of the train's other stops. "All abooaarrd!"

Kate gripped her brown leather armrest as the train doors slammed shut and the cars jerked into motion. Smoke and ashes billowed all around the railroad car, some wafting through open windows as they chugged away from the station. Despite her earlier bravado, it was a peculiar sensation to be moving through Tipton and its outskirts as the train gathered speed. She glanced out the window and decided it was more pleasant to see the countryside from a train than from a wagon.

"Comfortable?" Charles inquired.

"Thank you, I'm fine."

His lips turned up with humor. "You look terrified, gripping the armrest like that."

She loosened her hold on it. "I am not!"

"You do raise your chin when you're riled."

Hmmpf! she thought.

He chuckled. "In addition to a fine but stubborn chin, you have most intriguing lips, Miss Kate Talbot. I imagine the young men of Independence have also found that true."

"They have not!" she retorted, turning away. She'd only let one of them—Albert Morton—so much as kiss her, and little good that had accomplished in the end.

Sarah watched them from across the aisle, and Kate glanced out the window. It was disconcerting enough to sit so close to Charles McCourtney, without his making bold remarks. On the other hand, it made her more certain that he was still interested in her.

Eventually he opened the St. Louis newspaper he'd purchased in Tipton, and she felt him settle back. After a moment he quietly remarked, "Nothing about us reported. Only one small article about border strife."

"I'm glad to hear it."

"You're glad to hear about the border strife?" he joked.

She didn't bother to turn from the scenery outside the train window. "You know what I meant."

He chuckled again, and she kept her gaze on the countryside.

Once he was engrossed in the newspaper, she sat back in her seat, but his broad shoulder and arm were all too close to suit her. His black trousers hid strong, well-muscled limbs. . . .

She turned quickly and glanced out the window again, trying to concentrate on the pastoral view. It seemed a marvel to pass through the countryside so quickly. The main drawback to train travel appeared to be the smoke blowing into the car, making it smell like wet ashes. Likely it smelled worse in winter when they fired the iron stove.

After a while, he asked, "Enjoying the ride?"

"Yes, thank you, I am." Fortunately, her voice sounded as sane and sensible as she wished she felt sitting at his side. She kept her gaze on the hilly countryside where the grasses, bushes, and trees displayed their springtime light greens. Blossoming redbuds and apple trees brightened the land as they had in Weston and Independence—a thought that summoned bittersweet memories of leaving home and family. Yet there was a hopeful tenderness to spring, too—as hopeful as the flickerings of interest from Charles McCourtney. For a long time, she watched the train's shadow rushing alongside the tracks and the nearby grasses whipping about wildly in its path. Charles made occasional remarks about the scenery, not requiring her to say much in response, for which she was grateful.

The train blasted out warnings at crossroads, and the cows and horses in the pastures looked up from their grazing to see the huffing iron curiosity pass. She tried not to think of home. Once beyond that and the awareness of Charles's presence, it was a pleasure to ride along through the country at such a great speed. It seemed only a dreamlike interval before the conductor shouted, "Jefferson City! Next stop, Jefferson City! Capital city of the state o' Missouri!"

From her seat, Kate found Jefferson City an awesome sight. The train tracks ran alongside the wide, muddy river, leading to a substantial wharf; to her right, atop a great hill, towered the white capitol, topped by a Romanesque dome and fronted by a majestic portico.

"A fine edifice," Charles remarked from beside her. "It seems a long time ago since I stopped here en route to Weston."

"It's an even more imposing place than I expected," Kate replied. Indeed, the city surrounded the domed capitol, its buildings built downhill to the river. "Where's the Lohman Building?"

"There, just beyond the wharf."

As the train slowed, she viewed the approaching station and the waiting crowd, hoping to see Andrew. Charles still glanced past her, his nearness unnerving. Finally she said, "No sign of Andrew. We'll have to get off and wait at Missouri House."

"We have through tickets to St. Louis," Charles replied.

Kate stared at him. "But we were to meet Andrew here. That was the plan—"

"It's not necessary to wait for him," he replied in a most reasonable tone. "Stephen has a difficult time getting about, and I decided it was more sensible to buy tickets straight through to St. Louis."

"Why didn't you tell us?"

"Because I thought you'd be distraught, just as you are now. I'm confident Andrew can find his way to Natchez. He's quite competent. I made the decision with Stephen."

"But he's full of laudanum." She glanced at Sarah and Stephen. They showed no signs of getting up from their seats.

"I didn't know you were so interested in Andrew," Charles remarked, his silvery eyes awaiting her response.

"It was the plan we agreed to in Weston. We were to meet him at Missouri House or leave a message at the Lohman Building—"

"Is it so important to you?"

She drew a breath, then dropped her shoulders. In truth, she'd been counting on Andrew to join them, to bridle her attraction for Charles.

The train had stopped, and outside on the platform, Octavius ran through the waiting passengers. Suddenly a flaxen head of hair gleamed in the crowd.

"There's Andrew!" Kate called out.

He stood with his portmanteau and two trunks on the platform, delighted to see Octavius.

"I told you he could manage quite well by himself," Charles said. "Andrew has the uncanny knack of landing on his feet, no matter what happens. Good, he even has my trunk."

Octavius must have been telling Andrew their whereabouts on

the train, for Kate caught his eye through the window and returned his wave. He looked equally pleased to see them. As they watched, Octavius found a porter for the trunks, and Andrew headed for their railroad car. Before long, he beamed at them as he made his way up the aisle. His fawn-colored frock coat and trousers suited him well, and though not as handsome as Charles, he cut a fine figure as he approached.

"Good-day, ladies," he said to both her and Sarah, then added with a nod, " . . . gentlemen. I had a feeling you might make this afternoon's train."

Charles's voice took on a wry tone. "You and your confounded feelings, Andrew! Can't you manage like other mortals?"

Andrew gave him a lopsided smile. "Glad to see you're back in fine fettle, Charles. You had little to say when I last saw you in Weston."

"Finally came to my senses," Charles replied.

Kate asked Andrew, "Did you stop in Independence to see my family?"

"Didn't have time. I came straight to Jeff City."

"I suppose that was most sensible," she replied.

"Unfortunately."

Andrew turned his attention to Stephen as the locomotive gave its first warning blast. "I'm gratified to see you up and around again, Stephen."

Stephen had been growing increasingly weary, but he managed a pleased nod before turning solemn. "What do you hear of my family?"

Andrew drew a breath. "They know that Octavius was at Matthew's Tavern Landing, then went off with a wagon. I'm sorry to say they are bent on revenge. The word is that they're in full pursuit."

A lump of fear formed in Kate's throat. Aubin, Rodwell, and

Pa Bence suddenly reminded her of tenacious hound dogs. Between their humiliation and anger, they might never give up on finding them.

"What's my situation?" Charles asked his stepbrother.

"Jayhawkers don't give up easily, either. You're still on their list." They eyed each other silently before Andrew added, "The trunk you left in Weston is in the baggage car. Octavius is seeing to it."

Charles's thanks were nearly lost in the train's second warning blast, and Andrew turned to the grandmotherly woman occupying the seat in front of them. "May I sit with you, ma'am?"

" 'Course you kin," the woman replied. "My, ain't ye got yeller hair!"

Andrew gave a laugh. "That I do." Still grinning, he swung his portmanteau up onto the baggage rack with ease, then took the seat on the brown leather bench in front of Kate. By the time the train chugged forward, he had exchanged pleasantries with his seatmate and was closing the window for her.

Noting Andrew's sun-bleached hair and the breadth of his shoulders above the seat, Kate guessed he was more of an outdoor man than Charles might be. It also occurred to her that Charles most likely would not be friendly toward a grandmotherly woman, perhaps not even deign to speak with her.

Kate opened her handbag and found the letter Andrew had given her for his minister friend in Natchez. During a lull in his conversation with his seatmate, Kate handed the letter to him. "Under the circumstances, I thought you might like to have it yourself again."

Oddly, Andrew blushed as he accepted it. "Indeed. Appears it was a waste of ink. Thank you in any event."

She settled against her seat. From the corner of her eye, she saw Charles watching her, then his hand reaching for hers. Suddenly he was kissing her fingertips.

Raising his head, he smiled and murmured, "You're far too beautiful to fret. I promise to take care of you very well, Miss Kate Talbot." His gray eyes held hers for an instant, then she withdrew her hand from his.

"That's very kind," she managed.

Charles was jealous of Andrew! Surely that was why he was trying to win her favor again. Charles, whose splendid appearance drew every woman's attention, was actually jealous of his step-brother.

The streets of St. Louis, the vaunted Gateway to the West, bustled with carriages, buggies, drays, and even occasional ox carts and covered wagons. Its sidewalks were crowded with traders, merchants, harried clerks, fellow travelers, occasional riverboat gamblers, dance hall women, and a few bewhiskered fur trappers from the mountains. Likely there were no border ruffians here, Kate thought, since the federals controlled the eastern side of Missouri.

As the men bought their riverboat tickets, Kate and Sarah eyed the tumultuous joining of the blue Mississippi and muddy Missouri rivers. A conglomeration of vessels tootled, or blasted horns and whistles. In addition to ferryboats constantly crossing the rivers, there were rafts, skiffs, canoes, barges, pirogues, flatboats, broadhorns, keelboats, ordinary steamboats, and the great white side- and stern-wheelers.

"And I thought we knew river life, living so close to the Missouri," Kate remarked.

Sarah nodded with amazement.

While Octavius saw to their baggage, the rest of them boarded the *Mississippi Palace,* the most luxurious riverboat in sight. Instead of the squat, snub-nosed and brown-stained steamboats that traveled the Missouri River, the *Mississippi Palace* gleamed a sparkling white and was the finest boat Kate had ever seen. Its lively calliope music filled the air, adding to the excitement.

"First class," Charles McCourtney said as they started up the gangway. "Alas, we'll only see you ladies at mealtimes." He gave Kate a broad smile. "I do think that rules often stand in the way of good sense, don't you?"

She responded rather tartly. "I expect the rules are there for a good purpose."

"My, my!" He laughed, his silvery eyes shining at her. "At times you do surprise me, Miss Talbot."

"I'm glad to hear it," she responded.

In truth, until they'd purchased their tickets, she'd forgotten that the separation of the sexes was rigidly maintained on the finest Mississippi riverboats because so many of the lower class boats were known for dreadful debauchery. On the Mississippi River, even Stephen and Sarah were to be billeted apart—in different cabins on opposite sides of the ship. On the other hand, being apart would give her and Sarah a welcome respite from the men. Perhaps they could even request dinner in their cabin, just as Andrew planned to arrange for Stephen, who remained pale and unsteady.

They'd scarcely arrived on board before resonant blasts sounded from the *Mississippi Palace's* twin smokestacks, accompanied by twin clouds of black smoke. The calliope music played on as Kate stood at the railing with Sarah, watching the sailors take in the gangway. Much to Kate's relief, the male passengers were immediately separated from them by a heavy chain near the ship's sternwheel and doubtless by one in the prow. Charles was already gone. Octavius wheeled Stephen to the men's cabin, and Andrew went in search of the dining room steward on Stephen's behalf, since the old slave would have to stay in the ship's Negro quarters. As the *Mississippi Palace* slowly sailed away from its

St. Louis dock, three riders raced their horses to the wharf, looking wildly at the departing ship.

Kate felt her mouth drop open with dismay.

Aubin, Rodwell, and Pa Bence!

"Get back!" she warned Sarah, and she rushed back herself, but too late.

Rodwell's gaze seemed to lock onto her, then he shouted what sounded like a "Whooeeee!" above the calliope music. She and Sarah withdrew from the railing to hide in the crowd.

Sarah's face was ashen. "Did they see us?"

"I . . . I'm not certain," Kate replied.

Tears filled Sarah's pale blue eyes. "It's my fault you've been brought into this strife!"

"It's just as much mine! What's more, Pastor Armbruster would say that strife is the devil's doing," Kate told her. "You've done nothing wrong—"

"Except to marry into the Bence family," she interrupted with a sob. "Though I wouldn't give up Stephen for the world!"

Kate took her weeping sister into her arms, glad for the calliope's lively rendition of "Yankee Doodle."

"Hush, Sarah . . . people are beginning to notice us." She patted Sarah's back. "Doubtless they think you're just sad at leaving someone behind, but further crying will make them curious. We have to be careful."

Sarah drew away, pressing her lips together. "No more tears, I promise."

"Good." Kate turned and stood on tiptoe to peer over the crowd at the Bences. "They're leaving. They're riding off."

"They know we're aboard," Sarah replied. "I can feel it in my bones."

"How could they possibly? It looked to me as if they'd just ridden in to see if we were about."

But what she suspected was a different matter. The Bences were clever enough to check the ship's passenger list with the ticket master—even bribe him, if need be. In any case, she felt certain Rodwell had seen her. The question was: would they follow them beyond the state of Missouri?

That afternoon Kate seated herself on a wooden deck chair, trying to calm herself. She adjusted the writing paper box on her lap, took up a steel pen, and began to write on the white linen paper provided by the ship.

Dear Mama and Poppa, and my dear, dear sisters and brothers,

I am writing from under an awning on the deck of the stern-wheeler Mississippi Palace. Despite the excitement of our journey and the luxury of the ship, Sarah and I are homesick for you and our friends in Independence. Oh, how we miss each one of you! Just thinking of you opening and reading this letter at the mercantile or at home in the parlor brings tears to my eyes.

I shall try to put sentiment aside and tell you our news.

Sarah, Stephen, and I have made our way this far on the journey we discussed. We went by wagon to Tipton, then on by railroad, as Poppa suggested. (It is likely best for you not to divulge our destination for your own sakes, so I will not mention it myself.) In any event, this has turned into a memorable adventure. Stephen's health is still uncertain, and the medicine, food, and blankets you sent with us are much appreciated. Also, for your information only, the unconscious invalid accompanying us seems to be almost entirely recovered.

Sarah and I took our mid-day meal in our cabin. (Stephen, along with our other escorts, is doubtless asleep on the men's side of the ship.) At the moment Sarah is resting in the cabin, and I am contentedly watching the wooded land pass by—the state of Missouri on one side and the state of Illinois on the other. We shall sail past Ste. Genevieve and Chester, and our first stop will be on our side of the river at the famous Cape Girardeau, which you spoke of from your travels, Poppa. I am eager to see the old town. Perhaps there are still a few French trappers and traders about. Alas, we shall have no time to disembark for a proper perusal.

Kate stopped, wondering again whether Aubin, Rodwell, and Pa Bence would be among the oncoming passengers. If they were, what could be done to stop them? Ever since they'd left St. Louis, she'd pondered the problem and could find no solution. The crux of it seemed to be that the captain would probably not refuse anyone passage.

Trying to put the thought aside, she wrote on.

We shall soon have an opportunity to see a bit of Kentucky on the opposite side of the river. A large metal map adorns the deck wall behind me, so we can observe our progress and improve our geography in the process.

Some of the passengers seem to have no notion of where we are, nor do they show any interest in their whereabouts. Their lack of curiosity strikes me as astounding. It reminds me of what we often heard at school. I likely misquote. "Seize the moment of curiosity, for if you let it pass, the opportunity to learn may never return, and you shall be mired in ignorance."

Now, lest I be mired in ignorance, I should like to describe the river as I see it at this very moment. If my description sounds forced, it is only because school writing lessons have suddenly sprung to mind.

All around us, the winding river seems as vast and blue and depthless as the sky. Close to a thickly wooded island, a fish leaps up with a splash, sending circles spreading toward the shores. The forest that rims the water is a long, curving line of bright spring greenery against the river. On the Missouri shore, a fish-

erman sits in his boat, afloat between two islands. Nearer yet, just over our ship's railing, the mighty river rushes along as we steam through it. And there, coming around the bend, perhaps from New Orleans, is a smaller steamboat, its smokestacks billowing. Its low-pitched horn sounds at us, and now we return the melancholy salutation.

Enough description, but I do look forward to the changing scenes at sunset and in the moonlight, since Mississippi river-boats do not dock at night. Can you imagine, sailing onward as we sleep! I hope to see the missed sights soon on the return voyage to Independence.

Sarah and I each have two new cotton frocks that Stephen purchased for us at a mercantile in Tipton, so we are more neatly attired than when you last saw us. (Yes, Poppa, their prices seemed comparable to ours in Independence. I believe they receive their goods by both railroad and riverboat.)

We looked quite presentable on the train and in St. Louis, but wonder how we shall compare with some of the more fashionable ladies tonight at supper. A few boarded at St. Louis with several trunkloads of what must surely be clothing. Yes, you may laugh. This is indeed from Kate, who once cared so little about fashion. On the other hand, it is still far from my major concern.

She hesitated, her consternation about Charles McCourtney coming to mind. He seemed unpredictable, one moment enamored of her, the next moment backing off. She rethought the evening by the cook fire when he'd caught her by such surprise. Why had he turned his attentions from her after Sarah's intervention? Was it Southern gallantry? Vacillating interest? Octavius's playing hymns on his dulcimer?

She forced herself to write on.

On a more sober note, and as alluded to above, it remains important for you not to reveal our whereabouts. I must tell you that Stephen's father and brothers arrived at the St. Louis wharf as our ship sailed away. I'm unsure whether they saw us, but I am very sure they came for us, not to see the countryside. I don't wish to worry you, but to warn you in case they return to Independence. They are a vengeful lot.

The most important news is saved for last. Sarah sends her love and says I am to tell you that she and Stephen are to have a child before Christmas! They are most pleased. We should be home far sooner than that so we can all share the joy of the blessed event.

P. S. More good news: Stephen's injury is improving!

As she folded up the letter, she noted that the middle-aged woman on the next deck chair had been watching her. Nodding courteously, Kate rose to her feet to depart.

The woman, spindly as a stick, wore her red hair skinned back in a tight knot, and as Kate inspected her, a toothy smile came to the woman's face. Still smiling, she said, "Guess yer wonderin' why I bin watchin' ye."

"I hadn't actually noticed," Kate answered.

"Name's Ida Notzinger," the woman said. She stood up awkwardly, then smoothed the skirt of her bright green calico frock. "I was wishin' I could write a letter myself. Niver had a chance ter learn nothin' but workin'. What I wouldn't give to write a letter! Why, I bin prayin' an' prayin' on it!"

"Perhaps I can help you," Kate offered.

Ida's green eyes bulged with hope. "Bless my bones! Could ye, really?"

"I'd be glad to."

"Tomorry?" Ida asked.

"Why not right now?" Kate replied. "I have extra sheets of paper and envelopes here with me, and time on my hands."

"Well, bless my bones!" she repeated. "How'd we do 'er?"

Kate reseated herself on the wooden deck chair and took a

fresh sheet of writing paper. "You tell what I should say, and I'll write it down."

Ida nodded, drawing a nervous breath. "You won't tell no one on the ship what I say?"

"I won't tell a soul," Kate promised, her pen at the ready over the white linen writing paper.

Ida drew another breath. "Well then, let's begin with 'Dear Maudy,' " she said. " 'A lady is writin' this letter fer me.' "

She waited for Kate to finish, then began to dictate again. " 'I jist want ye ter know no matter what happened, we always love ye.' "

Her voice faltered. " 'Yer pa sold the house, an' he's gone ahead to his sister's in Cape Girardeau to find us a place ter live. I stayed a spell at Aunt Sari's an' then at Cousin Lotte's. Now I'm sailin' fer Cape Girardeau meself. Jist wanted ter let ye know we won't be on ye anymore. We looked fer ye, but ye weren't ter be found. Anyhow we love ye.' " Ida's eyes glistened. "Then jist sign it somethin simple, like 'yer ma and pa.' "

Suspecting that Ida ordinarily had to sign with an X, Kate signed *Ma and Pa* in her best penmanship. As it was, she had already made improvements on her shipmate's grammar.

Ida gave a St. Louis address where she hoped her daughter might eventually receive the letter, and Kate wrote it on the envelope. "Anything else?"

Ida shook her head, her green eyes filling with more tears. "Ain't no more. We raised 'er as good we could, but she turned from everythin' decent an' took up with bad men. Near broke our hearts, she did."

"I'm sorry."

Ida nodded. "Ye look like a lady. Probably ain't right to say it, but the truth is . . . I wish ye were my daughter."

Shaken by Ida's heartfelt expression, Kate said, "I'm far from perfect."

"But ye ain't took up . . . sinful with men?"

Kate shook her head, then remembered how she'd been affected by Charles McCourtney. *Not yet,* she thought. *And not if I can help it!*

In the evening, when they went into the dining room for supper, Kate wore her pale green cotton frock from Tipton. Sarah appeared more rested and was so beautiful in her new rose frock that Stephen beamed at her from his wheelchair.

After the five of them had settled at a table for six, Kate noticed Ida Notzinger venture into the dining room, still wearing her bright green calico. "May I invite that woman to join us?" Kate asked. "I met her on the deck this afternoon. She's alone."

Charles raised his brows with a show of distaste, but Andrew said, "Certainly. I'll fetch her." He rose immediately and started through the maze of tables for Ida.

The woman's eyes lit up with astonishment as Andrew explained his mission. She turned toward them and, seeing Kate, looked as if she might break into tears of gratefulness.

Charles had the good grace to stand as she arrived at their table, and Ida's expression shifted between awe and gratitude as Andrew seated her between Kate and himself. "Ain't ye folks fine ter ask me ter sit with ye? It's jist fine o' ye to make me feel t'home."

"It's our pleasure to have you here," Kate told her, and introduced her to Sarah, Stephen, and Charles.

Ida remained awestruck. "Pleased to meet all of ye, I'm sure. It's jist fine o' ye, lettin' me eat with ye. Don't know what I ever done to deserve yer kindness."

"It's our honor," Andrew assured her. "You know what Scripture says about widows and orphans—"

"I ain't widowed yet," Ida assured him, "but I was orphaned.

Me husband, Rufus . . . well, his folk rescued me from the misery o' bein' an orphan. And now ye rescued me from loneliness the first time I bin on a riverboat."

"Mrs. Notzinger's husband will be meeting her in Cape Girardeau," Kate explained to them.

"Rufus is findin' us a place there," Ida added. "I bin livin' around St. Louis from kin ter kin, an' let me tell ye, I'm more'n ready fer a place o' our own ter nest in."

With everyone's interest provoked, Ida waxed more and more eloquent, interrupted only by the waiter bringing them their soup and then their chicken dinners. Charles was polite, but barely hid his amusement. Even Sarah and Stephen, blissful to be together again, gave Ida a good bit of their attention.

As they sat eating and listening to her, it struck Kate that it might be Providential that Ida had come into their lives—especially since she was traveling to Cape Girardeau, where the Bences could easily reappear. Perhaps God had led the woman to sit beside her on the ship's deck this afternoon. An idea struck. Perhaps she would enlist Ida to help when she disembarked at Cape Girardeau—but only if the Bences were waiting to board, of course. The question was how to do it.

After eating their dried peach pie with cream and drinking their coffee, they left the table with Ida still grateful. "Don't ye gamble, whativer ye do," she warned the men in all seriousness. "Ain't no faster way o' losin' yer money than gamblin' on a Mississippi riverboat."

Charles gave a laugh, but Andrew and Stephen gave their promises. Sarah and Stephen looked as if they wished to be alone, so Kate accompanied Ida from the dining room.

"If there's anythin' I kin do fer ye," Ida said, "anythin' at all—"

"It may be that there is," Kate answered as they strolled to the women's deck. "Let's find a quiet place to sit."

"There, closer to the stern," Ida suggested. "Most o' these women won't trouble themselves to walk thet far."

Once they had settled on wooden white deck chairs, Ida sat at full attention while Kate explained Stephen's family as honestly as she could.

"Ye don't say!" Ida exclaimed at the enormity of the situation. "Ye mean Stephen's own pa shot him?"

"His father may not realize it," Kate replied, "but that's exactly what happened."

Ida shook her head. "I don't hold entire with either side o' slavin', but if there's one thin' I do hold agin, it's a drunk who shoots his own son!"

Kate swallowed. "If his father and brothers are at Cape Girardeau, I've been hoping you could somehow stop them from boarding the ship. I don't know how, and I wouldn't want you to lie. I know it sounds impossible—"

Ida proclaimed in full voice, "Don't ye worry yerself none. It'll be worked out, if it's the last thin' I do." Fortunately she looked about and quieted her voice. "Ye say it's a father and his two grown sons? What do they look like?"

Kate described them as best she could. She added, "I wouldn't want you to get hurt, or into any difficulties."

"Don't worry none on that," Ida replied.

"Don't endanger yourself," Kate told her again.

"I won't," Ida promised, "and I won't lie none, neither."

The next morning Ida ate breakfast with them, then scurried off to make arrangements for disembarking. It was kind of her to agree to help, Kate thought, but she wondered what Ida could possibly do. In the meantime, she sat on the deck with Sarah, trying to decide what they might do themselves in the event that the Bences boarded the ship. The only plan now was to retreat to their cabin as quickly as possible.

As they sat thinking, the Mississippi River made a westward bend through the wooded countryside. Behind a bluff, the town of Cape Girardeau came into view. "Does Stephen think they'll be there?" Kate asked.

Sarah nodded unhappily. "He says it's more than possible . . . it's downright likely. The fact is, they're more than just aggravated with us about slavery matters."

"What do you mean?" Kate asked.

"Stephen inherited his aunt's money. There's not much of it left, not after his trying to save the farm in Weston. But they'd be glad to get their hands on whatever there is."

"That certainly explains things!" Kate replied.

"In any case, he doesn't want us to bring Charles and Andrew into the Bence family troubles. He's adamant about it."

"Maybe Ida can stop them from boarding the ship," Kate said. "I told her about it all, and she's going to try—"

"I doubt anyone can stop them," Sarah replied.

"Then what can we do? What can we possibly do?"

Quite suddenly Sarah's eyes widened. "I have an idea!" She paused, considering it. "Yes . . . we can bribe the cabin steward into letting Stephen into our cabin so I can nurse him. We could ask for meals to be delivered to our cabin so no one will find us."

"I don't know—"

"We have no other choice," Sarah decided. "Come, let's find the steward."

Kate hurried after her, hope rising in her heart. If the Bences did board the ship, Sarah's plan might work. At the very least, they could keep themselves apart until the ship arrived in Natchez.

They rushed to their cabin and found the steward at his station in the corridor. He was an older black man, but quick of foot and mind. "Yas'm, kin Ah help you ladies?"

"We have a problem," Sarah told him, then began to explain

most plaintively how important it was that she care for Stephen. "Likely you've seen him in his wheelchair."

"Yas'm, I seed him," the white-coated steward replied.

"He's not getting proper care," Sarah said emphatically.

"You hab mah commiseration, ma'am . . . mah commiseration, but no mens is allowed in de women's cabins. Ain't no mens allowed."

Sarah took a pouch from her pocket and produced a small gold coin. She held it out for him. "Please, I beg for my dear husband's sake . . . please!"

The steward's eyes went from the gold coin up to Sarah's face, then down to the coin again. "How you think we git yo' husband ovuh heah to the women's cabins?"

"Octavius, who is down below, could wheel him here," Sarah replied. "Perhaps you could close off the corridor doors while he's underway. I expect everyone will be out on deck looking at Cape Girardeau when we stop there, just as they did when we embarked in St. Louis."

"Dat be true," the steward agreed. "We already slowin' fer Cape Girardeau. What else I got to do?"

"Tell Octavius when to bring my husband here, and then get meals to our cabin for the rest of the voyage," Sarah said.

The steward eyed the gold coin again. Finally, he shook his head. "It be agin de rules," he said. "Ah be losin' mah job. Cain't do it fer no amount of money, ma'am."

"I'm sorry," Sarah told him. "We don't know what else—"

"I be sorry too, ma'am," he said, then excused himself and hurried off down the corridor as if he were fleeing temptation.

On the verge of tears, Sarah looked at Kate.

"I'll go out on the deck and stay behind the other passengers," Kate said. "At least we'll know if the Bences are actually there and if they board the ship."

Sarah nodded, "Maybe you'd better."

Kate turned and rushed down the corridor for the women's deck. Outside, she positioned herself in a deck chair in the shade, well behind women who stood at the railing to witness the ship's arrival.

The *Mississippi Palace* was already approaching the wharf, sounding its low-pitched greeting and filling the air with lively calliope music, almost drowning out the excited shouts of the passengers to friends and families who awaited them.

As the ship was being secured to the dock, Kate stood up and peered past the women at the railing.

Aubin, Rodwell, and Pa Bence stood at the edge of the crowd, waiting to board the ship!

Kate swallowed. Judging by their determined stances, they'd find Stephen no matter where he was hidden.

The gangway clanked as it was let down to the wooden wharf.

To Kate's amazement, she saw Ida Notzinger in her bright green calico, her arm tucked into the captain's, ready to disembark. They were surrounded by an escort of ship's officers and sailors, and as they made their way off, the calliope music came to an abrupt stop.

Ida pointed a skinny finger straight at the Bence men on the wharf. "Them's the ruffians right there!" she shouted. "That's them! Makin' dire threats against yer passengers! Why, with such ruffians about, it ain't safe fer a woman to ride a riverboat, let alone git off!"

Everyone stared at the Bences, and immediately the sailors grabbed the three of them and wrested them off the wharf. Moments later, the calliope music started again, and the other passengers began to disembark.

Ignoring everyone else, Ida threw herself into the arms of a man who was surely her beloved husband. Except for a big round head, he was as spindly as she, but it didn't stop him from clasping her joyously, then spinning her about in a celebratory dance to the calliope music.

Still dancing with her husband, Ida glanced up toward the deck and gave Kate a wave. Through the calliope music, she shouted something that sounded like, "With God, all things are possible!"

8

Benjamin Talbot stepped up behind the counter of the Wainwright-Talbot Shipping and Chandlery warehouse, surprised to see the visitor before him. Thurmond Morse, a blond man with graying hair and a luxuriant handlebar mustache, had recently moved from South Carolina to California and set up a shipping and chandlery concern only two buildings away on the wharf. Morse was tall, an elegant man of about forty-five, well-dressed in a black frock coat and trousers. An expensive gold watch fob shone on his vest, matching the shine on his new wedding ring and adding to his air of propriety.

"Well . . . Mr. Morse," Benjamin said, extending his hand in welcome. "A pleasure to see you. We've been pleased to have you in church with your wife the past few Sundays."

"The pleasure is mine entirely, suh," Thurmond Morse replied. His southern accent was unmistakable, but his handshake seemed slack for such an affable man. "It's especially magnanimous of you, since my business is in some respects in competition with yours."

Benjamin gave a small shrug. "Others might disagree, but I feel there is sufficient shipping in California for men of good repute."

"You are kind, suh. Ah was uncertain as to whether you'd be

171

here at the warehouse today, but Ah thought to at least chance it."

"I no longer come in daily as I once did," Benjamin replied. "At my age, it's far more agreeable to stay at home and let younger colleagues attend to commercial matters here in the city."

"But you're here at work today, and Ah do salute you for it," Thurmond said. "You're a fine example for all of us here in California . . . an entrepreneur of good repute and a civic leader we would all do well to emulate."

Benjamin disliked flattery, but he gave a reluctant nod. "I thank you, Mr. Morse. You honor me far too much."

"Not at all," Thurmond protested. "Not at all! Your reputation precedes you. You captained one of the early wagon trains here, not to mention fighting for statehood and standing up against San Francisco's lawlessness."

Benjamin noted that the newcomer ignored what he himself felt was his most important contribution—that of starting churches before and during the gold rush.

"You're a man of renown in these parts," Morse added.

"I did none of it in my own strength—"

"You're a modest man, as well," his visitor interrupted. "But I come from a family of highly acclaimed men myself. One you may have heard of is Samuel Finney Morse."

"Yes, I have," Benjamin said with interest. "A Yale man. Famed inventor of the telegraph, the Morse Code, and far more."

"You know him?" Thurmond asked.

"We met several times in Boston, where my father had a church. Samuel was slightly older than I, and our lives veered in opposite directions—his to New York's Academy of Design and mine to the wilds of Missouri before I came here. Your relative is a man who, according to newspaper pictures, is taking on the look of a prophet. Now that I consider it, you share his fine Romanesque nose. How, may I ask, are you related to him?"

Thurmond's hazel-colored eyes had narrowed as Benjamin spoke. Now he said rather abruptly, "We're distantly related . . . on my paternal side, of course."

"Of course," Benjamin replied.

An old axiom came to mind: the haughty talk as if they had begotten their own ancestors.

But why had the man mentioned his relationship to old Morse and then been so eager to end the subject? Perhaps he only wished to use it as a mark of distinction. In any case, it seemed best to move the conversation on.

"Is your family getting settled in your fine new house, Mr. Morse?"

"Yes, indeed. Your kindhearted sister brought us a sumptuous roast beef dinner the day we moved in. We shall be forever beholden. Please thank her again for us."

"I shall. What can I do for you today, Mr. Morse?"

"An apt question, suh," Morse replied. "As a newcomer, Ah hoped you might be willing to introduce me to members of the city's old guard."

"Ah, but a gentleman like you won't require much introduction in California. There's not nearly the distance between old families and newcomers in California as there is on the Eastern seaboard and in the South. Nonetheless, I should be happy to help in any way possible."

"Perhaps you can recommend a bank," Morse suggested.

"Yes, of course. In fact, I'm taking my midday meal with my banker, Isaiah Meeker. Let me give you one of his cards. Shall I tell him to expect you to call?"

His eyes alight, Morse glanced at the card. "Yes, indeed, Ah would surely appreciate it. Thank you kindly." He hesitated. "Ah know you're an extremely busy man, and Ah don't wish to take up another moment of your valuable time, suh. Ah thank you most wholeheartedly and bid you adieu."

Benjamin thrust out his hand, and they shook hands again. It recurred to him that there was something tentative about Morse's handshake, and an evasiveness about his eyes. Even his Southern accent seemed too pronounced, but then, South Carolina was in the deep South.

"I hope to see you and your family in church Sunday," Benjamin said.

"Yes, indeed, suh. Ah do thank you for your welcome there, too. Mah dear wife enjoys it so."

As the man departed, it struck Benjamin that for a man of Thurmond Morse's age, he certainly had a young and beautiful wife. Moreover, she was a woman who, from all appearances, was devout in her faith. Likely that explained their move. It was a dreadful dilemma for many Christians on both the North and the South sides to live at peace with the institution of slavery.

That evening at the supper table, he told Jessica of the day's events, including Thurmond Morse's visit. "He says they are forever beholden to you for bringing their first day's dinner." He teased, "Jessica, despite your various flaws, you are good-hearted."

She smiled at his raillery, then shook her head. "We are the ones who are beholden. The Thurmonds arranged for Ada to work for us. It's she who cooked this dinner."

Benjamin forked up a bite of the succulent pork chop. "The Thurmonds arranged for her to come here?"

Jessica gave an incredulous laugh. "Don't tell me you've already forgotten, Benjamin. I do believe your memory is going even faster than mine . . . and you, the younger of us—"

"Now, now, Jessica, between my concerns at this place and our shipping dilemmas, I'm a man with a great deal on my mind." He should speak to her about letting Ada and Runnell go as soon as possible, but what could he say . . . that he disliked the man's looks? That he lacked patience with him?

Now that he considered it, he vaguely remembered something about the Morses obtaining Ada's services for them. Ada's sister cooked for the Morses . . . yes, that was it. And the sister's husband did general work, caring for the horses, chauffeuring and the like, though he had not driven them to church last Sunday in their fine carriage. Most likely the servants had Sundays off, just as Ada should.

"I couldn't be more pleased with her," Jessica said. "Not one bit more pleased."

She'd no more than spoken, than Ada bustled in from the kitchen. She was nearly as plump as she was tall, but she moved with amazing vigor, and it appeared that she hadn't overheard them discussing her virtues.

"Thought ye might like more of these buttered spring potatoes," she said. "California growed or not, they're as good any in Tennessee! And I brung in a few more pork chops."

"Thank you, Ada. I could be persuaded to have another chop and a few more of those delicious potatoes," Benjamin answered. "They melt in the mouth." He took up a forkful of a buttered spring potato with flakes of parsley. In truth, everything the woman cooked was delectable, and the entire house sparkled from her cleaning. It would be difficult to replace her. At the very least, he should sleep on the matter before upsetting Jessica.

On Sunday, Benjamin drove Jessica in the old buggy to their small white country church. "How is Runnell acting of late?" he inquired.

"What do you mean?"

"Is he still so insolent?"

Jessica retied the bow under her brown bonnet, absently glancing about the churchyard. "No, I think Ada warned him to hold his tongue. She implied as much."

"I am glad to hear it."

Jessica waved toward a fine black carriage. "There are the Morses now. Isn't that Annabelle a dear?"

"And a beauty," Benjamin replied with admiration.

He was not certain how dear she might be, although she gave every indication of it. Her husband was apparently in agreement, judging by his rapt expression as he helped her down from the carriage. Her dark blonde hair peeped from under a light blue bonnet, and her blue eyes sparkled as she glanced about. She wore a pale blue frock to match her bonnet, and her cheeks dimpled prettily as she called out a greeting.

"Good morning!" Benjamin replied, and Morse returned their salutation cordially.

They made such a charming couple that everyone in the church-yard took note of them. With such good looks, it seemed a shame they had no children, he thought. On the other hand, she was quite young . . . perhaps just over twenty. It occurred to him that despite her youth and sunny smile, she seemed somehow shy and private.

"Does Annabelle Morse have friends?" he asked Jessica.

"None to my knowledge," Jessica replied. After a moment, she added, "It's a shame . . . she seems so friendly. Still, it takes a long time for a woman to settle into a new community and even longer to make truly good friends. It's not as though she has any family here, beyond her husband. I remember how it was when Noah and I were newly married and by ourselves."

"I suppose they're like Elizabeth and I were as newlyweds," Benjamin said, remembering how sweet their love had been. His wife had gone to be with the Lord twenty-five years ago, but it took only a second to recall her lovely face, form, and manner. "We were an entire country unto ourselves. An entire continent! Oh, to be young and in love again."

"Why, Benjamin Talbot!" Jessica exclaimed. "It's a long time since you've waxed so eloquent on the topic of love. Likely because it's spring again. 'In the spring a young man's fancy turns to love.' "

"A *young* man?!" He gave a laugh and drove the buggy to the hitching post under the oak trees. Still chuckling, he got down next to the Morse carriage, where Thurmond Morse waited for him with his bride on his arm.

After exchanging pleasantries, Morse said, "Ah do thank you again for the banking reference. Isaiah Meeker seems to be a fine and upstanding citizen."

"That he is," Benjamin agreed. "And highly thought of in the banking community. I'm glad to have been of assistance. Let me know if I can help again."

"Ah shall, suh," Morse replied. "Thank you, Ah shall."

Kate Talbot looked out from the women's deck of the *Mississippi Palace* at the green, wooded states of Louisiana and Mississippi on either side, and wrote,

Dear Mama, Poppa, and dear sisters and brothers,

We have been sailing along on the Mississippi River for quite some time now and will soon approach Natchez. The river winds back and forth and up and around so much that it often seems we are sailing east and west as much as we sail in a southerly direction.

Since I last wrote, we have seen Thebes, Cairo, and Wickliffe in Illinois. At the roiling junction of the muddy Mississippi and the bluer Ohio, the two rivers looked so different, it seemed impossible for them to unite. The Mississippi River claimed its own valley and the Missouri shore; the Ohio River claimed the state of Kentucky and its bluffs. There, in the churning waters, the Mason and Dixon line seemed to be defined by nature.

Our last stop in Missouri was New Madrid, where it's said the river ran upstream during their great earthquake. In Memphis,

Tennessee, we saw the vast cotton fields, cotton exchange buildings, and warehouses. There were slaves everywhere, far more than we ever saw at home. After that came a hilly section of Arkansas. Now we sail between Louisiana and Mississippi. We have recently passed Vicksburg and will soon reach Natchez. The food is always good and served in generous proportions, and freshly-caught catfish is always on the menu along with many other selections.

Our own matters have gone well thus far, but Sarah, Stephen, and I feel peculiar about foisting ourselves on the McCourtney family at their Beaumont Plantation. If there is a change in the border situation, please let us know and we shall return home immediately. We are hopeful and heartened because in Memphis and the other large ports we purchased newspapers, and they mentioned nothing about our border difficulties. I wouldn't be surprised to find a letter from you at Beaumont saying to return.

Sarah and I are well, but Stephen's health is again uncertain. Andrew Kendall has been most helpful to him, as has Octavius, whom you met. Charles McCourtney claims to have no gift for doctoring. Nor do I have a calling for nursing. Stephen is able to get about on the men's deck in the wheelchair we purchased for him in Tipton. Since Sarah has written to you, too, there is no sense in my going into details about Stephen's situation. We will ask for a doctor immediately in Natchez.

She paused, wondering whether she should say anything about the romantic quandary that she had found herself in lately. Mama would be interested, as would her sisters—and even Poppa and her brothers. First, there was the matter of Charles's vacillating interest in her and the rumor that he stayed up to all hours in the gambling salon. Despite everything, at dinner last night, his fervent looks across the table had made her tremble and tear her eyes away from his.

Then there was Andrew's friendly attention. Last night when they'd been walking from the dining room, the ship had veered sharply, and he'd caught her arm to steady her. For an instant, at the door, he'd looked down into her eyes with such intense interest that she'd stopped with him for a prolonged moment. If she hadn't come to her senses, they might have stood there much longer for all to see. In any event, his attention to her sometimes seemed more than that of a mere friend and fellow traveler, but perhaps she was mistaken.

There was also the matter of Aubin, Rodwell, and Pa Bence, whom they hadn't seen since Ida's confrontation with them at Cape Girardeau. They weren't at the other riverboat stops, but for all she knew, they might be lying in wait in Natchez. In addition, there was the concern of Charles being on the Kansas jayhawkers' list. Fortunately, there'd been no sign of them, and one could only hope that the growing distance would cool their anger.

Although those problems seemed to have diminished, another had reared its head this morning on the women's deck. It came in the curvaceous form of a dark-haired beauty who had seated herself on the deck beside Kate. After a lengthy scrutiny, the woman had inquired with a slight French accent, "Are you with the McCourtney party?"

Kate had nodded. "Yes, I am."

"Are you one of his . . . how do you say it? . . . relations . . . his family?"

"I am not," Kate answered uneasily. Everyone knew there were gambling hostesses in the gaming salon, but they had never had the audacity to show themselves on the women's deck. Kate finally managed, "May I ask why you're interested?"

"It's important to know how matters stand," the woman replied, her brown eyes flashing. She was perhaps thirty years old, and even though it was mid-morning, wore a low-cut, bright yellow satiny frock—apparently unconcerned about the difference between morning and evening attire. The woman added, "He's a handsome man, your Charles McCourtney . . . very handsome."

"I suppose he is," Kate replied evenly.

"One could easily fall in love with him, could one not?"

A defensiveness rose in Kate's chest and she retorted, "I can't say!"

"With that, you have already told me," the woman replied.

The other women passengers on the deck watched them, and Kate asked, "What, may I ask, is your name?"

"Dehlia," the woman replied.

To fill in the awkward silence, Kate asked, "Where do you come from?"

"From New Orleans."

"I see."

The woman lifted her lovely chin, then spoke with some heat. "I see you, like everyone else, wonder about the shade of my skin, so I shall inform you. I am Creole, a quadroon." She smiled. "I doubt you even know the meaning of it."

"I do," Kate replied, meeting the woman's dark eyes. A Creole was of French or Spanish descent, and a quadroon was an off-spring of whites and a slave. A quadroon would have one Negro grandparent, and one could see it not only in Dehlia's exquisite *cafe au lait* coloring but in her sensuous lips.

Kate said, "You are very beautiful."

Dehlia gave a surprised laugh, then raised her shoulders with practiced voluptuousness. "So I hear, though seldom from a country woman like you. But flaunting one's beauty has its uses, does it not? Or are you too pure to know of it?"

Remembering the night at Halfway House when she'd worn the low-cut red taffeta frock, Kate felt heat rise to her cheeks. "Yes, beauty has its uses."

"Well, that I did not expect either!" Dehlia replied. She hesitated, her dark eyes examining Kate a moment longer. "With a man like Charles McCourtney, one must be careful. Especially with a man of his sympathies and sympathetic connections." She rose to her feet. *"Bonjour,* Miss Talbot."

"Good-day," Kate replied uncertainly.

After a courteous nod, Dehlia had swept along the deck in her yellow satin gown. In the doorway, she'd turned and smiled slightly, making Kate wonder all the more at their encounter. Had Charles made romantic overtures—and promises—to her? If so, the woman was clearly interested in him.

Best not to mention any of it in the letter home, Kate decided and continued with a safer subject.

The weather is sunny and warm now, but we have had many days and nights of hard rain, accompanied by ribs of whitecaps on the river. Today, however, nature is bright with spring color; dogwood, redbud, honeysuckle, and wild azaleas are in bloom. Yellow bitterweed and red clover make dazzling shows in the open spaces, of which there are many now along the river. We are told that "Natchez" means "wild turkeys in the woods" as well as being the name of early Indians. If that is the case, there may be a great many wild turkeys hereabouts, for there are woods along much of the way. More interesting to me, though, are the stretches of cypress swamps where trees live—and also die—right in the water.

The river has been rising steadily for some days, and here it seems alive with whole trees torn from islands and plantations upstream. Right now, a large cypress is crossing to the side of our riverboat; the tree jerks, zigzags, then goes smoothly down river for some time, spins around again, then heads for shore. It appears that the river has visited mile after mile in Louisiana, leaving it in islands and a jungle-like bottom. We sometimes see black bears on the shores, examining us as we examine them at a safe distance.

It is nearly time for our midday meal, and I shall finish this letter so I can freshen up and fetch Sarah from the cabin, where she is resting. She rests quite often now, which I suppose is to be expected.

With love for all of you,
Kate

When the dinner bell rang, Kate hoped to entice Sarah from her berth in the cabin, since her sister had not been eating well lately. "Do get dressed, Sarah. Eating in the dining room with Stephen will improve your appetite."

"Go on without me," her sister replied. Even her voice sounded tired, and she lay listless on top of the bedding. "I'm too weak and unsteady to be walking on a lurching boat."

"What will Stephen think? He's been so brave about his injury. Moreover, you're looking far too thin."

Sarah pressed her lips together, and tears filled her eyes. "I don't feel well, Kate. I truly don't feel well. Sometimes I think I must be fading away. . . ."

"You mustn't think like that!"

"But I do! Can't I confide in you?" Tears filled her eyes. "Surely you know I can't tell Stephen for fear it will bring his spirits down even further."

Kate drew a sorrowful breath. "Of course you can confide in me. You're right, it's best you share your concerns with me until his health improves." She hesitated, but Sarah made no reply. "I'll ask the steward to bring a light supper to the cabin for you."

She felt tempted to stay in the cabin and grieve with her sister, but reminded herself that one of them must be strong. That in mind, she decided to make a last attempt. "Stephen worries about you when you're not at the table. It heartens him to see you."

Sarah looked at her with petulance. "Let him worry a while then. If it weren't for him and his dreadful family, we wouldn't have been driven from Missouri—"

"Sarah! It's not like you to talk like that!"

"I'm tired. I'm simply too tired to deal with our difficulties."

Kate nodded, growing tired of them herself.

In the dining room, she was glad to see the menfolk were all present, since Charles was sometimes absent. Tonight, he rose to his feet more quickly than ever. "And how do you fare this evening, my lovely Miss Talbot?" he asked with a captivating smile.

The words sprung to her lips. "Perhaps better than your lovely friend, Dehlia, who came on deck to inquire about you."

His silvery eyes widened, but he recovered so smoothly that his astonishment seemed no more than her imagination. "It sounds as if the gambling hostess resents my winnings—"

"I don't know about *winnings,*" Kate interrupted.

Suddenly she realized she was jealous, and worse yet, Charles and Andrew knew it. Even Stephen seemed aware of it.

To her relief, their waiter arrived at the table to take their orders, followed by Andrew suggesting Stephen say grace. Stephen hesitated. Sitting in his wheelchair, he was already a pitiable figure, and now he was more saddened by Sarah's absence. Finally he bowed his head and gave a longer prayer than usual, one that included not only thanksgiving for their food, but a petition for Sarah's improved health and for godly wisdom for all of them.

Between spoonfuls of creamy mushroom bisque, Andrew remarked to Kate, "Tell us about what transpires on the women's deck. I fear the men on our side are a dreary lot, as men so often are."

She attempted an amusing description of events that took place on the women's side. Best to be entertaining to show Charles her lack of concern with the fascinating Dehlia. Now, if ever, was the time to use her dramatic bent.

Before long she had the men laughing, especially at how distressed some of the women became when the boat's whistle sounded at the river bends. One stout young woman, Miss Umlaut, always attired in flouncy pink frocks, seemed especially ridiculous. Kate rolled her eyes and waved her hands in alarm to imitate Miss Umlaut, who shrieked at all possible dangers and vowed that ghouls dwelt in the river. Despite Kate's best efforts to regale them, she could not shake her attraction to Charles.

After dinner, when they stood up from the table, Charles said to the others, "If you'll excuse us, I should like to have a word with our lovely Miss Talbot."

"Perhaps some other time," Kate replied.

Charles caught her elbow. "There is no time like the present," he replied most beguilingly. "This is a matter of some importance."

Both Andrew and Stephen looked uneasy. At long last, Andrew pushed Stephen in his wheelchair across the dining room toward the men's deck.

Charles escorted her toward the women's side, his hand warm on her elbow. To her consternation, he said nothing and only smiled warmly at her.

"What is it, Charles?" she finally asked. "What's of such importance?"

"You can see we have no privacy here," he murmured. "I should like to meet you at the ship's bow after sunset."

"You can't come to the women's side!"

He smiled. "We need only speak together over the dividing rope. Believe me, my lovely Miss Talbot, we'll not be the only man and woman there."

She gazed into his eyes and found herself nodding, albeit with reluctance. "Fine, then. I shall be there."

He squeezed her elbow, then spoke loudly enough for anyone who might be interested. "And, so, a good evening, Miss Talbot."

"Good evening, Mr. McCourtney."

She felt distressed at having given in to his request so easily—distressed but warm with anticipation.

When she returned to the cabin, she found that Sarah had dozed off. She'd eaten a bowl of beef broth and drunk half her tea, and looked less pale. After making certain that her sister was comfortable, Kate eyed herself in the mirror.

Perhaps she wasn't as strikingly beautiful as Dehlia, but with a sultry glance, she could pass. She smoothed back her hair and practiced a provocative look in the mirror. If only she didn't have to do battle with her conscience. . . .

Out on the women's deck, the sunset held a special brilliance. She paced the length of the deck twice, nodding at the other women passengers as she passed and never going quite to the bow. She pretended to admire the wonderful river views, and all the while wished the sun would set more quickly. Noting that the stout Miss Umlaut watched her, Kate sat down in the deck chair closest to the bow, her senses flaming with the magnificent sunset. She told herself firmly that to maintain any sense of decorum, she must wait until darkness fell. Already women were retiring to their cabins, including the ridiculous Miss Umlaut. Only three elderly women sat talking near the stern in the dimly-lit night.

A small cloud passed over the moon, and Kate stood, then quickly made her way around to the bow of the riverboat. As she came around, she saw Charles McCourtney looking out at the moonlit river.

She stopped for an instant, admiring his fine profile. If there had been a rope to separate the men from the women, it was down now. She stepped closer and touched his arm.

He turned to her, and a wondrous smile spread across his face. He caught her hands in his. "How beautiful you are, Kate."

Disarmed, she could only stand before him. He drew her closer before she realized another couple was embracing quite passionately behind them.

"Who is it?" she whispered.

"Only one of the sailors with your Miss Umlaut." He chuckled. "She is more sought after than one might expect."

Kate pulled back in distaste at the thought of a sailor courting the stout young woman right behind them. A picture of Charles with Dehlia suddenly presented itself along with the woman's warning: *With such men, one must be careful.*

"How do you know about Miss Umlaut's suitors?"

"Now, now—" Charles murmured.

Quite suddenly, Kate felt as sullied as the ridiculous Miss Umlaut, who was apparently desperate for love. "What is it you wished to tell me?"

Charles drew her closer.

"No . . . Mr. McCourtney," Kate protested, trying to regain her senses.

"Yes, Miss Talbot," he murmured.

Tearing herself from him, she turned and rushed away. She should have guessed this was what he wanted! she told herself as she hurried through the moonlight. She should have guessed! It occurred to her that this was the third time she'd escaped his romantic overtures—first, at the church social in Weston, then at the covered wagon cook fire, and now on the riverboat in the moonlight. Each time, someone had intruded or, like Miss Umlaut, had been on hand to discourage her. It was almost as if they'd been sent. And if they hadn't, she doubted she could have resisted him.

Lord, deliver me from this unseemly attraction to Charles! she prayed as she hurried to her cabin. I beseech Thee, deliver me from him!

The next day, she took her meals in the cabin with Sarah, trying to banish Charles from her thoughts. Absence, Kate found, did not cause her heart to grow fonder. Moreover, she recalled Dehlia warning of his sympathies and sympathetic friends. Hereafter, Kate vowed, she would be wary of him, just as one would be careful not to venture into the disease-ridden swamps that now lined the river. Hereafter, her only cause would be to turn him from slavery.

She was surprised when the steward arrived with a letter for her after the midday meal. She opened it and glanced down, finding Andrew's signature.

Dear Miss Talbot,

We missed you this morning at breakfast and then again at the mid-day dinner. Are you unwell? I hesitate to intrude into such a delicate matter, but I fear that my charming stepbrother may have tried to press his advantage with you. I questioned him, but he merely laughed.

You are a fine young woman, and I would do anything in my power to protect you from unwanted advances. I hope my suspicions are groundless, but I am here if you need me. I understand that young ladies are sometimes too embarrassed to request help, and so I have risked opening the topic for you. I pray I am mistaken.

If you would please reply, I would be grateful. Now that I have written, I am eager to be reassured as to your safety and comfort.

Your servant, Andrew Kendall

Kate stared at the firm black script, relieved and almost giddy. Andrew Kendall rescuing her! On the other hand, it was also reassuring to know he would take such a risk.

At length, she picked up her pen. What could she say? If nothing else, she must thank him. Perhaps Andrew Kendall cared for her more deeply than she'd guessed. Yes, she must reply.

Mr. Kendall:

I thank you for your note and your concern for my welfare. If ever I need assistance, I shall remember your kind offer. But rest assured that, to date, I have been quite successful at fending off unwanted advances. I do not foresee the need for help in the near future.

I have stayed with my sister today to keep her company in the cabin and to cheer her a bit. We sincerely appreciate your help with Stephen.

Thank you again for your concern. It is good to know I can depend upon you, should the need ever arise.

Yours truly,
Kate Talbot

That evening when she entered the dining room and saw Andrew, she felt slightly guilty. But she had definitely not written a falsehood. She had successfully fended off Charles's advances herself.

Andrew stood up as she approached the table. "Good evening, Miss Talbot. I'm glad to see you joining us again," he said, pulling out her chair.

Kate looked around the room. "Where are the others?"

"They should be along shortly," he replied, "but let me take this opportunity to thank you for your note and for easing my concern. I hope you'll forgive me for mentioning it."

Kate was struck with remorse for thinking his concern even mildly humorous. "Why, not at all, Mr. Kendall—"

"Andrew," he put in with a smile.

She returned his smile. "On the contrary, Andrew, I was quite comforted to know you are watching out for me." She put her hand out and he held it for a moment. "You are a good friend," she finished, looking into his blue eyes. It was unfortunate that she wasn't attracted to him in the same way she was to Charles, she thought. Andrew Kendall struck her as a true gentleman.

She was relieved to see Octavius wheeling Stephen into the dining room, and even more relieved to hear that Charles would not be joining them. At least her last evening on the riverboat would be peaceful.

As they ate supper, Stephen seemed dreadfully groggy, but Andrew was well-educated and could converse on all manner of subjects. He was, she decided, not only a gentleman but fine company.

The next morning, Sarah felt better and stood beside her to watch their approach to Natchez. As the *Mississippi Palace* sailed nearer, the river's deep blue water lightened to a paler shade, and Kate felt more warmth in the air. A steep bluff bent forward to meet the majestic river, and as the current drove them south, the world-renowned town of Natchez could be seen on its two levels—one sprawling out along the great landing, the other high in pine and magnolia hills.

From her history lessons she remembered that Natchez had been occupied by the Spanish, French, and English, then claimed by Americans, who made it the capital of the Mississippi Territory. Seeing its fine situation on the river, she was not surprised at the city's historical prominence. It seemed a shame that it had lost its distinction as the seat of government, which had gone to Washington and was now in the town of Jackson. Before long they approached the hundreds of vessels that ranged from flatboats to great ocean liners moored in a bobbing, shifting line.

As the disembarking passengers assembled on the deck near the gangway, Sarah said, "I didn't expect so many vessels!"

"Nor I!" Kate replied.

Others around them were equally impressed. At St. Louis one expected a great flotilla of ships since two immense rivers came together, but Natchez was only a well-situated town on the Mississippi, albeit a town on two levels.

Beside her, Andrew held Stephen's wheelchair and looked as if he had mixed feelings about his return. "Natchez-Under-the-Hill is a tumultuous place," he remarked about the landing. "I hate for you ladies to have to see it. Some claim the river, being shamed, altered its course and widened its banks to destroy much of the landing and that the tornado of 1840 was another act of retribution. Then there are the fires half burning the place down—"

"You think they're acts of retribution?" Stephen asked.

Andrew shrugged. "Some even say the epidemics of yellow fever are part of it. My late father, a physician, thought epidemics began down here with the sailors, then made their way up the bluff."

Stephen looked uneasily ahead at the landing. "We'd best stay close together."

"Believe me, we will," Andrew said. "Rest easy. I'll help your family."

The *Mississippi Palace* blasted a warning and the calliope music began, adding its liveliness to the tumult. As the riverboat approached the crowded wharf, the infamous Natchez-Under-the-Hill section presented its tawdry saloons, liquor shops, and shanties.

Kate felt increasingly nervous about disembarking. Even before hearing Andrew's talk of retribution, everyone spoke of the landing being the wickedest waterfront on the river—a place of cutthroats, drunken boatmen, and lewd women.

Octavius had taken charge of their baggage, and he motioned to a carriage-for-hire driver who waited on the wharf. The driver nodded, so at least they could depart quickly.

Charles stood not too far away on the deck, earnestly conversing with two New Orleans men, and Dehlia sat some distance away, observing everyone. On a sudden impulse, Kate gave the raven-haired beauty a small wave, taking her by surprise and making her smile slightly.

Finally the *Mississippi Palace* was secured. As Kate and the others disembarked, raucous hirelings called out, trying to lure them and the other disembarking passengers into gambling dens and pleasure palaces. It struck her as the sort of place the Bences would favor, and she was relieved at not seeing them. Perhaps it was safer to live here for a time, at least up in Natchez proper.

Strains of calliope music still drifted from the *Mississippi Palace* as they climbed up into the black carriage. Kate settled on the tufted leather back seat with Sarah and Stephen. Andrew seated himself across from her, and Charles sat down beside him, eyeing her with a repentant expression. He had been the last one off the gangway, having been deep in conversation with his New Orleans companions until the last moment.

"Are you ladies comfortable?" he inquired solicitously.

"Yes, thank you," Kate replied, the coolness in her voice making Sarah glance at her.

Andrew must have sensed that something was amiss between her and his stepbrother, but apparently chose to ignore it. "Octavius will be accompanying our trunks home by wagon."

"Thank you for making the arrangements," Stephen told him.

"Trust Andrew to do things well," Charles remarked with a show of magnanimity.

It wasn't until the horses and carriage clattered up Silver Street for Natchez proper that the riverboat gave its mournful warning blasts and maneuvered away from the wharf. The sight of it leaving flooded Kate with sadness, then a surge of anxiety. The riverboat had become a home of sorts, and now they would have to grow accustomed to another strange place. Despite Charles and Andrew's assurances, what if she and her family were unwelcome at Beaumont Plantation?

At long last they reached the bluff, and their horses clip-clopped along the cobbled streets of upper Natchez, passing fine specialty shops and mercantiles. Once beyond the business district, churches presented themselves, and Kate felt only slightly better. Next came streets with mansion after mansion. Deep in elms and live oaks, the fine houses looked out across wide ornamental gardens and splendid green lawns. Kate had glimpses of their impressive architecture between the spring greenery—domes, shuttered windows, balustraded galleries, columned porticoes and colonnades of white pillars, strips of black wrought-iron tracery.

Sarah looked out the carriage window past Kate. "It's beautiful. Nothing like Weston or Independence."

"No, not like Weston or Independence," Kate agreed.

"Natchez has more millionaires per capita than any city in the country," Charles told them with pride. "We have Shakespearean theater and famous singers like Jenny Lind coming through, not to mention celebrated visitors like the Marquis de Lafayette, and Louis Phillipe before he became King of France. Before our time, of course."

"Weston was a fine place in its own way until the river moved on it," Stephen answered defensively.

"It was," Sarah hastened to agree. "From its beginning, they tried to keep the riffraff out."

Charles inquired, "And did they succeed?"

"In the end, not entirely," Stephen admitted.

Fortunately, Andrew pointed out the attributes of a mansion across the road before Stephen went on. For the past few days, Stephen had seemed as angry at the Mississippi River as he'd been with the Missouri's damage to Weston.

Kate glanced out the carriage window past him and Sarah. In the mid-morning sunshine, her brother-in-law already appeared tired. She recalled the enthusiastic tour he'd given her of Weston not long ago and thought how his life had plummeted. What would Andrew and Charles do if Natchez's affluence fell like Weston's had fallen just twelve years ago?

"Do you ladies enjoy attending balls?" Andrew inquired.

Kate shrugged. "In Independence we only had the New Year's Ball. It took place at the courthouse, the most elegant building in town."

Sarah said, "We had few in Weston."

"I'm sure you'll be invited to balls at the mansions here," Andrew said, watching Kate with interest.

Kate darted a glance at Charles and found him watching her too. She looked away immediately. "I shall be glad to rest in one place for a while." She glanced out at an old twining wisteria with its pendulous lavender blossoms. "How lovely it is . . . especially the gardens. My, wouldn't Mama like them!"

"She would indeed," Sarah answered.

Andrew sounded almost apologetic. "It's been said that the planters of Natchez live like pharaohs, building monuments to power."

Charles shot his stepbrother a hard glance. "You've been living in one of those fine mansions yourself for some years, Andrew. I haven't noticed your moving into the slave quarters, despite your devotion to their inhabitants."

"I try hard to earn my keep," Andrew replied evenly.

"That you do, though you don't have to put it quite so baldly," his stepbrother returned. "What's more, you were not required to finish Uncle Namen's legal affairs in Weston. I had it all in hand."

Andrew drew a breath. "Believe me, I didn't like leaving in the midst of spring planting, but your father asked me to go. Everyone was concerned about your welfare."

Charles made no response, and the tension between them lingered in the carriage.

Kate was glad for the comforting clip-clop sounds of the horses' hooves and Stephen's occasional soft snores. She'd sensed Charles and Andrew's mutual resentment, but on the riverboat, she'd only witnessed them together at mealtimes. Was their rancor growing now that they neared Beaumont?

Best not to give the least appearance of taking sides, she decided. Best to remain entirely silent, then return to Independence as soon as the border troubles were over. Surely the interminable strife would end before long.

9

Once the town mansions and cobblestone roads of Natchez were behind them, the carriage clattered on through the dusty countryside. Kate caught glimpses of outlying mansions on great expanses of land, and of hundreds upon hundreds of slaves toiling in the cotton fields. It was known everywhere that nearly everyone in Natchez was connected to buying, selling, picking, planting, or supplying cotton, and that there was a voracious demand for it from Boston to England.

She felt troubled by the throngs of slaves working the fields around them. "Poppa claims that most cotton is produced on credit," she said. "The banks here must surely flourish with so much cotton growing."

"Not at all," Andrew replied. "Many went bankrupt early on. Most financial affairs are handled by the exchange brokerage. Charles and his father see to that end at Beaumont. I'm more interested in the planting."

"You like farming then, too?" Stephen asked.

Andrew's face lit with enthusiasm. "It's a pleasure to see the land produce and to improve the crops. I like experimenting with new agricultural methods."

His enjoying outdoor work wasn't surprising, Kate thought, for he was still bronzed by the sun, making his flaxen hair all the blonder and his eyes all the bluer.

"Andrew's our farmer," Charles mocked.

"I am surely not one of Natchez's army of lawyers, like you and your father," Andrew answered.

Charles replied with some heat. "Beaumont has benefited greatly by our work."

"That's so," Andrew said. "I won't argue that."

Kate looked out her window, unwilling to involve herself in extraneous disputes—not when she hoped to convince Southerners against slavery.

As the carriage passed small farms, she observed occasional white men and women toiling alongside two or three Negroes, just as one often saw in Missouri. Andrew had turned to look out the carriage window himself, likely deciding against a quarrel before their arrival.

After a moment, Charles remarked, "For all the Northerners' complaints, they seldom know that slavery is ardently defended by even the Southern whites who own no slaves. The fact is that slavery serves as a social mechanism to regularize behavior between the various classes."

Here was the chance she'd waited for, Kate thought. If ever she was to convince Charles to give up slavery, now was the time to speak. "No matter how slavery might 'regularize behavior' between classes, it can't last forever simply because it's wrong for one person to own another," she said. "It's absolutely wrong."

Charles shook his head. "Contrary to what Northerners claim, slaves are less than perfect themselves. Everyone knows they slow production, break tools, set fields afire, abuse livestock . . . even feign sickness to ease their work . . . and a good many of them dress better than our poor whites can."

Stephen started to speak, but Charles continued, "And what can you say about the free blacks who are planters and own slaves themselves? It's the Southern dream for both whites and blacks to own land and slaves, to become great planters. Everyone hopes for it."

"You don't find it immoral for one human being to own another?" Sarah asked.

"Immoral?" Charles almost laughed. "It strikes me as no different than the poorer classes slaving away in the North's factories. The plantation system produces a learned class of leaders who are able to prepare themselves for public service. I have no moral misgivings about someday owning Beaumont. No moral misgivings at all."

Kate argued, "In the North, the poorer classes at least have opportunities to advance themselves."

"Sometimes," he replied.

"Yes, sometimes," she had to admit.

"My dear Miss Talbot, don't worry yourself about this," he said solicitously. "You're far too pretty to think about such complicated matters."

Andrew shook his head. "A pretty woman she is, Charles, but you're mistaken about her intellect. She has good logic."

"Well, aren't you the expert on female minds!" Charles responded. "Tell me, Andrew, just when did you gain so much experience with young women?"

Andrew's color deepened. "There's no need to bicker about it. I simply know good logic when I hear it."

"Gentlemen, we're your guests, and we don't wish to cause disharmony," Sarah said firmly. "Let's discuss something more suitable. Please tell us again about your family, so we'll be ready to meet them."

Kate might have elbowed her sister if it weren't for her delicate condition, and if she didn't remind her of Mama, who was always eager to avoid trouble. Likely there'd be other chances to change Charles's opinion; perhaps some headway had already been made. After all, Andrew had mentioned her good logic.

"Our family is a rather complicated affair," Charles replied to Sarah's question. He turned to his stepbrother and gave him a mocking look. "I defer to you, Andrew. I should very much like to hear you explain our family."

Andrew ignored his brother's taunt and raised his brows thoughtfully. "To begin, there were eight children. On my side, Mother was married to Andrew Kendall, a physician, as I've mentioned. She was widowed when he died in a yellow fever epidemic. On Charles's side, his mother died in childbirth when he was two years old. His father, Charles McCourtney II, had known Mother in society years ago. He courted her after the deaths of their spouses, and they were married at Beaumont."

"Your mother for her security, Ah suspect," Charles said.

Andrew shot him a scathing glance. "Not to mention assuring your father's inheritance of Beaumont. Your great-aunt's stipulation, as I understand it, was that he marry a worthy Christian woman."

"True," Charles conceded, "and your mother is, above all, most worthy and most Christian."

"She is," Andrew said, then went on calmly. "Our parents' first child in this marriage was our sister Rebecca, who lives in town with her husband, a factor at the cotton exchange. Then came twins who died at birth, followed by another set of twins, Amanda and Alicia, who are sixteen and at boarding school in Charleston. Last there's Caroline, who's fourteen and being tutored, and still lives at home when she's not off visiting."

Charles added, "Don't forget our throng of visitors . . . aunts, uncles, and cousins, not to mention friends and dignitaries from far and wide."

"And Aunt Eliza Faye Ogleby, Mother's older sister," Andrew said. "She helped to rear us and is still hard at work trying to reshape Caroline."

"A noble project," Charles said.

"Is your aunt widowed?" Sarah asked.

Charles shook his head. "Aunt Eliza Faye claims she never found a man she'd risk her happiness for."

It was a common saying among spinsters, Kate thought. One that people in Independence likely expressed about her now that she was twenty.

"Aunt Eliza Faye was a beauty and a charmer," Andrew said. "In fact, she still is. In any case, that's the immediate family. And, of course Mammy, who came with Mother and me to Beaumont."

"Her one property of value," Charles added.

Andrew frowned. "My father was young and just establishing his medical practice in Natchez. In any case, Mother had her pick of suitors before both her first and second marriages. Aunt Eliza Faye says Mother was the most sought-after young lady and then the most sought-after widow in Natchez."

Charles raised his brows, but remained silent.

At length, the driver turned the carriage off the road and into a curving alley of moss-draped live oaks.

"Almost there," Andrew told them. "Mother should be expecting us. I guessed our arrival to the day in my last letter."

Kate craned her neck to see beyond Sarah and Stephen through the carriage window, wondering if Andrew had also mentioned their poor circumstances. She didn't like having to impose, even if Natchez mansions were famous for their hospitality. At home in Independence, now that covered wagon traffic to the West had slowed, they rarely had guests passing through town. She guessed Sarah had had even fewer in Weston.

Sarah said, "I'm sorry we're arriving just before dinner."

"There's always a meal being prepared at Beaumont," Andrew assured her. "One might say the kitchen never grows cold."

"And not long after dinner, there's afternoon tea for ladies who might come calling," Charles added. "Tea and gossip. Somehow I doubt they had teas in Missouri."

"Surely not at our house," Kate replied. "With such a large family, there was far too much work. Our entertainments were usually church and school socials, like the box supper in Weston."

Charles's eyes lit up with humor at the mention of it, and Kate quickly looked away out the window.

At the end of the alley of great live oaks draped with Spanish moss, a two-story white Greek Revival mansion slowly came into view, revealing itself like a magnificent painting. The house itself was an immense edifice with a Doric-columned portico facing the semicircular drive; on the second floor, graceful stone balustrades enclosed an upper terrace. Compared to the other mansions they'd seen in Natchez, Beaumont was a masterpiece of simplicity. Great mounds of pink azaleas and arbors of pendulous lavender wisteria softened its stark whiteness, and in the distance, between a screening of trees, Kate caught glimpses of the mighty Mississippi.

As the horses drew to a halt in front of the great double-doored entrance, two large white dogs came barking at them, and Andrew shouted through the open carriage window, "Alba! Elmo! We're home!"

The dogs barked even more excitedly, and a heavy-set, gray-haired Negro in shirtsleeves opened the wide front door. He peered out as the driver put down the carriage steps.

"There's Gabriel, our butler!" Andrew said with pleasure.

The butler called back to the house, "It's Mistuh Andrew an' Mistuh Charles come home! Mistuh Andrew an' Mistuh Charles!"

As they climbed down from the carriage, a silvery-blond

woman hurried out the door and beamed to see them. "Andrew! Charles!" she called out, then held up the skirt of her blue lacy frock slightly as she came down the stairs to greet them.

"Mother!" Andrew answered.

"Oh, I am so glad to have you two home!" She was a lovely blue-eyed woman with perfect features. Her silvery-blond hair was parted in the center and pulled back into a bun, a style more becoming on her than on most.

Behind her, a plump Negress ran out, smiling broadly.

Andrew hurried to the stairs to greet his mother, nearly sweeping her from her feet. Charles hung back, then gave her a polite peck on her cheek.

Andrew drew Kate forward. "Mother, these are our Missouri traveling companions, whom I wrote about . . . Miss Kate Talbot of Independence, and her sister and brother-in-law, Sarah and Stephen Bence, from Weston." In the course of introductions, it seemed equally natural for him to introduce the grinning butler, Uncle Gabriel, who shook hands with both Andrew and Charles, then the delighted gray-haired Negress, whom he called Mammy.

"We bid you welcome," Laurette McCourtney told them. "It's our pleasure to have you visit Beaumont."

She caught Kate's hands in hers and was so gracious that Kate felt thoroughly welcomed by the time the woman moved on to Sarah and Stephen. Standing back, it struck Kate that everyone regarded Andrew with a wonderful fondness. As for Charles, it appeared that Mammy and Uncle Gabriel watched him warily.

Before long, Uncle Gabriel helped the driver unload their hand baggage while Charles paid the carriage driver. Other Negroes arrived, their dark eyes flickering with curiosity at Kate, Sarah, and Stephen. As they were introduced, each bobbed a curly head and uttered a "How-do, ma'am," then set to work with the baggage.

Andrew explained to his mother, "Octavius, a slave from Uncle

Namen's, will be along with the trunks on a hired wagon."

"Fine," his mother replied, then said fondly, "Trust you to take care of matters."

Moments later, Aunt Eliza Faye arrived on the front door landing, eagerly greeting them as they made her way up the marble stairs. She was gray-haired and plump, but her facial features were lovely, like her younger sister's.

"I do hope you'll forgive me for not goin' down those steps to bid you welcome," she said, "but nowadays I have to conserve mah strength."

"Of course, I forgive you," Kate replied. "It's a pleasure to meet you."

"Caroline will be so sorry to miss meeting you, but she's in Charleston with friends," Aunt Eliza Faye explained. "Her tutor rushed off to Boston for a family crisis."

The rest of them made their way up the steps to meet her, Andrew and Gabriel supporting Stephen while one of the servants carried the folding wheelchair.

"I am so pleased to meet you," Aunt Eliza Faye declared to each of them, her eyes sparkling. She cocked her gray head and conversed with them in such a searching way that Kate guessed the woman missed very little.

"I'm delighted that you're here in time for dinner," Laurette McCourtney told them as they stepped into the white marble foyer. "There's just time to freshen up, so please don't bother to change your travel attire."

"The trunks are still to be delivered, Mother," Charles informed her rather abruptly.

"Thank you for reminding me, Charles," she replied. Her hopeful blue eyes met the hard shine in his, and she gathered him to her. "Oh, Charles, I do thank you for your patience with me. I know I must be a trial."

He stood somewhat stiffly as she held him, and Kate guessed that the very thing he lacked was patience with his stepmother—and that, unhappily, she knew it.

When Charles turned, the wave of his golden brown hair fell over his forehead, and he smiled warmly at Kate. "I hope you'll allow me to show you about the mansion myself. Uncle Gabriel will see to the baggage."

Kate glanced at Sarah for help, but she was busy assisting Stephen into his wheelchair. In any event, it would be ungrateful to deny Charles's request.

The white marble foyer led to a magnificent curved staircase, its wall lined with fine portraits. To the left, paneled double doors flanked by graceful palms stood open to reveal a spacious front parlor.

Charles led her into the parlor. "Good, the doors between the two parlors are open, so you can see the grand scope of it. We take up the carpets to use the space for balls and other entertainments."

Kate looked about in wonder, amazed at the size of the room. It eclipsed by far the space used for balls at the Independence Courthouse. Indeed, there was no comparison in size or grandeur.

A distance of at least sixty feet stretched between the two wall-sized mirrors inset by gilded carved frames on either end. Muted gold and blue Aubusson carpets covered much of the polished wooden floors, and a pianoforte and a gilded harp stood near the distant mirror. Love seats, armchairs, and tables stood in graceful clusters here and there, and the four white marble fireplaces held magnolia leaves for spring and summer.

"Well, what do you think of it, Kate?" Charles inquired with obvious pride.

"It's surely the largest parlor I've ever seen," she answered. "Also the most beautiful."

"There are larger mansions and parlors in Natchez, but these proportions seem to me the most beautiful." He offered his arm. "Come, I'll tell you about the furnishings and their histories."

She hesitated, then took his arm.

He smiled at her. "Shall we see how we look strolling along through the room toward the far mirror? I promise it will be a striking sight."

Uncertain, she nodded, and they started forward.

"Here's a French love seat upon which I would enjoy sitting with you," he said with a smile.

She blushed, but made no reply.

"The two carved chairs are from Italy, as are the white marble sculptures; their stone is said to be from the quarry where Michelangelo obtained his marble."

As he went on with his enthusiastic descriptions, she could scarcely take everything in. Instead, it seemed they were making their way through the fine furnishings towards the shimmering mirror as if they were master and mistress of the mansion.

When they neared the far wall mirror, he smiled at their reflections. "We do make a handsome couple, don't we?"

Yes, Kate thought, we do!

Stopping, he turned her slowly toward him, then cupped her face in his hands. "Fair Kate—"

"Please, Charles, I have to freshen up for dinner. Please—"

She tried to move, but he held her and she began to feel increasingly frantic. She was a guest in his house . . . in his parents' parlor . . . and now he was pressing that advantage. "Please, stop, Charles—"

"Kate, thou art fairer than the finest painting . . . lovelier than the finest sculpture . . ."

Surely he was jesting, she thought. In fact, they sounded like practiced words he'd spoken before.

From behind them, Andrew's voice crackled with emotion.

". . . and a godly woman, full of dignity and worth!" His reflection appeared in the mirror behind them. "Leave her alone, Charles. You have enough conquests. She's a decent young woman."

Charles hesitated, meeting his stepbrother's stern glare. Finally he dropped his hands from Kate's face and shrugged lightly. "In any event, I have to tend to some business concerns. I shall see you later, Miss Kate Talbot." With that, he brushed past her and headed for the door.

Kate felt weak with disappointment. He had to leave for business concerns? Had the stroll through the parlor been some kind of an act? What kind of a man was he? She was reminded again of Albert Morton leaving her for the gold rush. At least there gold had been an issue, and Albert had been far younger in life's experiences than Charles.

Andrew steered her over to a sofa. "I'm sorry to say that my stepbrother is a rogue. You can't let him upset you. He enjoys pretty women far too much, and I . . . feared for you."

"But I was so sure I could. . . ." She let her words trail off. In truth, she hadn't been sure of anything about Charles McCourtney.

"Don't worry about it."

Kate stared at the doorway where Charles had left, and a wave of humiliation swept over her. "I'm so embarrassed," she blurted, tears filling her eyes. "How can I face him again?"

"It's not as bad as all that," Andrew said, looking pained himself. "No one knows except the three of us, and Charles will forget it in no time. Matters will work out, you'll see."

Still humiliated, she rose to her feet and began to make her way back through the room, Andrew at her side. He said, "I've explained your flight from Missouri to my mother and stepfather as an escape from the border fighting and an injurious family situation."

"Thank you," Kate said. "It was not only thoughtful, but accurate on both counts."

Benjamin Talbot carried the mail to his whitewashed parlor eagerly. Settling into his horsehair armchair, he selected the letter from Matthew Hansel and slit the envelope. Taking out the linen paper, he was gladdened to see that Matthew had addressed both Jessica and himself as if they were truly an aunt and uncle, not merely related by marriage.

Dear Aunt Jessica and Uncle Benjamin,

Thank you again for the fine visit and your usual heartwarming hospitality. I regret not writing more promptly, but it has taken more effort than expected to investigate the status of the secret pro- and anti-slavery groups in Oakland and northern San Francisco. Worse, my information is still nebulous.

To begin, there are most definitely secret factions organizing for each side. Our pro-slavery legislature has drawn Southern hopes and apparently generous infusions of Southern money in their attempts to gain influence for what they are calling the Pacific Confederacy. Both they and the Northern faction would like to have California's support, not to mention a good measure of our gold and young men.

According to my informants, the desired support on both sides includes good will, legislative loyalty, and shipping facilities. (I suggest you keep a close watch on commerce at Wainwright-Talbot Shipping and Chandlery, not only in San Francisco, but at the other shipping offices, too. I should think they would be especially interested in the Missouri River connections in Independence and your various Mississippi River and Atlantic Coast offices.)

It was too incredible to believe, Benjamin thought. Yet, all great conflicts had been dependent on the movement of men and munitions—and such movements could mean defeat or victory. Unnerved, he read on.

How they plan to recruit our men and obtain our gold is still unknown, but they are most generous in their efforts at setting up channels. The Southerners are said to be taking a huge collection at the various plantations, amassing a large "war chest" to send on to California.

Benjamin drew a breath. True, the state had an excess of men from the thousands who'd arrived in '49 and later for the gold rush. As for gold, no matter how many articles were written to the contrary, the world wrongly thought that California was still awash with gold. Discouraged, he read on.

I regret to write that my informants were unwilling to give specific names, places, or dates, possibly because matters are still uncertain. The only certainty is that if a war between the states breaks out, California will be prepared for immediate action.

I regret to bear such tidings, but I've often heard you say that forewarned is forearmed. If we can find the warmongers, we must stop their influence as rapidly as possible. Like you, I see evils on both sides, and I believe that of the two evils, it is best to chose neither and, rather, to fight to halt both.

We have other news—I hope good news—to temper the bad. I will take the summer pastorate at your fine church. I shall be writing to inform the committee as soon as I have sealed this letter, so I ask that you don't mention it at this time.

May God bless the two of you and keep you and your family, and may He shed His light upon all concerned for wisdom.

Sincerely,
Matthew

Benjamin shook his head. It seemed that no matter how far away one lived or how old one became, there were evils to fight. If good men did nothing, evil prevailed.

Kate lifted her russet cotton frock decorously as she descended the grand staircase to the foyer. After Andrew had come to her rescue, there'd been little time to freshen up, barely enough to wash away the dust from the carriage ride and smooth back her French twist. On the way down the marble stairs, she passed portraits of richly-dressed men and women who had presided over Beaumont, and felt most improperly attired for the mansion Charles would someday inherit. It occurred to her that he might be betrothed to a Southern belle with a great inheritance. Such arrangements were customary for plantation owners' sons.

Best to dwell on other matters.

For one, it was a blessing to have a bedroom of her own after sharing the *Mississippi Palace* cabin with Sarah—not to mention sleeping under the wagon en route to Tipton. She felt uncertain, however, about her bedroom being just across the hallway from Charles's room.

Laurette McCourtney stood at the dining room entrance in her lacy blue morning frock and greeted Kate. "I hope you're feeling somewhat refreshed."

"I am, thank you."

The gleam of a crystal chandelier caught her attention, and she glanced beyond her hostess at the luxuriantly-appointed room. The table was set with gleaming silverware, crystal goblets, delicately flowered china, and a crystal vase of yellow and white roses. The pale yellow linen tablecloth matched the yellow silk of the draperies and upholstered French curved chairs, adding a warmth of welcome.

"What a beautiful room," she said.

"Thank you," Laurette replied. "But I have no right to accept any compliments on the decor. With the exception of the draperies and chair upholstery, the room is furnished very much the way it was years ago when my husband's aunt willed Beaumont to him.

She had experts travel to France and Italy to buy furnishings. I've only tried to make it warmer and more welcoming."

"Then the house suits you well," Kate said.

Laurette beamed. "Why, Kate, thank you. I do believe you mean it quite sincerely."

Kate nodded. "Sarah can assure you that I'm not known for flattery."

Laurette laughed. "I'm glad to hear it. One hears far too much flattery as it is nowadays."

It struck Kate that the last time she'd been invited into a family's dining room had been at the Davisons' house in Weston, Missouri. There she had been welcomed with equal graciousness, but hidden intentions. She wondered if Mrs. McCourtney had her own reasons too.

A new thought came to mind. "Do you have someone here named Randall?"

Laurette McCourtney shook her head. "No."

"I only ask because before Charles's memory returned, he referred to Octavius as Randall."

"We once had a slave by that name," Laurette said unhappily, "but he's no longer with us."

Did that mean he had run away or been sold off? Kate wondered.

"Here come the rest of your family now," Laurette hastened to say. "And there are Andrew and Eliza Faye. My dear sister was kind enough to direct final kitchen arrangements for me."

Kate turned and saw Sarah and Stephen coming along the lengthy hallway from their downstairs suite. Octavius pushed Stephen's wheelchair just behind them. Andrew and Aunt Eliza Faye had joined them from a doorway off the hallway, Andrew lending an arm to his aunt with obvious pleasure.

"And here comes Charles from his office," Laurette said.

For an instant, Kate thought the man striding through the foyer was the one who had humiliated her just a short time ago—but this man's dark blond hair had streaks of gray, and he was slightly shorter. Of course—this was Charles's father.

"I'm afraid my stepson had to ride into town for an urgent matter," Laurette was saying.

What urgent matter? Kate wondered.

Laurette turned to her husband. "Charles, allow me to introduce our guests."

As Charles McCourtney II's silvery gaze held Kate's, she knew immediately that his interest in her was as a woman—and he was at least thirty years her senior.

"A pleasure to meet you, my dear," he said, kissing her fingertips with gallantry. "Our pleasure to have such a beautiful young lady here. Our pleasure entirely."

Laurette gave her husband a warning glance, then led him toward Sarah and Stephen with gracious ease.

At length, they were all seated at the beautifully set table, and Kate was glad to be sitting between Laurette and Andrew. Several servants carried in platters of fried chicken, roasted beef, potatoes, vegetables, breads, and relishes; others poured white wine or well-iced lemonade.

"Won't you please say grace, Andrew?" Laurette suggested.

The servants stopped their serving to bow their heads.

In the fleeting second that Kate was lowering hers, she caught their host surveying her, and she closed her eyes quickly. How could he scrutinize her in such an ungentlemanly manner while everyone was bowing in prayer?

When the room grew silent, Andrew gave thanks for their food, the safe journey back to Natchez, and Charles's recovery from amnesia, then petitioned God for peace in their household and across the land. "We pray in the name of our beloved Lord and Savior, Jesus Christ. Amen."

"Amen," Laurette and Eliza Faye echoed quietly.

"Andrew," his stepfather began, "I believe you are embracing more and more extraneous matters in your prayers of late."

"I'm sorry if prayer offends you, sir," Andrew replied.

"Offends me?" his stepfather echoed. "I should like to know how prayer could offend." He allowed his remark to hang among them for a moment, then hastened on, "In any event, let's have some of that peace you prayed for." He took a long drink from his wine glass. "Now, then, tell us in full detail about Charles's accident."

Kate feared that Andrew might also go into detail about the slave-freeing enterprise at Halfway House. Nervously spreading a biscuit with scuppernong jelly, she saw no way to stop him from relating what he knew.

"It was apparently a wide-ranging fight outside a country tavern not far from Uncle Namen's property," Andrew replied. "Somehow in the heat of it, Charles was unhorsed. I wasn't there, and he recalls little about it."

Relieved at the sparseness of detail, Kate took a bite of the biscuit.

"Charles unhorsed!" his father exclaimed. "I never thought to hear of such a day. Nonetheless, he appears to have recovered."

"Thanks to these ladies' nursing," Andrew informed him.

"You have our gratitude," Mr. McCourtney said sincerely to Kate and Sarah. "Our heartfelt gratitude. It would only be fitting if we could reward you in a suitable manner."

"It's reward enough, you takin' us in," Stephen said.

Charles's father shook his handsome head. "That's merely Southern hospitality, as you must know, coming from Missouri's 'little Dixie.' Charles told me your clothing was left behind in your flight from Weston and that you were all reduced to buying ready-made attire. I should like to have Addie and Lelah, our seamstresses, make up for your loss."

211

"Thank you," Kate said, "but we couldn't accept—"

"I beg your indulgence in such a small matter," he insisted. "We would be ingrates if we didn't help you. Moreover, there will be teas and balls and dinners for you to attend in Natchez. Yes, we surely wish to provide you with some frocks, don't we, Laurette? It seems the least we can do."

"Of course," his wife answered. She smiled at him carefully. "We did lend Lelah to the Manions—"

"We won't hear otherwise," he pronounced.

Sarah gave Kate a quieting glance, then turned to him. "Thank you, Mr. McCourtney; we appreciate your kindness. Perhaps we can ease our Missouri consciences somewhat by helping with the sewing as we did at home. We do enjoy sewing."

"If that's what you wish," he answered. "Now tell us about your family in Independence. Charles informs me that you're connected to the Talbots of the Talbot-Wainwright Shipping and Chandlery family."

"Yes, we are of that family," Kate replied.

Their host raised his brows, impressed. "I met the founder, old Wainwright, in Boston some years before he died. In fact, he recommended railroad stocks in both Pennsylvania and Ohio, and we are also greatly beholden to him on that count."

Kate thought she must have looked amazed, for he added, "Yes, I'm among the numerous Southern planters with Northern holdings. But I also own stock in the Natchez railroad, which I maintain will someday replace the riverboats for carrying cotton, no matter what others say. I'm a pragmatic man in business matters." He took another long drink of wine from his goblet. "Old Wainwright was a fine gentleman. Interesting indeed that your family is part of the firm."

Their host surely placed great importance on their shipping connections, Kate thought. Oddly enough, shipping had never been of utmost importance to her side of the family. In fact, Poppa had a hired man to deal with Missouri River shipping. Just recently they'd hired a new one—Thomas Meeker—a Southerner, to prove that they maintained a political balance.

Sarah said, "Poppa isn't too involved with the shipping side of the business."

"A shame," Mr. McCourtney remarked. "Ah have always thought shipping was one of the most fascinating aspects of commerce. In any event, Charles has met your Thomas Meeker—" He stopped abruptly, as if he'd blundered, then hastily added, "Yes, I for one do enjoy travel."

Something was amiss, Kate thought. It dawned on her that their host might not know they were abolitionists; after all, he'd mentioned their living in "little Dixie." Just as quickly a new thought struck. Might Charles be interested in her for her family's shipping interests? Perhaps his family would think marrying into her family would be useful to Beaumont!

She glanced at Andrew, feeling as if she'd missed something, but he only gave her a pleasant smile.

"Well, then," his mother said, "we ladies shall have a fine time looking through our yard goods after dinner. I don't know how we ever collected so many bolts of it."

"Likely Amanda and Alicia ordered most, then changed their minds about them," Andrew answered drolly.

"Likely," Aunt Eliza Faye replied, and Laurette nodded with hopelessness at her daughters' indulgence.

By the time the servants cleared the table and carried in the pecan pie and coffee, it was decided that Kate and Sarah would each need at least three new frocks for coming events—a tea dress, a dinner frock, and a ball gown.

From the head of the table, Charles McCourtney II said, "I should not want you ladies to suffer with no more than the minimum requirements. Beaumont can well afford to outfit you most handsomely. I should consider it an honor . . . the least we can do to repay you for your kindness to Charles. I promise you, it is our pleasure . . . our honor and pleasure."

Kate decided not to argue. If nothing else, it would be pleasant to have suitable clothing for their stay in Natchez. Just so it wasn't another red taffeta gown.

Benjamin Talbot stepped into the San Francisco Trust Bank with anticipation. It was a fine, sunny spring day to take the mid-day meal in the city's best restaurant with his banker.

"Benjamin!" Isaiah Meeker said. He stood with another man, whose back was to him. "Ah had no idea that you were in the city this morning."

"I came in unexpectedly, even to myself," Benjamin confessed. "I thought you might take dinner with me if you hadn't made other arrangements."

Isaiah hurried over to him to shake his hand. "Ah am so sorry, but Ah have indeed made other arrangements."

Benjamin thought that his old friend might explain, but he made no attempt at it, nor did he offer to introduce the man, who was now headed for a back office. He was a tall, well-dressed man, closely resembling Thurmond Morse.

"Another time?" Isaiah asked.

"Yes, another time," Benjamin agreed, still thinking it might be Morse. "I had nothing in particular to discuss. My regards to your family."

"And mine to yours," Isaiah replied cordially.

Benjamin left the bank uneasily. If the other man had been Morse, surely he'd have turned and greeted him. Something felt sorely amiss.

Upstairs in the sewing room, Kate and Sarah were introduced to the seamstress, Addie, a beautiful young mulatto who had thin lips, a narrow nose, and other Caucasian features. She sat sewing in a ladderback chair by the window and wore a tight yellow gingham frock over her provocative form. At last she put down her work and rose to her feet.

"Don't let us disturb you, Addie," Laurette McCourtney said kindly. "Do go on with your work."

"Yes'm," Addie replied with resentment. She sat down and, chin raised, resumed sewing on a white embroidered gown.

Kate recalled Charles's words on the carriage ride to Beaumont—about slavery being "a social mechanism to regularize behavior between the various classes." What sort of behavior between the various classes had been regularized by Addie's mixed parentage? And was it this "regularized behavior" that made her so sullen?

Laurette led them to a large walnut armoire and opened its doors. "Here are the extra yard goods," she said. "Just take out what you like. None of these goods are spoken for. Am I right, Addie?"

"Yes'm," Addie replied, her eyes on her sewing.

"Ah do declare, it's an embarrassment to see how many yards of goods we've amassed heah!" Eliza Faye chattered as if she were nervous in Addie's presence. "We don't dare let the menfolk see such a profligate stock!"

"We did buy most of them at reduced prices last summer," Laurette replied. "And here we have the latest *Godey's Lady Book,* as well. So, ladies, all we need are decisions. One advantage of your situation is that you can start all over with new clothes. I wish I could myself."

"But you can and you should," Eliza Faye told her. "Beaumont can well afford it."

"But I won't," Laurette replied. "Papa brought us up frugally—

and upbringing is hard to overcome."

As they spoke, Kate darted a glance at Sarah, wondering again if they should accept clothing as gifts, but her sister was looking through the yard goods. If Sarah thought it appropriate to accept these generous gifts, then likely it was. Kate began to sort through them herself.

After making preliminary decisions, they pored through *Godey's Lady Book* and saw that hooped skirts remained stylish. They narrowed their selections, listening to Laurette and Eliza Faye's helpful suggestions. Through it all, Kate felt certain that Addie was not only listening to their every word, but judging them harshly.

In the end, Kate chose a lightly flowered yellow voile for a full-skirted morning dress, a green watered silk with a small hoop for dinners, and an ivory organdy for a hooped ball gown.

Sarah chose a pale pink voile for morning, a rose silk for dinners, and a pale lavender organdy for a ball gown. She made no mention of her delicate condition, though she was beginning to look as voluptuous as Addie.

Laurette told the seamstress, "We shall need the two dinner dresses as soon as possible, then the ball gowns for next week. The morning dresses can be made last."

"Yes'm," Addie replied evenly. "I sews 'em up jist as fast as I kin. I needs an old dress fo' a pattern. I gots lots o' work, an' you went an' sent Lelah off to sew for de Manions' wedding—"

"Lelah is Addie's older sister," Aunt Eliza Faye explained with embarrassment. "The Manions lost their seamstress last month, and just before their daughter's wedding!"

Addie shot them a self-righteous glance.

"Sarah and I will help," Kate told her, not wishing to add to the seamstress's burden. "We have plenty of experience, even if we aren't fine seamstresses."

Addie sewed on without speaking.

"I enjoy sewing with Addie myself," Laurette put in. "She is a very talented seamstress. Though I am not always sure of my welcome here in the sewing room."

Again Addie made no reply, and Eliza Faye said quickly, "We can expedite matters. We'll take the yard goods and sewing supplies with us. It will be enjoyable to help our guests. After all, they did save Charles's life in Missouri."

Addie darted peculiar glances at them, all the while drawing the needle and thread through the dress. Behind her, sunshine streamed through the window and made the shade of her skin appear even lighter. There was something else, as well. Something Kate couldn't quite put a finger on. Then with a shocking suddenness, she understood. The shape of Addie's face resembled that of Charles and of his father. . . !

Kate hurried from the room, unwilling to contemplate the thought further. Better to consider which dress to use as a pattern for the sewing. . . . This russet fit well enough, but with shorter sleeves for summer. Yes, it would be wisest to bypass Addie as much as possible.

Sarah insisted that they cut the pieces of green watered silk for Kate's dinner dress first. They used her pale green ready-made dress from the Tipton mercantile for a pattern, adding fullness to the skirt, removing most of the sleeve length, and cutting the neckline moderately lower.

That accomplished, they chattered gaily as they carried the pieces with them to the shaded second floor verandah. There they settled into the white wicker chairs and began to sew, first darts and then bodice and skirt seams. The weather was pleasant, and birds sang from the tall magnolias and the great live oak trees.

Laurette observed companionably, "One thing about sewing

summer frocks, they have easier necklines and no difficult collars."

"Indeed," Eliza Faye replied. "But I dread contemplating summer and the fevers."

"We have them in Missouri, too," Kate said. Nonetheless, she earnestly hoped to be home by summer. In the downstairs hallway this morning, she'd glanced at the *Natchez Courier* and the *Natchez Free Trader,* and neither mentioned border strife. Surely the strife would end shortly, she told herself. She wouldn't have occasion to wear these new frocks here more than a few times. The sewing, however, would be a pleasant pastime. As for the lower neckline these ladies claimed were common in the South, she was glad she had relented only slightly.

"Tell us about your home in Independence," Laurette urged, and Kate and Sarah began to describe their spacious log house and equally large family.

At length Eliza Faye said, "They must miss you."

Kate nodded. "Even with so many of us, I'm sure they do. Sunday they'll go to church, and I know they'll pray for us. Maybe our sister Jocie will sing." Just thinking about them brought tears to her eyes.

"Do you girls sing too?" Eliza Faye inquired politely.

"We all have different talents," Sarah replied. "Like Kate . . . she has a bent for drama."

Laurette sounded shocked. "You mean as a stage actress?"

"No, it's mostly entertaining the younger children," Kate assured her. She shot Sarah a warning glance, hoping she wouldn't reveal her dramatic presentation at Halfway House.

At three-thirty Alba and Elmo began to bark, and a carriage rattled up the alley of mossy live oaks. "Oh my, tea time!" Eliza Faye exclaimed. "I was enjoying your company so much, I'd nearly forgotten. Well, if it isn't Mona-Anne Snelling come to visit."

"It is," Laurette replied, pleased. "We'll just lure her up here to join us, and forget about entertaining in the parlor unless someone else comes." She explained to Kate and Sarah as she rose to her feet, "Mona-Anne attended boarding school with me in Charleston. We're very different, but dear friends."

Not long afterward, Mona-Anne Snelling was brought up and introduced to them on the verandah, and one of the servants carried up tiny iced fruitcakes and three kinds of tea.

Mona-Anne had dark hair and was slim and spirited. "Ah declare," she said, "only you two would think of turning tea time into a sewing party. Of course, you've loaned your sweet Lelah to sew for the Manions. If that isn't like you, Laurette, to deprive yourself! Heah, y'all give me some of the work to do, and we'll see if I remember how to sew. I expect I'll recall the basics."

Laurette handed her two sections of the skirt to pin together. "You're certain you want to, Mona-Anne?"

"Can't think of anythin' Ah'd rather do than make use of my time while I'm tellin' you about Saturday night's dinner dance," she replied, setting to work. "Of course, Kate and Sarah, you and your family are invited. And Charles and Andrew, of course. We'll have twenty at the dining room table and three tables for eight on the verandah. Let's hope the sunny weather holds."

As she spoke, they heard hoof beats, then saw Charles riding up to the house on a shiny black stallion. He doffed his hat and saluted the ladies, smiling broadly.

"Oh my, won't Marvella Montclair . . . and Sally Mae Semper . . . be delighted to see Charles is home!" Mona-Anne exclaimed. "Of course, Marvella will just be arriving from Paris. In any event, Ah do wish he'd settle down. As for Andrew, he's a fine catch, too. Everyone says he's an honorable man and an outstanding planter."

"Albeit a planter without a plantation," Eliza Faye offered.

Laurette shot her a dismayed glance. "Eliza Faye!"

"Everyone knows," her sister returned, undaunted. "Why, there's not a soul in the South who doesn't know Beaumont is Charles's inheritance, and that his best match in all of Natchez is Marvella. But if I were a woman in a position to choose, I'd take a reliable husband like Andrew in a minute. I do like reliable men."

Laurette determinedly changed the subject to President James Buchanan in the White House. From there it moved to the abolitionist, Lincoln, running for president in November.

"Can you believe he claims slavery has no place in a democracy?" Mona-Anne exclaimed with vexation.

Kate pressed her lips shut.

Mona-Anne went on with indignation, "You know what he said two years ago when he ran for Illinois senator. 'This government cannot endure permanently half-slave and half-free. It will become all one thing or all the other.' And those are his exact words and his exact sentiment. He means to ruin us! To ruin the South entirely!"

"Let's not speak of it!" Aunt Eliza Faye said determinedly. "I am heartily sick of politics. What is important now, as I see it, is cotton futures."

Before long, Mona-Anne returned the subject to Natchez gossip. It seemed that Marvella Montclair was not only wealthy and beautiful, and despite reaching the advanced age of nineteen unmarried, reveled in being pursued by wealthy suitors. Sally Mae Semper, the overseer's fifteen-year-old daughter, was another matter. It appeared she'd set Natchez tongues wagging over her pursuit of Charles. Kate felt oddly jealous.

At five o'clock, the Snelling carriage arrived to take Mona-Anne home. "Well, didn't we make good progress on your dress, Kate!" she proclaimed. "How beautiful you'll be in green with your wonderful reddish-blond hair. Ah'd be mighty disappointed if you don't wear the dress at tomorrow night's dinner dance. Ah do hope it is finished in time. And Ah do wish Ah could help with your dress too, Sarah."

Later, when it was nearly time for dinner, Charles arrived on the verandah to find them still sewing. Kate realized that Andrew had been right, for Charles acted as if nothing had gone amiss between them just a few hours earlier.

"It's one thing to see you ladies doing needlepoint or embroidery," he said, "but such wholesale production? Addie must feel displaced, at the very least."

Aunt Eliza Faye cocked her head and shook it. "Addie claims she's too busy to help, and your own father has promised frocks to Kate and Sarah. You know they brought very few, leaving Weston so quickly."

Charles's gray eyes sparkled. "Then I shall have to talk some sense into Addie."

"Do, Charles," his stepmother said. "In truth, Addie is becoming more and more difficult. If only she were sweet-tempered like Lelah. Charles, perhaps you should take Kate along, so no one can malign your intentions. As it is, tongues are wagging over you and that scandalous Sally Mae Semper. You know her reputation—"

He gave a laugh. "What gossiping women won't concoct! I promise you, ladies, no matter what Mona-Anne Snelling might say to the contrary, I am innocent. Entirely innocent of her usual contentions."

Kate glanced at his stepmother.

Despite his adamant protest, Laurette appeared more hopeful than convinced. "Charles, please be more careful. What you do reflects upon Beaumont . . . upon all of us."

"Like Father's reputation?" he inquired archly.

Laurette's face paled. "That's going beyond the bounds of propriety."

He drew an exasperated breath. "I'm sorry. It's just that these cursed gossips are so vexing. What will they conjure up next?"

An uncomfortable silence filled the verandah, and Kate wondered where the truth lay. In any case, Andrew was likely right. No matter how attracted a woman might feel to Charles, he was not to be entirely trusted.

"Come along, Kate," Charles said to her. "I don't believe you're so easily taken in by malicious gossip. Let's appeal to Addie's finer sensibilities. Bring the pieces of your dress."

Kate stepped away, glancing at Sarah, who looked at her encouragingly. Likely she was considering their awkward situation and hoping that Charles wouldn't make matters more difficult for them.

"Kate . . . ?" Charles repeated.

"Yes, just let me get the pieces together."

It seemed there was nothing to do but go with him and pretend that matters were fine between them. She managed a small smile for the others as she joined him, then even one for him. Now, if ever, she needed her so-called dramatic talent.

10

Neither Charles nor Kate spoke as they started up the third floor stairs to see Addie. Kate expected him to mention the incident that had taken place between them at noontime in the parlor, but he didn't so much as give her a halfhearted apology. Had he truly forgotten it already, as Andrew had suggested? Perhaps he'd been prone to amnesia before his accident in Weston.

Halfway up the stairs, Charles said, "You'll look lovely in green, Kate. I do hope your frock won't be too sedate. Our Southern women dress with sophistication, though I do know you'll look charming in anything."

"Even in a ready-made dress?" she inquired.

He smiled and put his hand under her elbow solicitously. "In anything I've ever seen you in, you have looked lovely."

She tried to tug her elbow away, without success. "You're never at a loss over what to say, are you, Charles?"

He looked at her with mocking incredulity. "Why, Kate Talbot!"

"Why, Charles McCourtney!" she echoed.

"You look mighty tempting with that sweet chin of yours in the air. It emphasizes the curve of your delicious lower lip." Smiling, he halted her beside him on the stair.

"Charles!" She pulled away and hurried up the remaining steps. If only he weren't so handsome and tempting himself. And if only she'd never set her eyes on him! Little wonder the women in Natchez were interested in his return.

The sewing room door stood open. Addie must not have heard them approaching, for she stood before the oval mirror swaying back and forth, humming a romantic tune and holding the embroidered white gown up to her body as if she were far away dancing.

"Are you attending a ball, Addie?" Charles inquired with a chuckle.

Taken aback, she glanced at them, then turned haughtily back to the mirror. The virginal white gown before her made her look all the more provocative. "Could go to the ball myself if I was jist a mite lighter, couldn't I?"

"You could at that," Charles agreed, "but wouldn't all the field bucks be upset if you deserted them?"

"I got no truck wid dem, Mistuh Charles, an' you knows it!" she replied. "It ain't no field hand dat got me in trouble!"

"Now, Addie!" he countered, and she raised her head even higher.

"Addie," he said, "this is Miss Kate Talbot."

Addie turned and gave her a perfunctory bob of the head. "Miz Kate," she said, then immediately turned her attention to settling the white gown on a padded satin hanger. "I done mets her before."

"Hello again, Addie," Kate said. She held the green watered silk pieces, and Addie's eyes flickered past them as if they were of no consequence.

"I understand you don't have time to sew for Miss Talbot and her sister," Charles said curtly. "I am here to inform you that their work takes precedence over anything else to be sewn at Beaumont. That is, unless you'd prefer to find yourself working elsewhere."

Addie's eyes widened, then she concentrated on hanging the white embroidered gown's hanger on a wall peg. "I gots so much work, Mistuh Charles! So much work without Lelah heah! You gots no idea . . . everybody saying, 'Addie sew dis an' Addie sew dat!' Jist ain't no end to it. I ain't got no he'p—"

"Then bring in some of the younger girls to help you. It's high time we train up others to sew, don't you think? Just in the event you are called upon to help out in the fields. . . ."

Addie's mouth dropped open. "Me work in the fields?!"

Charles nodded. "That's what I said."

"I . . . I jist finished Miz Caroline's gown, so I ready to work on dere dresses next, Mistuh Charles! I jist finished an' I be glad to work hard—"

"Good," Charles interrupted, "but I want you to bring in at least two other gals, starting tomorrow morning. Make sure they know how to sew already. I'm certain they'll be glad to get out of the kitchen or out of the fields. I'll come by first thing to be sure they're here."

"But how'll I train 'em?" she asked in alarm. "I doan know nothin' 'bout trainin' up he'p!"

"The same way you were trained," he replied firmly. "You show them how to do a thing and then you make sure they do it well. Bring in competent girls if you value your work here."

She wailed, "But they sold my mama off when I gots trained up! And her bein' such a favorite wid yo' daddy, too. Ever'body knows he an' Mama—"

Charles interrupted smoothly, "Your mother became uppity, Addie. In fact, she turned sullen just as you have lately. Uppity . . . and full of complaints. You know Beaumont is a working plantation. You look very well fed, as do all of our people. I see you're wearing a clean dress and you have shoes on your feet."

"Shoes on mah feet!" Addie echoed. "You ain't gonna take 'em? I ain't gonna run away!"

"I know that, Addie. You're too well off here at Beaumont to run away."

Addie must have realized it was true, for now she asked with fear, "You mean you think 'bout sellin' me, Mistuh Charles? Sellin' me when I gots two babies to look after heah at Beaumont?"

Two babies?! Kate marveled.

Charles replied, unperturbed. "You're the one who mentioned selling, Addie . . . not I. Now, your sister, Lelah, she never complains. She's always pleasant and agreeable."

Gulping, Addie quickly took the green watered silk goods. She even bobbed her head politely. "Yes suh, Mistuh Charles. I be workin' on Miz Kate's dress dis very night, eben if I doan git a lick o' sleep. Yes suh . . . yes'm, Miz Kate, I be sewin' it up right now . . . right away. And we sew up all de others as soon as we kin."

"Remember, I'll stop by tomorrow morning to see how your training program is progressing," Charles told her. "Be sure that your helpers' work is excellent."

"Yes suh, Mistuh Charles! Yes, suh! It be de best sewin' you eber seen at Beaumont. De best sewin' you eber seen in all o' Natchez!"

Kate swallowed hard herself.

Once they were out of earshot and had started down the stairs, Charles said, "I regret you had to see Addie being so difficult. Sometimes subtlety isn't sufficient to remind them of their positions, and one simply has to put it quite plainly—do your work well here or you'll do it elsewhere. I understand it's exactly how they handle troublemakers in the mills and factories up North. And there, most workers don't even receive room and board, or medical attention."

Kate disliked hearing him say so, but it was true. The North was harsh on its workers too.

"It's a centuries-old maxim heard the world over: Do your work well if you value your position!" he added before she could mount a protest. "But enough of such serious talk." He smiled at her again, his eyes lingering on her lips.

She could see he planned to stop here on the stairway again, likely because it was a hard place for her to protest. For an instant, she was as tempted as she had ever been.

"I'd best get busy," she said quickly. "I-I have to write a letter home."

He gave a warm rumbly laugh. "Kate Talbot, you drive a man to distraction. I expect my lips are just as interesting to you as yours are to me. It seems a pure waste not to enjoy each other as a man and a woman should with a kiss. Look, there's no one about—"

"That's enough, Charles!" she protested and raced down the remaining steps. Luckily, a maid was stepping into the hallway and eyeing them, and Kate had a feeling that Addie was listening.

Charles laughed again from behind her. "Kate, you are priceless!"

He was only trifling with her affections, she told herself as she headed for her room. Likely he knew of no other way to converse with women. Best to put him out of mind quickly—and to stop her heart from pounding so wildly.

In her bedroom, she closed and locked the door against him. It took the writing of the entire letter to put the matter back into perspective, but she did it. She was a guest here at Beaumont; before long, she would be returning to her family in Independence.

When the letter was folded and in an envelope, her thoughts returned to Addie. It occurred to Kate that Andrew would have handled the sewing difficulty with more kindness.

It was late afternoon when Benjamin Talbot stepped from the stable, where he'd been for some time with a young foal. As he strode out into the California sunshine, he glimpsed a movement of bushes under the parlor window.

He halted mid-stride.

His first inclination was to avoid trouble and retreat to the barn, but Jessica and Ada were in the house alone. There was no one else to protect them. He gathered his courage, then moved on quietly, staying behind the trunk of the pepper tree. Unhappily he slid his gun from its holster. Strange that he'd even worn it today, but of late there had been more and more worrisome noises around the house. Watching the bushes as he edged closer, his boot crunched on a bit of gravel, and the trespasser must have heard, for he ducked more deeply into the greenery.

Benjamin stood behind the tree, noting that Runnell's horses and wagon were at the hitching post. "Runnell!" he shouted fiercely, "I've got a gun on you. Put your hands up. I'll shoot into the bushes if you don't show yourself now."

The scrawny fellow rose slowly from the bushes, hands in the air, the expression on his bony face vacillating between fear and anger. "I ain't done nothin', Mr. Talbot! I ain't done nothin' wrong!"

"You've been spying at our windows . . . and for some time," Benjamin stated. "Come over here with your hands up." The man apparently carried no gun, for which Benjamin was grateful. "Stop there," he told him when he was about ten feet away. "Just stand still and answer my questions. First of all, when did you start this spying?"

"I ain't got nothin' ter say," the man replied, his words slightly slurred and likely by drink. But he had no more than refused comment than he added, "I was lookin' fer somethin' in the bushes. Ada lost her weddin' ring, that's what it was—"

"Don't aggravate me further by lying," Benjamin returned.

"Your wife, Ada, is a good cook and fine housekeeper. She seems like a decent woman, as well. It's you who's going to make me fire her. It's you who's causing her to lose her position."

"We don't need yer money no more!" Runnell returned.

"Why is that?" Benjamin asked. "Have you been stealing?"

"I ain't no thief!"

Benjamin kept the gun trained steadily on him. "Then I assume you're spying, and the only spying being done around here lately is for the Southern and Northern causes. Are you receiving some of the money being funneled into California?"

Runnell stared at the gun nervously, but managed a truculent, "How would I know about such money?"

"Because you strike me as a man who looks for easy money . . . illegal money." He jerked the gun as a further threat.

"It ain't illegal!" Runnell protested.

"Then where does it come from? Or don't you even know?"

"Don't ye think bankers know how to git Southern money here?" Runnell babbled. "Don't ye think money cain't be brung in, right under yer nose?"

Benjamin recalled being at San Francisco Trust to invite Isaiah Meeker to dinner and thinking the man who kept his back to him was Thurmond Morse. No, it couldn't be. Isaiah Meeker was a friend, a reputable banker, a man who'd come to California some ten years ago. Still, he was a Southerner—

"The South is richer'n ye think!" Runnell yelped.

Benjamin recalled observing that Thurmond Morse's wealth appeared recent—from his fine new carriage and house to his gleaming gold watch fob and wedding ring. "Runnell . . . are you saying the South is rich enough to support Thurmond Morse and his new shipping venture?"

"I ain't niver told 'bout that!" Runnell retorted.

"What about his wife?" he asked, wondering if they had been

taken in by her, too. "She claims to be a Christian."

Runnell narrowed his eyes. "Women kin be led around by their noses easy if ye say ye love 'em an' buy 'em things."

"Then Mrs. Morse isn't part of the conspiracy?"

"I ain't talkin'!" Runnell replied.

Didn't the man know how much he'd already given away? Benjamin wondered.

Now Runnell was blabbering, "Ye kin shoot me, but I ain't talkin' 'bout nothin'. I ain't talkin'!"

"Well then, since you're not talking, go on over to your wagon and wait for Ada," Benjamin told him. "And if I see you around here again, I am not going to kill you. I'm going to shoot off your scrawny kneecaps."

Runnell grunted, then turned and hurried to his wagon.

Benjamin holstered the gun, glad the confrontation was over. He'd never shot a man and hoped he'd never have to. Heading for the kitchen door, he drew a deep breath. Now for the difficult part of the matter . . . to let Ada go and to explain the entire matter to Jessica.

Saturday afternoon, Kate rested atop the white crocheted coverlet on her walnut sleigh bed and savored the loveliness of her room at Beaumont. A narrow strip of white wall covering with pale rose flowers and light green leaves edged the ceiling, defining the color scheme. Carpet, draperies, wall coverings, and the bed canopy were all a pale rose, trimmed with light green. Rose and green fringe hung from the swagged draperies and bed canopy, and the matching draperies fluttered behind a fine walnut desk and chair by the nearest window. Pastoral paintings made the room even more pleasant.

She recalled their arrival some days ago, and how Charles's father had been impressed by her family's shipping connections.

For her part, a woman would be foolish not to consider living in such a fine mansion. More than foolish.

As the week had passed, she'd realized the importance of tonight's dinner. Apparently Mona-Anne Snelling was an accomplished hostess who brought celebrated national and international visitors to Natchez. One never knew who might come, Andrew had informed Kate at their midday meal.

"And you're going?" she'd asked him.

"Of course," he'd answered. His lopsided grin emphasized the engaging curve of his mouth. "Despite the gossip and matchmaking, I wouldn't miss it. It's usually a memorable evening."

He'd looked as if he wanted to say more, but his stepfather had interrupted with questions about the state of the fields and the crops.

Now, lying on the bed, she considered the slavery question. It was true that people worked like slaves in the Northern mills and factories. A good many of them starved, and there was no money for doctors as they had here at Beaumont. Why, just this morning, Laurette McCourtney had been out visiting the sick at the slave quarters with the very doctor who'd seen to Stephen. Nor did Northern factory workers receive food, clothing, or quarters on a spacious estate like Beaumont. Certainly plantation life was imperfect, but was it truly as bad as she'd assumed?

To begin, it was apparent that the McCourtneys were not idle aristocrats. There were endless business and legal matters to attend to beyond the growing of cotton. And despite having an overseer, the family was constantly occupied with the slaves' welfare; then there was the land, the crops, the sale of cotton, and far more. The time and energy devoted to plantation business and to the lives of the workers made the entire enterprise seem more like running a small nation than like living idly.

What's more, at Beaumont she was safe from the border

ruffians. Indeed, she felt completely secure. Despite her earlier stance, slavery didn't seem quite so conclusively right or wrong, but more of a tangle of complex issues. On one point, however, she felt adamant: owning other people was wrong.

As she pondered the matter, she heard birds twittering in the trees. The afternoon humidity made her lethargic, and she was drifting off into sleep when Alba and Elmo began to bark. Next there were hoof beats pounding up the driveway and Uncle Gabriel quieting the dogs from the front door. Rising from her bed, Kate leaned across the desk and glanced out the open window.

A dark-haired young woman, perhaps fifteen years old, stood angrily holding her unsaddled chestnut in the curve of driveway near the front door. Instead of proper riding attire, she wore a damp cotton dress over her lushly proportioned form, and her hair streamed wildly down her back.

"Mistuh Charles ain't heah, Miss Sally Mae," Uncle Gabriel told her. "He ain't home now."

So this was Sally Mae Semper, the overseer's daughter who'd set tongues wagging all over Natchez, Kate thought. Judging by the girl's wanton appearance, it wasn't surprising.

"I don't believe you!" Sally Mae told the butler. "You been sayin' it over a month now. It's all you eveh say. 'Mistuh Charles ain't heah . . . Mistuh Charles ain't heah'! Well, I know he's been back from Missoura for days now!"

Uncle Gabriel's voice turned hard. "He *is* back from Missoura, Miss Sally Mae, but he be in town on business."

Sally Mae hesitated. "Well . . . then tell him I'll be waitin' fer him tonight. Waitin' . . . an' he better be there!"

"Tonight he be attendin' a big dinner party with his family, Miss Sally Mae."

"Oh, you are stupid!" she called out. "Stupid!"

Her large eyes traveled up to Kate's window. Seeing her, Sally

Mae smiled up with contempt. "You can tell him, too, Miss Kate Talbot. Tell him Sally Mae Semper knows he's home, thet she knows about everythin' . . . and thet he'd better come see her if he values his hide!"

"I will," Kate responded uneasily. Something about Sally Mae reminded her of Addie, the seamstress. Contentiousness . . .

Sally Mae seemed surprised to have received an answer, but she turned it to immediate use. "You hear thet, Uncle Gabriel? Now you got to tell him. No more o' yer lyin'!"

She quickly remounted the unsaddled chestnut, her skirts hiked high over her bare limbs. With disdainful glances at Kate and then at the butler, Sally Mae kicked the horse's sides and, holding onto its mane, rode off like a wild thing.

Kate wondered how his visitor fit into Charles's theory of slavery "regulating the classes of society." She had an uncomfortable feeling that Sally Mae Semper—like Addie—had overstepped the bounds of her social class, and that Charles had gladly aided and abetted her to some degree.

Standing at her bedroom window, Kate realized her own plight. No matter what Charles McCourtney's bond with these Southern women might be, and no matter how many times she'd renounced him, she was filled with envy.

That evening they rode in the McCourtney carriage to the Snelling mansion, Cypress House. From its tree-lined driveway, the mansion resembled a great yellow-painted Greek temple whose white shutters at the windows and tall white columns helped to achieve a precarious architectural balance.

"Cypress House is one of Natchez's first mansions," Mr. McCourtney explained. "It overlooked the cypress swamps along the Mississippi until the river changed its course." He sat on the backwards-facing seat of the carriage beside Andrew; Kate and

Laurette sat facing them. Charles had other matters to attend to and would ride in later, and Sarah had stayed at Beaumont with Stephen, who felt poorly again.

"Cypress House is a bit overdone, I fear," Laurette said, "but Mona-Anne loves it. It was in her family, and she's as a fine plantation mistress as we have in Natchez."

"And you are as fine a plantation mistress as one can find in the entire South," her husband pronounced.

It was a splendid compliment, but Laurette said, "Thank you, Charles. You know, though, that anything of value I might do is because of the Lord."

"Now, now," her husband protested.

"It's true," Laurette stated firmly.

Her husband drew a deep breath, then shrugged with hopelessness.

As they drove up to Cypress House, Andrew remarked, "I prefer simplicity in architecture." He gave Kate a smile, his blue eyes on hers with interest. "I'm sure that your log house in Independence is more agreeable than some of our mansions."

"It did look more welcoming," Kate agreed. "I feel as if I'm. . . ."

"An outsider?" Andrew suggested. "I often feel like one myself in many of these mansions." His hair was still slightly damp from washing, making him look charmingly boyish in his black tuxedo. He'd been so busy catching up on his work since they'd returned to Beaumont that she'd scarcely seen him.

"Do you miss your home in Missouri?" he asked.

"I do," she admitted. Tears welled in her eyes, and she had to blink them back.

"I shouldn't have mentioned it. Leave it to me to say the wrong thing."

"Now, Andrew, that's rarely true," his mother protested.

Nonetheless, his stepfather shook his head at him, and just then the carriage came to a halt.

"At any rate," Andrew added to Kate, "you look very beautiful in that frock."

"Thank you." She made herself smile a little.

The driver opened the carriage door, and Andrew got to his feet quickly. "Here, let me help you." He climbed down from the carriage, then stood waiting for Kate to gather up the skirt of her green watered silk frock. As she stepped down, he murmured a hopeful, "Forgiven?"

She nodded. "Easily forgiven."

He offered his arm. "I hope you'll save the first dance and several others for me, Miss Kate Talbot."

"With pleasure, Mr. Andrew Kendall."

His blue eyes sparkled, and she noted an inner strength about him again.

As they approached the marble steps, he said in a confidential tone, "I'd have been happy to stay at Namen Ormand's house in Missouri instead of returning."

"You'd have stayed in Missouri?"

Andrew glanced back at his mother and stepfather, who were instructing the driver about parking the carriage. "I thought that would surprise you. But, yes, I'd have been happy to stay."

"Is your uncle's house sold?" Kate inquired with perplexity.

Andrew shook his head. "Not yet. It's difficult to sell anything in Weston, especially with Halfway House so close by."

Perhaps he could accompany them when they returned to Independence, Kate thought. It would be good to have him near-by as a friend. She was eager to learn more, but his mother and stepfather were approaching.

"May I escort you in?" Andrew asked, offering his arm.

"Yes, I won't know anyone. . . ."

"You'll know us," he said reassuringly.

Inside, the foyer was adorned with a gilded chandelier and sconces, a black-and-white checkered marble floor, and red velvet draperies, settee, and chairs—so extravagantly adorned that the furnishings seemed in ruthless competition. From the back of the house, however, came the lovely sound of stringed instruments playing a familiar melody.

The black tuxedoed butler had already presented Laurette and Charles McCourtney II to the Snellings, who stood receiving their guests in the foyer. Now the butler proclaimed, "Miss Kate Talbot and Mistuh Andrew Kendall!"

Despite the formality, Mona-Anne Snelling caught Kate's hand in hers with delight. "My dear, don't you look lovely in *our* frock? I don't know when I've enjoyed sewing so much. Oh, it does look beautiful with the reddish highlights in your hair."

At length she passed Kate along to her white-bearded husband, a jovial patriarch. "A pleasure to meet you, Miss Kate," he said. "Ah declare, you Missoura ladies are beautiful beyond words."

"Thank you, sir," Kate replied, "and you Mississippi men are quite gallant."

He laughed, then turned to shake Andrew's hand. "Aren't you a fortunate fellow to be accompanying such a beauteous young lady this evening!"

"Indeed!" Andrew said, smiling broadly.

As they moved on, Kate glimpsed herself in the entry mirror. She did look nice in the green watered silk, which set off her upswept hair. What's more, she could see Andrew admiring her in the mirror. She hadn't realized he would be considered her escort, and found herself comfortable with the idea.

He introduced her to the other guests with unmistakable pleasure, then accompanied her out to the back verandah, where a string quartet played and three festive tables were set for the younger guests. For a moment they stood alone overlooking the distant river, and Kate asked, "Were you serious about staying in Missouri?"

He watched the river winding along toward New Orleans. "I shouldn't have spoken. But knowing you've left your home behind . . . and considering my situation. . . ."

"You'd leave Natchez?"

"I think of it. Being in Weston after the rest of you left gave me an opportunity to reflect." He hesitated. "I've been here at Beaumont as long as I can remember . . . part of a family, but always in the awkward role of a stepson and stepbrother. If it weren't for Mother—" He gave a quiet laugh, then shook his head. "As I said before, I shouldn't have spoken."

"It goes no further with me," Kate told him.

"I thought not," he replied, his blue eyes holding her gaze. "From the moment I met you, I knew you'd be trustworthy. How I wish that—" He stopped.

"What is it you wish so fervently?" Charles asked from behind Kate. "Not to have Marvella on your arm, too, in addition to our beautiful Kate Talbot?"

Kate turned to see Charles in his fine black tuxedo, an exquisite honey blonde woman on his arm. The woman was boyishly slim, and her bare-shouldered ice blue taffeta frock bespoke Paris and utter sophistication. Her pale blue eyes and slightly parted lips held the most sensuously haughty expression Kate had ever witnessed.

"Kate, may I present Marvella Montclair?" Charles said. He turned to the woman at his side. "This is Miss Kate Talbot of Independence, Missouri."

Kate forced herself to say a pleasant, "How do you do."

"Enchanté," Marvella replied.

It was a most appropriate response, Kate thought, for the woman looked like an enchantress. Even without her inheritance, her beauty and sensual manner would lure streams of suitors to the Montclair mansion.

Marvella turned to Charles and, lifting a bare shoulder, murmured something further in French to amuse him. Her shimmering honey-colored hair was done up in an elaborate twist, and she smoothed it back over an ear, drawing attention to the diamonds sparkling on her earlobes and her lovely fingers.

Kate's heart sank. No woman—not even a wild thing like Sally Mae Semper—could compete against Marvella for Charles's affections, likely because she appeared so unattainable. As for giving him Sally Mae's message, this was no time for it.

"If you'll excuse us," Charles said eagerly. "Marvella has just returned from Paris and has been missing our dear Mississippi River. We're going down to the arbor for a good view."

"Of course," Andrew replied. "Marvella, it's nice to have you back in Natchez."

Marvella turned a teasing smile on him. "I'm glad you think so, Andrew. I do believe you've grown more handsome. I daresay the girls in Natchez must all be making eyes at you."

He laughed. "Not that I've noted."

Kate made herself smile, trying to ignore Charles's annoyed look at Andrew, then his proprietary manner as he escorted Marvella down the steps from the verandah. They turned immediately onto the flagstone walk to the scuppernong vine-entwined arbor.

Exactly what she'd feared, Kate thought. He'd only been trifling with her affections. Only trifling with her, when something in her still held hope for him.

Andrew turned to Kate with concern. "Shall we find our place cards at the tables?"

"Yes, thank you."

Charles must be just as enchanting to her as Marvella was to him, Kate thought. They probably deserved each other, but thinking so didn't stop her pain.

As they passed other guests who were already seated, she overheard bits of conversation about the Pacific Confederacy and collecting money.

Andrew found their table, and she was glad to see that Charles and Marvella were not to sit with them.

"Tell me about your home in Independence," Andrew was saying nervously. "I'm sorry! Forget that I've brought it up a second time!"

"No . . . I . . ." Kate hesitated.

To her amazement, she felt her eyes fill with tears, and she spoke the thought that suddenly came to mind. "I don't know if I'll ever return to Missouri! I don't know, Andrew! I really don't know what will become of me!"

His hand gripped hers, and he glanced about. "Look," he said softly, "let's have a walk ourselves, but in another direction. I have . . . no ulterior motives."

She pressed her lips together and nodded, grateful that he understood.

"Come, we'll go over to the orchard and see how the fruit is setting."

Glad for any excuse to escape, she took his arm and accompanied him down the steps. Once they were out of sight at the edge of the orchard, the hot tears ran down her cheeks.

"I'm sorry," Andrew apologized. "You've had so much to endure, and now I say all the wrong things, and Charles treats you shamefully. If only I'd traveled with you from the beginning!"

Kate began to sob, her body shaking. It seemed she was to lose everything—her home and family and now what was left of her dignity. Seeing Charles with Marvella had made her feel not only spurned, but entirely abandoned.

Andrew took her into his arms and patted her shoulder. "Worst of all, Kate, it's untrue about my not having ulterior motives. I do have ulterior motives . . . God help me, I do."

Weeping against his shoulder, she scarcely heard his words. Everything was hopeless . . . utterly hopeless.

When she finally stepped back, she accepted Andrew's folded handkerchief. "I'm so sorry to weep all over you."

He looked grief-stricken himself. "If only I didn't say all the wrong things when I want to help you. And if only there were something I could do."

"You're here, Andrew," she replied as she blew her nose. "You're here. That's what helps me now."

Looking hopeful, he drew her into his arms again for an instant, then awkwardly patted her shoulder and stood back. When she finally pulled herself together, he said, "I think we should pray."

"Yes, please pray."

It struck her that this was exactly what Poppa would say in such a situation. It occurred to her, too, that neither Mama nor Poppa would have approved of a man like Charles for her. As she quieted, she heard Andrew pray for her protection, then ask God to lead her into a new and abundant life. It seemed that he knew the One to whom he prayed.

When they returned to the verandah, everyone was congratulating Marvella and Charles—and admiring her magnificent sapphire and diamond betrothal ring. Andrew held Kate's hand as if to give her strength.

"I can't believe you two are settling down!" laughed one of Charles's friends.

"Now, now," Charles protested, grinning himself.

"When is the felicitous event?" another asked.

Marvella reveled in the acclamation. "This fall. I brought home a wedding dress from Paris."

"Marvella!" a woman exclaimed. "You already knew, then?"

Marvella laughed. "Oh, I knew . . . I simply didn't know to whom. Dear Charles convinced me . . . and most forcefully . . . that it was to be he."

The men laughed and clapped Charles on the shoulder.

Kate turned away, grateful for Andrew's presence.

In the midst of the excitement, a commotion had risen inside the mansion, and Mona-Anne Snelling ran out onto the verandah, white-faced. She could scarcely choke out the words. "A slave uprising at Rivermont! Right over the river in Louisiana!"

Everyone quieted, for scores of planters owned property on both sides of the river.

"They're burning the outbuildings!" she cried. "And burning their own quarters! What can they be thinking?"

Someone blurted, "And outsiders say they don't need caring for! Outsiders have no idea!"

In the rush of excitement, Andrew turned quickly to Kate. "Under the circumstances, perhaps we should go home. We can say you're not feeling well, but they'll know that it's for me to check on Beaumont."

"Yes. Yes, that's fine. Let's go." As it was, her emotions were barely under control.

Minutes later they made their excuses, as did several other guests, and the Beaumont driver drove their carriage up to the front steps. "Jist you two, Mistuh Andrew?" he inquired, climbing down to open the carriage door.

"Yes, just us," Andrew told him. "Miss Talbot isn't feeling well. I'm afraid you'll have to return later for Mother and my stepfather."

"Yas, suh," the driver said groggily. "Yas, suh."

He had obviously been sleeping and, still not quite awake, he was clumsy in helping them into the carriage. In the midst of Kate's distress, his clumsiness brought to mind a stream of pro-slavery expressions: *Negro labor was necessary to farm large*

plantations . . . their strength and endurance made them well suit-
ed for the work . . . they needed caring for . . . couldn't make it on
their own . . . hadn't the background nor the intelligence . . . they
were surely better off than those left behind in the jungles of
Africa at the mercy of each other in tribal battles and of the wild
beasts that lived there . . . abolitionists were impractical idealists
with no regard for the consequences for their ideas or actions . . .
the world was less than perfect in many ways and always would
be. . . .

She recalled the bits of conversation she'd just overheard about
a Pacific Confederacy in California and the vast sums of money
collected. She recalled Charles's intent discussions with the New
Orleans men on the *Mississippi Palace*.

No! Surely she was leaping to conclusions.

The carriage had already jolted forward and was now rattling
along the road. Andrew inquired into the silence, "May I ask what
you're thinking of so seriously?"

"About the institution of slavery," she replied. "I wish it had
never begun!"

"You're not alone in that," he said, "but to put it into perspective, there were slaves in the time of Christ . . . in Roman and
Greek times . . . in ancient Egypt and Babylon. Slavery has existed throughout most of the world's history. It wasn't until the late
1700s that a movement started by Christians in England con-
demned the slave trade and all forms of human bondage. Sadly, in
much of the world it's still an accepted way of life."

"That doesn't make it right."

"No, Kate, it doesn't. All kinds of sin have been about since the
beginning of man, but it doesn't make a one of them right. Not a
one in God's eyes."

"Now you sound like Poppa and likely my Grandfather Talbot."

Andrew raised his flaxen brows. "Is that a compliment?"

"It is," she assured him.

He smiled, his face backlit by the magnificent sunset. "Then I consider it an honor. And if all is well at Beaumont, I would also be honored if you'd take supper with me, though it's likely to be ham, biscuits, and fried tomatoes in the kitchen."

"It would be my pleasure," she found herself saying. Suddenly she wondered why she hadn't fully noticed how attractive he was. Had she been that mesmerized by his stepbrother? That obsessed by him?

As they rode along, a sudden thought struck. "Charles called Octavius 'Randall' when he first came to in the wagon."

"He did?"

She nodded. "Who is this Randall?"

"When Charles was growing up, Randall was his manservant," Andrew explained. "The man was somewhat of a rascal, and unfortunately he aided and abetted Charles in all manner of mischief. Or perhaps it was Charles who aided and abetted him. In any event, Randall was let go."

She dared to ask, "Did it . . . concern Addie?"

Andrew hesitated, then answered solemnly. "Yes. Yes, the final straw concerned Addie."

"I see," Kate replied.

At Beaumont, Uncle Gabriel greeted them at the door with uncommon grimness. "Yo' sister be waitin' fo' you, Miss Kate," he told her solemnly. "A black-borduh letter from Missoura."

A black-bordered letter?

Kate caught up her skirts and rushed through the foyer. She ran through the hallway to the back of the house and, moments later, knocked on Sarah and Stephen's door. Andrew stood a discreet distance behind her.

Sarah opened the door, her face stained with tears. "Shhh . . . Stephen's sleeping," she whispered, catching back a sob. "Let me get the letter."

Seconds later, she hurried out with the black-bordered envelope, her lips pressed together.

"What is it?" Kate asked.

"It's from Poppa. You have to read it yourself. Poor Stephen was so shocked, I-I had to give him more laudanum."

Kate's heart pounded wildly as they sat down at the verandah table, where the lingering rays of sunset still provided dim light. Who might have died? The family's most elderly members, Grandfather Talbot or Aunt Jessica in California?

Andrew glanced at the letter, then at Sarah's tear-stained face. "I expect you need some privacy. I'll be out with the overseer for a while."

Kate nodded, then opened the letter and read,

My dear Kate, Sarah, and Stephen,

I scarcely know how to begin this letter, but it is my sorrowful duty to tell you our heartbreaking news. Last week, border fighting erupted again all about us. It seems only a small matter that windows were shot out of the mercantile and it was looted, for far worse harm was done. Indeed, it is a harm that will forever haunt us.

Kate swallowed, then pressed on.

There was shooting all around the house, too, and to put the matter as quickly and painlessly as I can, a bullet came through the parlor window and killed Jocie on the sofa, right where she sat mending clothes.

No! Jocie was only eighteen years old . . . she'd scarcely had a chance to live. . . .

Kate could imagine her sister sitting on the sofa in the spacious log-walled parlor, then a bullet blasting through the window and Jocie falling forward over the mending in her lap.

Drawing a breath, Kate recalled the last time she'd seen her, the night by the cabin when she'd had the dreadful premonition that she'd never see them again. Jocie had looked so beautiful; the gold cross hanging around her neck had gleamed in the moonlight.

Kate sat stunned as another thought hit. Could the Bences have done the shooting? They were just the sort who would take pleasure in riding about wildly and shooting through windows. She noted the date on top of the letter and mentally worked her way back. No, the Bences would have been in Cape Girardeau just then or, at most, returning to Weston.

Nonetheless Jocie was dead . . . killed as she sat in the parlor. Across the table, Sarah had dropped her head onto her arms at the table and wept. Hot tears rolled down Kate's own cheeks as she forced herself to read on.

As it must be to you, it was a dreadful shock to us. A heartrending shock that has kept us in tears for days. We are only grateful that she was a believer, that she is now in a better place, and with the Lord. He will keep evil from her now, far better than a mere father can here on earth.

In church, we had some of the dear old hymns played, although for the most part, we wept too copiously to sing ourselves. The funeral service ended with "Amazing Grace." Both slavers and abolitionists attended the service, and Jocie's dear body lies buried in the churchyard with a stone cross over it. She is the first of our family buried there, and we are determined that she shall be the last.

While my faith was never as strong as your grandfather Benjamin's, nor his minister father's, God has granted us an abundance of faith now. Verses your mother and I read in the Bible over the years leap to mind, and we know we shall someday see Jocie on the other side. She is indeed "a treasure in Heaven."

It is strange that we, a family of moderate abolitionists in "little Dixie," might have been shot at by some who profess the same stance. We feel certain that our assailants cared more about carousing and shooting than they did about abolishing slavery. As Pastor Armbruster said, riding about and shooting is caused not by the pursuit of freedom for all, but by the darkness that lurks in man's heart.

The violence here continues unabated, and we have become prisoners in our homes, endangered by those on both sides of the dispute. It is no longer mere slavery and anti-slavery passions that rage on the Kansas-Missouri border, but hatred, killing, plundering, lying. While it seems evil to own another person, there is far more to it. The breaking of all ten of God's commandments is rife. Evil reigns here as never before. Evil. No other word suffices.

Having read thus far, you may not be surprised to hear that we have made a hard decision. As soon as is possible, we are moving on to California to join your grandfather Benjamin and the rest of the family. For some time, we have had a standing offer for the mercantile, and we have sold it. Only the final signing of papers remains. We also have a party interested in buying the home place at an almost fair price. We are proceeding as quickly as is humanly possible so as not to draw out the agony.

I never thought your mama would agree to go to California, but she is eager to leave before we lose more of our family here. We are selling all but our most treasured belongings, and shall be underway as quickly as we can, taking Missouri and Mississippi riverboats, then traveling via the railroad through Panama, and up the Pacific slope by coastal steamer. The Atlantic and Pacific steamer departures and arrivals are now coordinated, so train travelers can debark and board on the opposite coast the same day. Rail travel from Aspinwall to Panama City takes only four hours—thus it's not as arduous as it once was.

We yearn to see you, but we are all too exhausted with grief to stop at Natchez and visit with strangers. We think the violence will grow rapidly, and we pray most fervently that you will travel on to California as soon as you receive this letter. In the event you lack sufficient funds for the journey, I am enclosing a bank draft. We beg you, leave immediately.

Now that we are moving forward, we feel more hope. We shall have a new life in California. Your grandfather speaks of those who come only to bring their problems and bitterness with them. We are determined not to be among them, but among those who come with open and godly hearts. Do not hold hatred for those who killed Jocie, nor for those who have driven us out. You must not be bitter, but pray for God's tender mercy to take root in your hearts. This is what we have been praying for ourselves. He has given us peace in the midst of our heartbreak. It's as if He is here with us as He promises in Scripture. His presence is the tenderest mercy we have ever experienced.

Please write immediately to tell us of your plans, for we shall not remain here much longer. It would be wise also to write Grandfather Benjamin in California to advise him of the details of your journey.

All send their love and keep you in their prayers.

With a father's great love,
Your Poppa

Kate looked up through her tears and saw Andrew approaching. She handed the letter to him, then like Sarah, dropped her arms onto the table and wept.

11

The morning drizzle turned even the graceful grounds of Beaumont into a gloomy gray-green expanse. Nonetheless, the news from slave quarters was good: no sign of unrest and no new uprisings elsewhere. In light of Jocie's death, the unsettling Louisiana slave uprising was now the least of Kate's concerns. It was all she'd been able to manage to dress for church. Even eating breakfast had been impossible.

In the carriage, her soul seemed grimmer than the mourning frocks and bonnets Laurette had found for her and Sarah. And darkening matters even more was the news that Charles and his father rarely attended church. Kate couldn't help thinking Charles had attended in Weston only to gain the people's confidence. He'd taken in not only her, but likely other Missourians.

Laurette patted Kate's arm as the carriage bumped along. At breakfast she'd expressed her sympathy with great compassion, and even wore mourning now to share in their grief. As for California, they'd buy tickets tomorrow, then await a Panama-bound ship.

Riding along, Laurette remarked, "It's a sad commentary on Natchez's endless Saturday night dinners and parties that only the most determined attend church on Sunday mornings."

"I thought the deep South was religious," Sarah said.

Laurette shook her head. "Not in Natchez. Many don't go to church at all. I suppose it's also true in other places that those with power, riches, and intellect often rely upon themselves instead of upon the very God who formed them and their universe."

"A preacher has put it most succinctly," Andrew remarked. "I quote, I hope precisely, 'The people of Natchez in general are very rich, very proud and very polite—exceeding all for compliments—but they have little religion, and little piety.' "

"That does put it succinctly," Laurette answered.

As they rode on, it occurred to Kate that she herself had little humility, little meekness. Poppa had said, "You step out in boldness without praying"—which was all too true.

"What did Kate and I miss at the Snellings' party by leaving early?" Andrew asked his mother.

"Your stepfather formally announced Charles and Marvella's betrothal. Nothing else of note happened. The music and dancing were going on apace when we left. One would think nothing had gone wrong across the river."

Kate was thankful to have missed further ado about Charles's engagement. In the face of a formal announcement, she might have broken down in tears in front of everyone. It was bad enough that Andrew had witnessed her heartbreak.

Stephen had been glancing out the carriage window at the dreary weather, and now he turned to them. "We have an announcement of sorts to make ourselves." He hesitated, then glanced at Sarah, who nodded her encouragement.

It'll be the news of their child, Kate thought. He hopes to cheer us.

But Stephen gazed down at his cane soberly. "Dr. Hardy says my wound is almost mended, but he believes I've got somethin' worse . . . that I'm . . . I'm dependent on laudanum."

250

Kate was stunned. "Dependent on laudanum!"

"The doctor feels it's why he's been so weary and listless lately," Sarah added, and Stephen nodded balefully.

Sarah's eyes shone with tears. "We're asking for your prayers this morning at church. Dr. Hardy has reduced the dosage, and it's very trying for Stephen."

"What's the affliction like?" Andrew asked with concern.

Stephen's voice shook. "I crave the foul stuff endlessly. Been better if I'd shouldered the pain than bein' like this now. Anything would be better!"

"We'll pray for your deliverance," Andrew declared. "Scripture tells us that God can deliver one from anything, and I'm convinced of it." He placed a hand on Stephen's shoulder. "Come, let's pray now."

Kate folded her hands quickly, once more taken aback by Andrew's spontaneous praying.

"Heavenly Father," he began, "Thou who didst create heaven and earth, we praise Thee for Thy lovingkindness in sending Christ to be our propitiation for sin . . . for sending Thy own Son to take our sins upon Him at the cross, to take those dreadful stripes for our healing. . . . Father, we praise Thee and are grateful for Thy power and might."

He hesitated as if he awaited leading, then went on. "We pray for Stephen, that Thou wouldst deliver him from the desperate craving for laudanum now. In Christ's powerful name and under His mighty blood we pray. Amen."

Tears filled Stephen's eyes, but he stamped his cane and pronounced, "I'm more than willing to be delivered of it."

Kate glanced blindly out the window. Just last week, God had allowed Jocie to be killed in the family parlor. How could He be expected to help Stephen . . . or anyone else for that matter?

"How do you feel?" Andrew asked Stephen.

Stephen's voice held a tinge of surprise. "I don't know. I expect maybe more hopeful."

Kate darted a glance at Stephen's long face and saw no change. Perhaps Andrew and his mother were too religious. Miracles took place during Jesus' time on earth, but that was eighteen hundred years ago.

"We'll continue to pray for you," Andrew assured him.

"We certainly shall," his mother agreed. "And we'll pray that, as impossible as it might seem now, your family's grief would eventually turn into . . . almost a gladness at your dear Jocie being with the Lord."

Never! Kate thought. Never!

"Considering what you've said about her faith," Laurette added, "she is a treasure in Heaven for you."

What good did it do for her to be in Heaven? Kate thought, still angered. The only good she could imagine was that her family would no longer live in the midst of the border strife.

Laurette went on kindly. "I believe God sees death very differently than we do. It is, after all, the homecoming of a soul to Him. I wish it hadn't taken me so many years after Andrew's father died to arrive at that conclusion."

"It took me some time too," Andrew confessed.

At least his father's death hadn't embittered him, Kate thought.

Before long, they joined numerous other carriages and worshippers arriving at the white stone church. The light drizzle had stopped, but immense dark clouds loomed in the sky, reminding Kate of her grief. Not that she needed more reminding, with all of them in their black mourning attire.

Andrew helped her down from the carriage. "I'm eager for you to hear Paul Thompson, our minister. He makes the entirety of the gospel clear. He preaches yielding ourselves as fully as we can to the indwelling Christ."

His mother joined them, adding, "And making Him the true Lord of our lives . . . of glorious, victorious lives."

Kate had heard similar words, but this struck her as a different teaching. "In our church, we learned that He is our Savior, that He redeems us."

"Then you'll surely enjoy hearing Paul Thompson," Laurette said. "For a young man, he has a great depth of wisdom about intimacy with Christ."

At the phrase, "intimacy with Christ," Kate glanced at Sarah and Stephen, who looked as apprehensive as she felt.

They stepped into the church, and she took note of the white sanctuary's grandeur. Gothic spires . . . great stained glass windows . . . a fine altar with a magnificently sculpted white marble altarpiece of Christ and the apostles. The parishioners were richly dressed too. It was all quite different from the simple wooden church in Independence. The title of the sermon, "Mercies So Tender," was not too unusual, however, and the organ prelude was familiar, as was the anthem, "Come, Thou Almighty King."

Kate stood with the congregation, but felt too grieved about Jocie's death to even try to sing. From beside her, Andrew's deep baritone lifted her spirits slightly. Despite his status as a mere stepson at Beaumont, he seemed to possess a great joy.

When they sat down again, an elder extended a welcome to the congregation, then read from St. Paul's letter to the Galatians: "I am crucified with Christ: nevertheless I live; yet not I, but Christ liveth in me."

A familiar verse, Kate thought with relief.

The organ music began again, this time with the hymn, "O Worship the King," which was also sung in Independence. Kate made herself mouth the words about God's might and grace. Despite her dispassionate singing, the words thundered in her mind and heart—"His mercies how tender, how firm to the end, our Maker, Defender, Redeemer, and Friend."

Friend? Kate thought. *Was Christ truly her friend?*

Sometimes He did seem like a friend when she sang in church. Only sometimes. At home, Pastor Armbruster said one should often address Christ Himself, to speak His name and use it tenderly, prayerfully, powerfully. Perhaps that's what was meant here in Natchez by "intimacy with Christ."

The Reverend Paul Thompson, a young auburn-haired man, stepped to the pulpit. He was a tall man, with a fine bearing and a beatific smile. It was to this man that Andrew had written the letter, Kate recalled—the letter she'd returned to him on the train.

"My dear friends," Paul Thompson began.

Kate glanced at Sarah beside her, who listened with interest. Likely she thought the same thing: this minister was surely not old and somber like Pastor Armbruster in Independence.

"Most Christians know that Christ died for their sins," he began, "but few have learned of their own deaths in Him." He glanced about the sanctuary, a radiance about him. "Yes, their own deaths in Him. As we heard from the Scriptures, St. Paul said, 'I am crucified with Christ: nevertheless I live; yet not I, but Christ liveth in me.' "

He paused for emphasis. "Christians have been set free from the penalty of their sins, but many do not live lives from which Christ shines out with love and power."

As does Laurette . . . and, yes, Andrew, Kate thought. Christ did seem to shine from their lives, even through their difficulties.

The minister went on. "This message of the believer's identity with Christ has been lived and preached down through the years by great men and women of faith . . . believers who have abundant, adventurous lives. . . ."

As the sermon went on, Kate recalled the purposes of a Christian's life. They were as this young minister explained: "to serve the Lord in all we do, to obey Him, to love Him, to glorify Him." She knew of helping others, doing good deeds, obeying the Ten Commandments. But serve Him in all one did? It seemed impossible. As for loving Him, sometimes in church when she sang with the congregation, she felt a love for Him, especially when Jocie had sung so joyously beside her. As for glorifying Him—

"It is Jesus Christ expressing His life in and through us that gives God His greatest glory," Paul Thompson told them. "What hinders most of us from glorifying Him is that we glorify ourselves through selfishness . . . being self-willed . . . overly self-reliant . . . and seeking self-gratification."

At the word *self-gratification,* Kate recalled her obsession with Charles McCourtney. Heat rushed to her face. She focused her eyes on the spray of red roses by the pulpit. Slowly the minister's words began to penetrate her thoughts again. He spoke of mankind being born apart from God . . . of Jesus being the source upon which one should depend.

"The greatest mercy . . . the most tender mercy of all," he said, "is to be in total communion with God through prayer . . . conversing with Him and listening for Him. Let the depths of your spirit be in communion with the depths of the Spirit of God. Out of this can come instruction, guidance, even a burden to pray for certain people or matters. Adore Him . . . hearken unto Him . . . abandon yourself altogether to Him."

Kate squirmed on the wooden pew. Surrendering so totally seemed impossible, but she finally made herself pray, *Oh, God, if this is Thy wish, help me to be in closer communion with Thee!* A thought presented itself, a curious impression, and she added, *Lord, I ask Thee to deliver Stephen from laudanum!*

Then came a greater surprise yet—the loving voice that others sometimes mentioned. It was neither still nor small, but deeply stentorian and a declaration.

I AM.

She sank against the pew, stunned.

Kate, Sarah, Stephen, Laurette, and Andrew settled at the far end of the long dining table, and the servants carried in dishes and platters of ham, buttered beans, black-eyed peas, mashed potatoes, cold greens, and steaming biscuits. Charles and his father were absent, a situation apparently quite usual. In fact, it was increasingly clear to Kate that Andrew's mother had made an unfortunate marriage, perhaps for his sake. "Like father, like son," also came to her mind. Charles would likely be the same kind of husband.

Sunshine streamed through the window, warming Kate's neck as Andrew said grace. Since God had spoken, it seemed as if a spark had been planted, a spark that flared into hopeful joy.

Once they'd begun eating, Laurette McCourtney asked, "What's taking place, Kate?"

"I see why Jocie had such joy," Kate answered, "and why Poppa writes of their extraordinary peace and faith. And, strangely, somehow I no longer dread going on to California. Despite everything, it's more as if an adventure awaits us."

Laurette closed her eyes. "Lord, how we thank Thee for answering our prayers! Oh, how we thank Thee!"

"As if that's not surprising enough, I no longer seem to have the craving for laudanum," Stephen said. "Ever since Andrew's prayer in the carriage, I've had peace. Then in church, I felt sure as could be I was delivered from the dreadful stuff. Delivered in a moment!"

"Oh, Stephen!" Sarah exclaimed.

Despite everything, Kate could scarcely believe it.

Stephen took Sarah's hand shyly in front of them. "I wanted to be free of it for your sake and for our child's."

"And the pain in your limb?" Sarah asked him.

"Not quite gone," he replied, "but I can endure it."

Kate shook her head in wonder. "When we were in church, I was praying about another matter altogether when suddenly it came to me to pray for you. It's as if . . . as if God is proving Himself, though I'm sure He doesn't have to."

"God still performs miracles when we pray," Laurette said with a joyous smile. "It so often happens. I believe if we prayed more, much in this world could be changed."

"I believe it now," Kate said. "I can truly believe it."

"You must come to the slave quarters after dinner," Laurette told them. "Andrew and I read from the Bible, and answer our people's questions the best we can. Believe me, they understand all too well about bondage."

"Shall we?" Kate asked Sarah and Stephen.

"Jocie would want us to," Sarah answered, her pale blue eyes aglow with faith and certainty.

"Yes," Kate replied. "Yes, Jocie would!"

At length, Andrew turned to Stephen with a slight smile. "Pardon me, but you made a passing reference to a child. Were you merely speaking in generalities, or do you have an announcement to make?"

Stephen beamed. "Sarah and I are going to have a child in California . . . a little Californian!"

In the ensuing excitement, it occurred to Kate that Stephen was not only going to be a father and had been delivered from laudanum, but that he was being delivered by distance from his earthly father and brothers, which was surely another blessing.

That afternoon, during the Sabbath service for twelve slaves, sunshine streamed through the leafy branches of the sprawling oak tree. The sun's rays were especially bright on Laurette and

Andrew as they took turns reading Scripture, then retelling the morning's sermon. Every one of them, even the dogs who lay nearby under the tree, seemed to enjoy the informal service.

Anyone from unlettered slave to intellectual could understand the Gospel if he wished, Kate thought. What's more, the message could be understood in the great outdoors as well as it could be in the most glorious manmade sanctuary.

Lelah, Addie's older sister, who resembled her closely, listened with joy, and Kate wished that Addie were there. "Contentment comes from more than salvation," Laurette was saying. "It comes from close companionship with God. He hopes so much for friendship with us that He became human and died for it. He wants to walk and talk with us."

"Amen, Lord!" Lelah called out. "Amen!"

"Amen, Lord," Octavius echoed. He accompanied them on his dulcimer as they sang "Sweet Little Jesus Boy," "Oh, We'll Walk Around the Fountain," and "Go Ring That Bell."

When the service under the oak tree was over, the slaves began to make their way back toward their quarters—some joyous and others more quietly content.

"Wait, Octavius!" Kate called behind him.

"Yas'm?"

"You've been such a great help to us," she told him, "I want you to hear it from us that we're going to California."

His eyes bulged with astonishment. "To California?"

Kate nodded. Simply speaking the words helped her to believe it herself.

"Kin you take me?" he asked. "Bad times a'comin' heah! Bad times a'comin'!"

"I don't have money enough left to buy you," Stephen told him with regret.

"Ah be old," Octavius replied. "Cain't cost much."

"I have funds," Laurette said. "I'll see if I might buy your freedom. I'll ask my husband."

"Thank ya, Miz Laurette!" the old slave said, tears in his eyes. "God be blessin' you through an' through. God be blessin' you forever."

"That must be one of the finest benedictions ever given," Laurette told him which pleased him greatly.

As Octavius headed off to the slave quarters, Andrew said, "Mother and I have prayed over and over about this matter. If I'm welcome, I would like to sail to California with you."

"You . . . sail to California with us?" Kate repeated.

His blue eyes were on her as he nodded. "Octavius isn't alone in sensing troubled times ahead. Mother wants me to prepare a safe haven for the family in case such times do come."

"My husband doesn't know our plan, nor does Charles," Laurette warned them. "We ask you to keep this quiet. They're rabidly pro-slavery. Charles may wish to go also to accomplish their own purposes in California. It's charged that they're forming a Pacific Confederacy to enlist California in the South's cause."

For an instant, it was all too overwhelming.

Finally Kate spoke up. "In Weston, it appeared that Charles was inquiring into the Underground Railroad. Perhaps even trying to find a way to stop it."

"Precisely what I learned," Andrew said. "Best not to speak further of it until we're long gone."

Kate turned to Laurette. "I hope you'll also come with us."

"God has given me no direction to leave," Laurette replied. "Perhaps eventually, or perhaps I'm meant to remain here. I await His leading."

It occurred to Kate that if God could speak to her in church this morning, it seemed likely that He could lead Laurette, too.

"You must buy your tickets to San Francisco tomorrow,"

Laurette told them. "Five tickets."

"Five?" Sarah inquired.

"The fifth ticket for Octavius. My husband knows your news. I'll simply say that in addition to everything else, Sarah is with child and your party will require help. We'll make no mention of Andrew's departure until you're all ready to leave."

"How can we ever thank you?" Kate asked.

"There is a way . . . a very special way," Laurette replied quietly. "I'm going to leave it in God's hands to someday show you."

Monday morning, Andrew and Stephen rode down to Natchez-Under-the-Hill and returned with tickets for a Wednesday sailing on the *Pearl,* an ocean liner stopping in Panama. A faster ship, the famous *Corinthian,* sailed the next day, but all cabins were expected to be occupied when it reached Natchez. Kate had sent a letter for Grandfather Talbot to town with them, although it seemed unlikely he'd receive it before they arrived—unless, of course, it sailed to San Francisco more swiftly than they could.

By Tuesday morning, Addie and her two nervous assistants had finished Kate's and Sarah's frocks. When Kate bid the seamstress farewell, the young woman snapped, "Good riddance! Good riddance to Octabius, too! Dat no-good hymn-singer say God done freed 'im. Huh! He jist lak mah sistah Lelah, since she gots religion!"

Kate stood before her, understanding freedom more fully now herself. "I think it's probably true about their being freed, Addie. It appears to me that only God gives true freedom."

Addie clenched her fists. "Ain't got no freedom when yo' father be master o' de plantation an' sell yo' mama off when she doan please him no mo'!"

It was true—Charles McCourtney's father was Addie's father too, Kate thought with horror. Charles was Addie's half-brother.

And his sisters were her half-sisters who were not only educated and established in society, but likely enjoyed everything money could buy. Little wonder at her rage.

"Why you look at me like dat?" Addie asked.

Kate hesitated. "I was thinking how hard it must be for you to understand God's love when you've never experienced love from an earthly father."

"High n' mighty Mistuh McCourtney be my sistah Lelah's daddy, too! Be daddy to a passel o' babies hereabouts! And dat Charles ain't no bettah!"

Kate's mind rebelled, unwilling to contemplate the matter further. Finally she said, "Addie, you'll have to forgive him and anyone else who has wronged you. One thing I do know is that we can't be forgiven unless we forgive others."

"Ain't forgibin' none o' dem nebah!" Addie returned. "An' Miz Laurette know about my mama, too. Eben so, Miz Laurette help deliber me . . . deliber her own husband's baby when she jist hab one herself a few months befo'. She an' Andrew be de only good white folks heah at Beaumont!"

Kate stared at the woman and began to understand more. "Your mistress must have forgiven everyone involved, or she wouldn't have helped. I-I hope you'll consider forgiving him, Addie. It appears your sister has. And no matter how much you dislike us, I am grateful for your fine work. Truly grateful."

The seamstress spun away. "Ain't nebah forgibin'!"

Lord, help Addie forgive, Kate prayed. Help Addie!

Later, as they packed, Laurette gave Kate and Sarah fragrant dried flowers from the garden for a remembrance. "To remind you of my prayers for you," she said. "We'll go into town with Andrew to have daguerreotypes made too."

On Wednesday morning, Beaumont's carriage awaited them at the mansion's front door, and everyone gathered outside to bid them farewell. Charles and his father rode their horses over from the stables, and their eyes widened with anger and amazement to see Andrew dressed for travel, baggage at his feet.

"What's this?" Charles demanded. "You're not going with them?"

"I am," Andrew replied evenly. "I'm going to California."

"Did you plan this, Laurette?" her husband asked furiously.

She held a hand up. "My dear—"

"It's high time I leave," Andrew said. "I appreciate your caring for me all of these years, even seeing to my education. It's time for a life of my own."

Anger burned in his stepfather's eyes. "And who's supposed to see to the growing of the cotton at Beaumont?"

Charles erupted. "I won't have such work imposed on me! I have far more important responsibilities already."

"Be that as it may," Laurette said, "it's time to bid Andrew and our guests farewell. Please, let's present a loving scene for their last memory of our family at Beaumont."

Despite his anger, Charles's face lit up. "Wait . . . let me get something for you to take with you—"

"Hurry, then," Laurette said. "The ship won't wait."

Kate's eyes clouded over as she and the others embraced Laurette. "We'll never forget you. Never."

"Nor I, you," Laurette returned, holding each of them for a long moment.

Charles returned in no time with a thick, sealed envelope, and handed it to Kate. "For Thurmond Morse in San Francisco."

"And if I can't find him?"

Charles's father said, "Then give it to the banker, Isaiah Meeker, at San Francisco Trust. It's a large bank there. Should be easy to find."

For an instant, Kate wondered if Isaiah Meeker were related to

Thomas Meeker, the new shipping man Poppa had hired in Independence. Their sharing the same last name struck her as a strange coincidence.

"On the ship, keep the letter in the safe," Mr. McCourtney said with concern. "I doubt they have safes on the Panama Railroad, but do your best to keep it secure."

Kate hesitated, then thought of how kind and generous he and his family had been to them.

"I'll do my best."

Charles's gaze awaited hers, his silvery eyes dancing with a hint of amusement before he kissed her hand. When he looked up, one would scarcely guess he was betrothed by the way he murmured, "I hope to see you in California."

She decided not to encourage him, but smiled at him openly for all to see. "Thank you, Charles, for your kindness and assistance to us."

Before long, she and the others were in the carriage and the door was closed behind them. As the carriage moved forward, they waved a sorrowful farewell. It occurred to her that some matters in their lives had improved since their arrival at Beaumont. Stephen was not alone in being delivered from an affliction. She was free of her obsession with Charles McCourtney!

When they boarded the ocean liner *Pearl,* Kate immediately asked the purser about her family and learned that they were not on the ship's passenger list.

"Perhaps we'll find them on the Panama Railroad," she told Andrew. "It would have taken Poppa's letter some time to arrive at Beaumont."

Andrew nodded, looking unconvinced. "Just so you're not disappointed if they're not there."

"I'll try not to be."

Lord, she prayed, they're in Thy hands . . . in Thy hands! Surround them with Thy angels of protection.

"Come, let's get settled on the ship," Andrew suggested.

She and Sarah would share a cabin, and Andrew was to share another with Stephen. Octavius had to travel below in steerage, but he went in good spirits, dulcimer under his arm. Laurette had indeed purchased him and given his ownership to Andrew, who had immediately freed him. But instead of fleeing, Octavius wished to travel with them to California.

The Pearl held high standards of decorum, but unlike the reputable Mississippi riverboats, did not require men and women to be lodged on opposite sides of the ship. The first few hours of sailing established the custom of Kate and Andrew being together on the hurricane deck. In the wooden deck chairs and at the ship's railing, they discussed the passing regions of Mississippi, Louisiana, the Gulf of Mexico, and their crops and histories, as well as endless other topics about which he was knowledgeable. As the days passed, she realized she'd never known a man of his age who took such a lively interest in everything.

On Sunday morning, the ship's captain conducted a worship service on the sunny aft deck. Passengers participated, and the Scriptures and hymns seemed especially hallowed as the ship sailed through the turquoise Caribbean Sea.

Andrew read from the Psalms, "The heavens declare the glory of God; and the firmament sheweth his handiwork. . . . Blessed is the man that walketh not in the counsel of the ungodly, nor standeth in the way of sinners, nor sitteth in the seat of the scornful. But his delight is in the law of the Lord. . . . I will praise Thee, O Lord, with my whole heart; I will shew forth all Thy marvelous works. I will be glad and rejoice in Thee: I will sing praise to Thy name, O thou most High. . . ."

Joy flooded Kate's heart, and she recalled how God had

changed her heart about this journey. She rejoiced as well to see Andrew stand before the shipboard congregation with such glowing faith.

When the service ended, she told him, "You did splendidly, Andrew. Splendidly! I'm so proud."

"I thank God for using me at all," he replied. "That's the greatest adventure." He smiled at her as beatifically as his friend Paul Thompson had at his congregation in Natchez last Sunday morning, though it now seemed a long time away.

Later, at the ship's railing, Andrew inquired, "What will you do about delivering Charles's letter in California?"

"I'd almost forgotten about it." The letter was in the ship's safe, and she hoped Andrew didn't expect her to give it to him. He looked most appealing—his flaxen hair blowing in the breeze and his eyes even bluer against his sun-browned face.

He said, "I'm uneasy about anything Charles might send."

She remained firm. "I gave my word to deliver it."

The uncomfortable moment ended with his understanding smile. "So you did. I appreciate your being a woman of your word. There's a great deal to be said for faithfulness."

She returned his smile, and another letter came to mind. "If I may be so bold as to inquire, what was in that letter you gave me in Weston to deliver to your minister?"

His color deepened. "I can't say."

"Can't or won't?" she replied with a laugh.

He grinned despite his embarrassment. "Perhaps I'll tell you someday."

Their ship blasted a resounding salute to a ship that was overtaking them some distance to the starboard. "The *Corinthian!*" someone shouted. "Look at 'er go!"

The *Corinthian* returned the sonorous salutation, and Kate wondered if her family were aboard it. The ship was too far away to recognize the tiny passengers who waved at them, and in no time, the *Corinthian* disappeared in the haze.

As usual that evening, a string quartet played romantic music, and Kate stood at the ship's railing, looking up at the starry sky with Andrew. In the quiet of the night, she knew she cared for him. It wasn't as if she had fallen from Charles's arms into Andrew's, she told herself. This was different—an admiration of Andrew's character, and a sense of sweetness and rightness before God. This caring had grown since she had first met him, and was far deeper than the vague hope she'd once had to marry Albert Morton . . . and far deeper than her obsession with Charles.

When they disembarked at the Panamanian port of Aspinwall, *The Pearl* was the sole ship at the dock, and Kate saw only dark Panamanian stevedores whose shaggy donkeys were tied to the trees. There was no sign of her family. What if they'd been killed in the border strife in Missouri like Jocie? she thought. Or what if they'd been killed in one of the endless steamboat explosions?

Lord, I beseech Thee to keep them safe, she prayed over and over.

The Panamanian railroad had been built with money from the California gold rush and, as Papa had written, the train was scheduled to make the journey in four hours. Their ship's captain, however, warned, "Four hours barring hurricanes, unloading at Cruces, or *banditos*. It's always chancy."

The air at Aspinwall was steamy and still, seemingly eliminating the likelihood of hurricanes, and someone gleaned from the stevedores that there would be no unloading at Cruces—leaving only the possibility of *banditos*.

The train tracks ran almost to the docks, and the farthest siding was only fifty or so feet from the ship; behind the tracks loomed the dense green jungle. Already the puffing black engine maneuvered freight cars to the siding for *The Pearl's* cargo.

When the cargo was finally loaded, the passengers boarded. The train itself was shorter than the one they'd ridden on in Missouri: a smoking black locomotive followed by coal, baggage, passenger, and freight cars. In their passenger car, Andrew sat on the wooden seat with her, and Sarah and Stephen in front of them. Poor Octavius and his dulcimer were consigned to a freight car, but he headed back to it happily, as if he were bound for adventure.

At length the train gave its warning blast, then clickety-clacked slowly into the fetid jungle. Thick vines hanging from trees held brilliantly colored birds and curious monkeys. Here and there, great ugly lizards Andrew called iguanas crept from the undergrowth.

As they passed through the greenery, Kate felt certain he enjoyed her as a traveling companion, but he still showed no romantic inclinations. Did his caution have to do with her carrying Charles's letter? With her being in mourning? Or was there something else? Something in her that he found amiss?

The train's engine blasted warnings as it huffed through the lush jungle. They watched out the windows, and fortunately there were no *banditos*. Finally the lowlands gave way to cooler mountains on the western edge of the isthmus, and Kate was reminded of family members she had yet to meet. "Eleven years ago, in '49, my cousin Louisa from Virginia rode through these mountains by donkey," she told Andrew, "and that was after going through the jungle in a bungo canoe poled by natives."

"The tales of miners making their way through here to California were horrific," he said. "Hundreds died of snakebite and cholera. We're blessed to have a train."

She nodded, liking to hear the word "blessed" from him. She smiled hopefully, and he returned her smile.

"You look as if you're feeling blessed," he said.

"I am. I am now." Couldn't he read her thoughts? Couldn't he guess how she had grown to feel about him?

"Tell me more about your California family," he suggested.

She felt discouraged, then decided to be glad for his interest. She told what she knew of the family stories: Grandfather, Aunt Jessica, and Cousin Abby traveling to California by covered wagon from Missouri. . . Abby's best friend, Rose, rounding the Horn by clipper ship into the beginnings of the gold rush . . . Cousin Louisa trekking through Panama . . . Betsy, teaching in a one-room gold rush town school . . . and Callie, traveling partway from New York City on an orphan train. . . . And then there were the equally adventurous Talbot men. It struck Kate that Andrew would fit in well with them.

When they detrained on Panama's west coast, she looked again for her family, though she no longer truly expected to see them. She was less disappointed. There was, however, a Pacific steamer waiting.

"The first steamer here took Cousin Louisa to California," she told Andrew. "It was a twenty-day sailing then."

"And a mere twelve days now. Though I doubt I'd mind twenty days aboard—" He stopped abruptly, and she thought he had almost said *with you.*

As the ship plied its way up the Mexican coast, he seemed as interested in her as ever, but unlike his stepbrother, he remained a gentleman. She found herself ardently hoping that he might declare himself. It wasn't as if she'd fallen in love with him at first glance, she told herself. It wasn't as if she didn't know him quite well now.

Andrew, don't you love me? she wondered again and again. Perhaps he was waiting to declare himself on their arrival in San Francisco, she decided. Or perhaps he wanted to ask Poppa's permission. Whatever the reason, it seemed a shame to wait when sailing up the Pacific Slope under the night stars was so wonderfully romantic.

In their steamer's cabin, Sarah asked no disconcerting questions, but watched them with expectation. How different from their Missouri wagon journey, when she'd warned her against Charles's advances.

As the ship docked in San Francisco, Kate retrieved Charles's envelope from the purser's safe, and once on deck, looked about at the waiting crowd. The city appeared to be a wealthy, civilized place with fine marble banks and other prosperous buildings— unlike the aged Panamanian and Mexican ports the ship had visited, and unlike the riotous San Francisco one heard of during gold rush days.

When they walked out onto the wharf, gusts of damp air buffeted them, and Sarah called out, "Hold onto your handbag, Kate! The captain warned of pickpockets—"

Her handbag did feel strangely light, but when she looked down, the black bag hung exactly where it should against her black mourning dress. Another gust of wind lashed them, and she called back teasingly, "Hold onto your bonnet, Sarah!"

Making her way through the crowd, she was glad her sister had weathered the journey well. Just as encouraging, Stephen had grown robust and hopeful about their prospects in California. Kate still felt hopeful herself.

While they were hiring a carriage at the edge of the wharf, a policeman suddenly shouted, "Halt there! Halt, you!"

Kate turned to look with the startled crowd.

The policeman nabbed a tall, scrawny man, then nearly lost him as a blast of wind blew papers from the miscreant's hands into the water. Finally, the policeman's efforts prevailed, and everyone slowly moved on, muttering about lawlessness.

At length they found a carriage driver who would take them to Grandfather Talbot's home at Rancho Verde southeast of the city. Octavius, as usual, was quick to help with their luggage, then enthusiastically clambered up to sit with the driver on his seat. In moments, they were off. Once the city of San Francisco was behind them, the carriage clattered along through sunlit hills with blowing green grasses, then through flat-bottomed valleys with clusters of dark live oaks.

"Gold or not, it's no wonder people come to California," Andrew remarked. "It's a beautiful place. Mother will surely like it."

"Yes," Kate agreed, "I think she will too. There's a strange sense of both newness and permanence about the countryside."

"Yes, exactly."

It seemed a long ride, but at length, Octavius shouted down from beside the driver. "Here we be!"

Kate glanced out the window. In the distance, a vast ranch presented itself. In its midst was a white stucco, red-roofed compound of houses, and behind it stood numerous white outbuildings. As they rode toward it, the white houses and outbuildings gleamed in the sunshine, and great bursts of red flowers arched over the surrounding walls.

"Casa Contenta," Kate said. "Exactly as Grandfather Talbot described it in his letters. It does have a rustic splendor about it."

Before long they drove through the gateposts to the main house, and Kate wondered if she would recognize her grandfather. She hadn't seen him since 1846, when he'd left Missouri by covered wagon—and she had been a mere six years old. At home in Missouri, there'd only been a daguerreotype of him and Aunt Jessica with the California family.

As the carriage driver jumped down from his seat to let them out, a white-haired man came running and waving from the front door, a thin white-haired woman behind him.

"Grandfather Talbot and Aunt Jessica!" Kate exclaimed. "They seem to know who we are! They must have received our letter—"

In moments, she was climbing down from the carriage and

being enfolded in her grandfather's old arms. "So you're Kate . . . the reckless-mouthed one!"

"Not anymore," she assured him. "I hope not anymore!"

He laughed. "You and your family have filled our prayers for months now. The others arrived two days ago. They took the *Corinthian* from St. Louis."

"They're here?" Tears burst to Kate's eyes.

"They're here. At Abby and Daniel's house now."

Within moments, Mama and Poppa came running from one of the white houses, sisters and brothers behind them. They all wore black mourning, too, but their dear faces shone.

"Oh, Mama . . . oh, Poppa . . . I thought . . ." Suddenly Jocie came to mind, and the dreadful truth tumbled from Kate's lips as if she were a child. "I thought I'd never see you again!"

That evening they made their way into the dining room for a joyous supper. Once they were all seated at the massive dark oak table, Grandfather Talbot stood. "My heart is so full of gratitude, I can only thank God for bringing us together again."

He wiped his wet eyes and cheeks. "Look at me . . . weeping like a child, though I see I'm not alone at it! Enough! Let's all stand and sing 'O For a Thousand Tongues.' "

Kate held Poppa's hand on one side and Mama's on the other. Glancing around the table at their family circle, Kate saw tears running down most faces, but the gratefulness springing from their hearts filled the room with adulation.

O for a thousand tongues to sing
My great Redeemer's praise,
The glories of my God and King,
The triumphs of His grace!
Jesus, the Name that charms our fears,
That bids our sorrows cease;

'Tis music in the sinner's ears,
'Tis life, and health, and peace.

As they sang the third verse about "setting the prisoner free," Kate glanced at Stephen, who sang out a most fervent, "His blood availed for me!"

She closed her eyes, and it seemed as if Jocie were among them singing the last verse most joyously:

Glory to God and praise and love
Be ever, ever given
By saints below and saints above,
The Church in earth and heaven!

Fresh tears ran down everyone's cheeks, but as they sat down, their embarrassed laughter brought them back to themselves.

While they ate, Kate slowly became acquainted with her San Francisco aunts and uncles: Abby and Daniel Talbot, Martha and Luke, Jenny and Jeremy. Rose and Joshua Talbot lived some distance away in the small town of Oak Hill, as did Louisa and Jonathan, her minister husband, and Betsy, who was married to a doctor, Adam Buchanan. Callie and her professor-minister husband, Matthew Hansel, were moving nearby for the summer. Rena, a wonderful singer, was with Jocie in Heaven.

Abby, Martha, and Jenny had prepared the meal, but Aunt Jessica had directed it all with aplomb. "Not too long ago, we had a fine housekeeper," she explained, "but Benjamin had to let her go. Her husband is one of those political interlopers bent on bringing strife to California."

"Seems like there are troublemakers everywhere nowadays," Poppa remarked.

"I feel like an interloper myself," Andrew said, " . . . a Mississippian, the stepson of a Natchez plantation owner, sitting at your table. I've been concerned at how you might feel about me."

"You're altogether welcome," Aunt Jessica assured him. "Just think how hospitable your mother was when Kate, Sarah, and Stephen were in dire circumstances. We are forever beholden."

Grandfather added cordially, "We hope you'll stay as long as you like."

Andrew heaved a grateful sigh. "All I care about is buying land and having a quiet country life. At least as quiet a life as is possible here on earth."

"Exactly what I wished for," Grandfather Talbot said, "but life didn't turn out quite that way." He examined Andrew down the length of the table. "Do you have political intentions?"

"None for warmongering," Andrew replied. "The fact is, I'm more interested in finding a good minister and church. I've come to the conclusion that it's only through God's grace that mankind can be changed."

Grandfather nodded his agreement. "Now that Matthew is coming as pastor, we'll have a superb minister this summer. He and Callie arrive next week, and we hope to keep them with us forever. As for the church, it's been a good one. Unfortunately, we suspect several newcomers tried to use it for their own purposes. Nonetheless, God is faithful—and sovereign."

He hesitated, then added, "A neighbor's land is for sale if you like this locale."

"I do," Andrew replied. "I like the rolling hills for cattle. I'd like to try a few crops too, but I'm done with cotton . . . and with slavery."

"You can see the land as soon as you wish," Grandfather told him. He smiled at Poppa, then rose with some difficulty.

When everyone quieted, Grandfather Talbot announced, "You'll all be pleased to know that Adam has agreed to take over my work at the warehouse in town. With his vast experience at the Missouri trading post and mercantile, he'll be a great help to us. We propose to build another house here in the compound for them."

"Praise *Gott!*" Mama said, tears in her eyes as she applauded with the others. "Praise *Gott!*"

"It's exactly right for you, Poppa!" Kate put in amidst the congratulations. And exactly what Grandfather had promised if they came to California. If only it hadn't taken Jocie losing her life to make them leave Missouri.

Grandfather still stood at the head of the table. "I have more good news. Stephen and Sarah have agreed to move into this house with us, Sarah to see to the housekeeping with Jessica, and Stephen to help run Rancho Verde. As you all know, he too enjoys working with the land."

The family applauded again.

It seemed to Kate that everyone's concerns except hers were being addressed. At length she rose with cousins Abby, Jennie, and Martha to clear the table, then helped to carry in the glazed strawberry tarts for dessert.

When everyone was reseated, Kate asked her grandfather, "Do you know a Thurmond Morse? I have a letter for him from Andrew's stepbrother. I can also give it to an Isaiah Meeker."

A stunned silence fell over the California relatives.

Finally her grandfather said, "Thurmond Morse is a neighbor . . . and Isaiah Meeker, a banker. You have a letter for them?"

"Yes," Kate said, realizing that something was amiss. "I am only carrying it for the McCourtneys—"

"I see," her grandfather replied. "You likely don't know that Morse and Meeker are thought to be in the Pacific Confederacy here in California. Warmongers. It would surprise me greatly if your letter didn't contain vital information or a bank draft for their cause."

Aghast, Poppa exclaimed, "A Thomas Meeker is now in charge of shipping in our Independence office!"

"We'd best investigate him," Grandfather said.

Kate sat appalled. Even though the similarity of names had occurred to her in Natchez, it didn't seem possible that someone who worked for them could be involved in the conspiracy. Her mind moved on with suspicion to Charles McCourtney. "It might be that it is such a letter. What shall I do?"

"Where's the letter, Kate?" Poppa asked.

"Upstairs in my handbag."

Mama's hands had flown to her lips, and she removed them only to say, "Best to give the letter to your grandfather."

"I gave my word. . . ."

Her grandfather drew a thoughtful breath. "That being the case, I believe we should pray for guidance."

Kate's traitorous situation caused her to toss and turn all night in bed. At the breakfast table, Mama and Poppa were for burning the letter, its contents unread, then decided such an act would be deceptive and dishonest. Grandfather Talbot and Aunt Jessica continued to pray about it, and Andrew said only, "You took it in good conscience, just as you took the letter from me to our minister in Natchez without inquiring about its contents."

She considered returning the letter to Charles by mail, thus putting it at risk and delaying its delivery rather than confiscating something that wasn't hers to destroy. But even that was deception.

When she returned to her bedroom, she berated herself. How could she have become embroiled in such a dilemma? How could God have allowed her to have gotten into it?

At once she knew the answer. Instead of praying and listening for His reply, she had agreed to take the letter. Another bit of rashness.

Lord, forgive me for causing this trouble! she pleaded, feeling increasingly dejected. *Forgive me for not praying about it, for not seeking Thy will. Oh, Lord, I am so reckless and unworthy, but I ask Thy forgiveness. Also in the matter of my feelings for Andrew, I've been self-willed. I haven't even asked Thee if He is to be my husband. I haven't even asked Thee! I always barge ahead. . . .*

She hesitated, then forced herself on. If ever she'd been reckless, now was the time for it. *I give him up . . . I give up the entire matter.*

For the first time in a long time, she truly listened. Eyes closed, hands clasped in prayer, she waited for the still, small voice.

Nothing came.

Instead, she sensed that she should retrieve the letter from her handbag.

She went to the dark wooden armoire, took out her handbag, and looked inside.

No letter.

No letter anywhere in it!

The letter was missing . . . as was her small coin purse!

Quite suddenly she recalled Sarah calling out about pickpockets on the wharf, and her handbag feeling so light. Surely it must have been stolen then. No one had been in her room since Aunt Jessica had brought her to it. No one.

Carrying her handbag, Kate ran through the hallway, then down the stairs to the large whitewashed parlor, where everyone sat. "It's gone! The letter and my coin purse! I thought I felt something peculiar at the wharf—"

Sarah's eyes widened. "Remember the warning about pickpockets? And that ruffian the police caught was near you—his papers were blown into the water."

Kate recalled the scene with clarity. "It must have been Charles's letter blowing into the water. The more I consider it, the more certain I am. The thief must have torn the envelope open."

Grandfather Talbot drew a breath. "Was this ruffian a tall, scrawny fellow?"

Sarah nodded. "Yes. Yes, he was."

"Runnell . . . it must be," he said. "We heard he was jailed. Likely he knew you were coming with the letter and wanted to insure their receiving it. It would have been simple for someone in Natchez to send word ahead of you on a faster ship, or even upriver and then by Pony Express."

"You know the man?" Kate asked.

"Indeed," Aunt Jessica replied. "His wife was the very house-keeper I mentioned. We think Runnell was spying us out to see if we were forming an abolitionist society, which we have not."

Grandfather drew a deep breath. "How often evil is done in by its very participants."

After a joyous dinner, Andrew rode out with Poppa and Grandfather Talbot to see the property for sale. At the table, he had been attentive beside Kate as usual, but still displayed no romantic interest. She reflected on it as she washed dishes with Mama and Aunt Jessica. Why was he so reticent? Perhaps because he was unsure of his reception?

The men returned hours later, apparently pleased with their outing. Poppa called Mama from the kitchen to have a word with her, and she returned, only to take Kate aside.

"I have something to say, Kate, and I will not answer questions," Mama said. She paused and added meaningfully, "Mourning isn't as strictly observed in California as it is in the East. It is not necessary for you to concern yourself overly with it. After all, Jocie would want our lives to go on happily. She would wish us the best."

"You mean because I'm wearing my green dress?" Kate asked, perplexed. Surely Mama knew that her one black dress from Laurette McCourtney had been washed this morning and flapped like a crow out on the clothesline at this very moment.

"No, it doesn't concern the wearing of mourning . . . not altogether," Mama answered. "No questions. You'll see."

When they all gathered again in the parlor, Aunt Jessica asked Andrew, "How does the land suit you?"

"It looks very good indeed. I offered a price, and the owner found it acceptable."

"What fine news for all of us," Mama said to Andrew. "It will be good to have you living nearby."

Andrew thanked her, then turned to Kate. "Octavius is hitching a horse to the buggy. I should like to take you out to see the land."

"Now?" she asked. "It's almost time to start supper."

He nodded, his blue eyes shining.

"We'll save you something to eat," Aunt Jessica assured her rather meaningfully.

Everyone was watching as Kate took off her apron and nervously accompanied Andrew out the kitchen door.

"A fine day, isn't it?" he inquired on the way to the buggy.

"Yes, a fine day," she replied, looking about at the blue sky.

He is going to propose, she thought. That was why Mama had spoken of mourning practices not being strictly adhered to in California, and why everyone else had watched them so expectantly. At long last Andrew was going to propose, and she was free to accept.

A new problem arose, however. She had given him and herself up to God! How should she answer?

Andrew handed her up into the buggy solicitously, then went around and climbed up on the driver's side.

"Comfortable?" he asked.

"Yes, I am fine, thank you."

He smiled, then urged the old chestnut mare to set out.

At length, he told Kate, "Don't look so concerned. I'm a careful driver, and this mare doesn't look like a racer."

His driving and the mare's speed had little to do with it, she thought. She wasn't sure if God wished her to be married . . . nor, now that she considered it in this light, if she even wished to marry such a careful and subdued man.

The swaybacked mare pulled the small buggy up the driveway. Inside the house everyone would be speculating about them, Kate thought, just as they had done when Stephen courted Sarah. Andrew was so restrained, he'd probably already asked Poppa for permission, and Poppa had said she could make the decision, then told Mama to speak to her about ignoring mourning practices. Suddenly the entire matter of marrying Andrew struck Kate as a lackluster prospect.

Andrew's flaxen hair shone in the late afternoon sunshine. "The land isn't too distant," he said companionably.

He was somewhat appealing after all, she decided, then was just as quickly unsure.

Next came two wildly disparate thoughts. First, she could wear the ivory organdy frock Addie had made for her in Natchez as a wedding gown! It would please Laurette enormously. She could even tell Addie how much her work was appreciated, thus encouraging her.

The second thought was less exhilarating: Under no circumstances did she wish to have a dispassionate husband. Whomever she married would have to be a bit reckless—within God's dictates, of course.

"There's a house on the land, too," Andrew remarked as the horse clip-clopped up the dusty road. "Spanish architecture like Casa Contenta, though not in a compound. The house needs work, but it's entirely repairable. Even Mother will like it when she comes from Natchez."

So that was it! Kate thought. *This house was for his mother and family!* As much as she loved Laurette McCourtney, she felt not only shocked, but outright jealous. Perhaps he was one of those men who would never marry! She'd been wasting her time and heart on him.

At length Andrew reined in the horse by a huge oak tree some distance from a Spanish-style house that clearly needed a good whitewashing. He tied the horse's reins to the tree, then smiled at Kate and came around to help her down from the buggy. "Please, Kate, let's go to the shade."

She managed a smile as he led her under the oak tree.

In the shade, he turned and stood before her, his hair blowing slightly in the breeze. Squaring his shoulders, he said, "Kate, despite your being in mourning, your father has given me permission to ask for your hand in marriage."

She stared at Andrew's earnest face, and her words came in a confused rush. "I-I don't think we are suited to one another."

"Not suited?" he repeated, his blue eyes wide. "What do you mean, 'not suited to one another'?"

"You are so dispassionate," she began unhappily, "and I suppose as long as I am alive, I shall always be somewhat reckless."

Slowly an incredulous smile began to spread across his face. "You truly think I'm dispassionate?"

She nodded, backing up slightly as he approached, for quite suddenly he did not look so restrained.

"Let me prove myself to you then, Kate," he said, his eyes holding her gaze. "You have no idea how I have been reining myself in because of your mourning . . . and until I could ask your father's permission and offer you a home. God has made it clear to me that I'm to marry you. Even Mother hopes for it. Now it appears I must declare my love in a way I'd only dared dream."

He paused, "To begin, I love you, Kate Talbot . . . love you most passionately. . . ."

Before she knew what was happening, his strong arms enfolded her and his lips neared hers. Their mouths met with a tentative tenderness, then slowly warmed to such a fiery passion that Kate finally had to pull away, breathless.

"Shall I quote the Song of Solomon to you?" Andrew inquired with his lopsided smile. "It's the book of Scripture most often on my mind since the moment I saw you in that red frock at Octavius's cabin in Weston. I can imagine you starting the Halfway House uproar."

"You knew I'd been there? You knew my role in it?"

He nodded, his eyes brimming with amusement. "Let me tell you what was in the letter I gave you for Paul Thompson in Natchez. I charged him that under no circumstances was he to marry you to Charles . . . nor to anyone else! Because I wanted you for my bride!"

"That's what you wrote even then?"

"I did."

"Why didn't you tell me?"

He shook his head. "You were so obviously smitten with Charles, it would only have damaged my cause. I knew Charles would eventually do himself in. He has a long record of it."

"I'm . . . I'm not surprised at that."

She noticed that Andrew had a very slight dimple in his chin when he smiled at her so fondly. And judging by the determination in his eyes, it appeared he might be somewhat reckless himself.

"Shall I recite the Song of Solomon to you?" he asked again.

"From what I hear of it," she answered, "best to save it for later . . . a little later."

He beamed. "Does that mean you'll marry me soon?"

She hesitated, and such a peace, love, and joy overcame her that she knew it was of God. She reached her hands around Andrew's neck and pulled his head down to hers. "Would next month be soon enough?"

"Not quite," he murmured. "I was thinking more recklessly . . . like tomorrow if we could arrange it."

"Maybe next week, since I already have a wedding frock," she said before his lips met hers. With wedding preparations to make, next week would likely be reckless enough.

EPILOGUE

That October of 1860, Sarah bore a fine baby, little Laurette—
a first niece for newlywed Kate. The next month Abraham
Lincoln was elected President, and just before Christmas, the
Talbots read with despair that South Carolina had seceded from
the nation.

"It's tantamount to a declaration of war," Grandfather Talbot
pronounced. "Other states will follow."

A letter from Laurette arrived, asking for prayer. She enclosed
clippings from the Natchez newspapers. The *Courier* editorialized
against Mississippi's secession; the *Natchez Free Trader* held for it.

In January, Mississippi seceded and, according to Laurette's
next letter, most of its citizens, including her husband and steps
on Charles, gave allegiance to the new Southern nation.
Mississippi's action was followed by the states of Florida,
Alabama, Georgia, Louisiana, Texas, Virginia, Arkansas, North
Carolina, and Tennessee. More heartening, the slave states of
Delaware, Maryland, Kentucky, and Missouri, as well as western
Virginia repudiated the actions of the Confederate Convention.

Also heartening, while some California men and gold went into
the fray, it was not a major effort. On the local front, Thurmond
Morse and his wife had sold their house and, like Runnell and
Isaiah Meeker, disappeared. Octavius, for his part, had married a
fine middle-aged Negress he'd met while playing his dulcimer at
a tent revival meeting.

In the spring of 1863, General Ulysses S. Grant laid siege to
Vicksburg; on July 13, Natchez was occupied without resistance,
and a large cache of arms and ammunition was captured. The
Mississippi River was entirely in the possession of the Union
armies, and President Lincoln proclaimed, "The Father of Waters
goes unvexed to the sea."

Laurette managed to get a letter through the military lines to California. Her husband lay at home badly wounded, likely dying. Her stepson, Charles McCourtney, had died in battle. Most of the slaves, including Addie, had deserted, but Addie's sister Lelah had stayed. Daughter Rebecca and her wounded husband had moved out from town to Beaumont. Together they were trying to keep the plantation from ruin. Daughters Amanda, Alicia, and Caroline were without beaus at present, and reluctantly helping Aunt Eliza Faye with a vegetable garden upon which the family's survival was greatly dependent. Sally Mae Semper was said to have been shot as a spy, and Marvella Montclair, who'd postponed her wedding to Charles, was in Paris, recently married to a marquis.

As a postscript, Laurette wrote, "We shall survive. Expect me and as many of the girls as I can bring to California when this dreadful war ends."

Enclosed was a letter from Greta Davison, who relayed the news from Weston, Missouri. Pa Bence had died quite suddenly, and Aubin and Rodwell had been killed in border warfare. Greta and her family had fled the Missouri blood bath to live in Michigan. It seemed impossible that so much could happen in the space of three years, Kate thought, but war changed matters so quickly.

On the brighter side, she and her grandfather had grown close. She often joined him on the wooden bench in the courtyard, under the shade of the California pepper tree. Today, she sat with her hand on his, saddened to see him suddenly looking so much older.

His blue eyes remained lively, however, and he asked, "Are you happy here, Kate? I know how you loved Independence."

She patted his thin, wrinkled hand. "It would be impossible for a woman to be happier. Any unhappiness I feel is for our friends in Missouri and Mississippi, living in the midst of such carnage."

"If only they'd come here until the war ends," he said.

A hopelessness over the war tugged at her heart. "After so long, it seems as if the war will never truly end."

Benjamin Talbot shook his head. "Eventually the battles will cease, but the warring will end only when each side asks for God's love and forgiveness for both themselves and the others. Everyone argues about North versus South . . . or South versus North . . . or the so-called war of emancipation, but it's about far more than slavery. Far more."

"What then?" she asked, though she already could guess his answer.

"It's our endless sins that cause such hatred," he replied. "For one, our pride . . . demanding to be right, demanding to regulate matters our way. Then there's anger, thieving, and debauchery, so prevalent on the Kansas-Missouri border before the war even began. And, of course, greed. Hatred comes from all kinds of sinfulness. This war, like most, is the outworking of man's inhumanity to man."

He closed his eyes, and raised his old head skyward. "O Heavenly Father, forgive us . . . forgive us . . . forgive us! In Christ's holy name, I implore Thee to forgive any part I might have had in it, whether sins of omission or commission. Forgive all of us, Holy Father in Heaven."

He was like a prophet of old, Kate thought, a prophet who asked forgiveness for himself and for his nation. She watched his thin lips curve into a smile, his wrinkled face radiant against the sky.

At length, he opened his eyes and spoke the words like a benediction. "God forgives us. Despite everything, God forgives us. His tender mercies prevail."

He turned to her, his white hair blowing in the soft breeze. "I shall be with Him soon, Kate, and with my dear parents and Elizabeth . . . with Rena and your sister Jocie. I am eager for Heaven."

Now was the time to tell him, she thought, now before the moment was lost. Tears welled in her eyes. "Grandfather, Andrew wanted you to be the first to be told . . . we are going to have a great-grandchild for you. A little Benjamin . . . or if it's a girl, a little Elizabeth, for your wife."

Tears filled his eyes, and he gathered her in his arms. "I am honored . . . truly honored, Kate."

When he drew away, his words were fervent. "Tell your children how much Christ loves us . . . that He will walk with us if we only allow it."

"I shall, Grandfather," she promised. "And I'll pray more myself . . . and listen. Andrew's mother and his minister friend in Natchez say that God's listening and speaking to us is His tenderest mercy of all."

Benjamin Talbot beamed. "Indeed it is. God yearns for communion with us. Imagine it, Kate . . . He yearns for us to be His companions."

Kate was drawn up in the wonder of it herself. "It took me a long time to understand," she said, "but oh, how I do know it now. The God of the universe yearns for us to be His close companions."